TIME OF DEATH

TIME OF DEATH

GARY MADDEN

FIVE STAR
A part of Gale, Cengage Learning

GALE
CENGAGE Learning

Detroit • New York • San Francisco • New Haven, Conn • Waterville, Maine • London

GALE
CENGAGE Learning

Set in 11 pt. Plantin.

LIBRARY OF CONGRESS CATALOGING-IN-PUBLICATION DATA

Madden, Gary, 1967–
  Time of death / Gary Madden. — 1st ed.
    p. cm.
  ISBN-13: 978-1-4328-2513-3 (hardcover)
  ISBN-10: 1-4328-2513-5 (hardcover)
  1. Pittsburgh (Pa.)—Fiction. I. Title.
  PS3613.A28348T56 2011
  813'.6—dc22   2011022039

First Edition. First Printing: September 2011.
Published in 2011 in conjunction with Tekno Books and Ed Gorman.

Printed in the United States of America
1 2 3 4 5 6 7 15 14 13 12 11

For my lovely wife, Kelly, without whose
hours of proofreading, editing, and catsitting
this book never would have reached completion.

1

The dead come to me without ceremony. They show up on my doorstep like a deranged gang of Christmas carolers, lingering long enough to pine their off-key songs. Spirits whisper to me from behind closed doors and dark alleys. The presence of ghosts chills me on bright summer days. And when I turn out my bedroom light I know they're lurking in every shadow, begging for my attention. Until Virginia came into my life I denied it to them.

I first saw Virginia Beal on a quiet Thursday night. She appeared in my kitchen. I looked up from mulling over the contents of my refrigerator to find her standing by the table, shimmering and terrible. Her whispers were desperate and lonesome and they echoed an emptiness I'd felt the day I learned my father had died. Every lost girl with a broken heart has a legion of sisters in the world. Virginia showed me the sisterhood extended to the afterlife too. That moment I knew I couldn't be a spectator any longer. She gave me her name and in return I swore I'd find her killer. That's how our fates were joined.

I watched her story disappear from the front page of the *Pittsburgh Daily Democrat,* fading behind the deluge of news about striking steel workers and the end of the occupation of Japan. When I read Virginia made her living turning tricks in Manchester, the editorial tone had shifted. The reporter made his opinion clear: the murder was an example of the price of virtue spoiled and a warning that women shouldn't let themselves fall prey to their inner moral shortcomings. After that I called an old friend, and for the price of an evening spent having dinner with him, I got a copy of Virginia's file. I examined her tragedy over a strong cup of coffee in my favorite booth at The Quarter.

In the photographs she looked like a swimmer caught in mid-breaststroke; her head was turned as if she were drawing a breath. One palm faced skyward, emerging from the dirty Monongahela River, while the other arm was cast above her head to dig back into its depths for another stroke. The scene would have been utterly unremarkable if she hadn't been caught up on a pier of the Point Bridge, locked in the city's frozen jetsam. The police report said a barge pilot had reported seeing a body when he'd maneuvered a load of coal upriver. Soon after the first report, homicide showed up with cameras to record the details in crisp black and white. The two dozen photos I thumbed through captured the moment with coldness that rivaled the early spring day they'd been taken. There were snapshots of her blank stare, of the blood caked under her nails, of the bloodstains that muddied the pattern of her floral dress, and of the nearly decapitating slice that had ended her life. Sitting safe in my coffee shop booth I could almost smell polluted river water mingling with the ripeness of death.

Through the summer, Virginia's case drove me on. I walked the seedy streets she'd worked, unraveling the story of the last few days of her life. I spoke with the prostitutes who'd shared street corners with her and dealers who'd sold her dope. I followed trails that the police had decided weren't worthwhile and put in the time they didn't. By August I felt like Virginia's sister. By the end of November I was frequenting the sleazy bars where she picked up her "dates" until I found the pimp who brokered her flesh.

His name was Richard Fleck, and one snowy, early December

night I sat down the bar from him at a Western Avenue dive called Fakey's Taproom. He wasn't altogether sinister looking. Maybe a little rat-faced, with a long nose that was too narrow and too pointed and a washed-out complexion accented with pockmarks. His eyes were cold, though, and they lurked under stringy blond bangs in a way that let you know he was trouble. From a distance I knew Fleck had answers about Virginia, and I meant to have them. So when he headed for the tavern door I paid my bill and followed.

I endured salacious looks as I crossed the barroom; Fakey's wasn't the kind of place "nice" girls went and I'm sure the low-lifes and drunks who were regulars figured me for Virginia's replacement. It didn't matter. I could deal with being thought of as produce long enough to get the information I needed. I grabbed the door handle and braced myself for the inrush of cold air. Too bad I wasn't prepared for the fact that Fleck hadn't continued down the street.

When the door swung open he was standing just outside, lighting a cigarette. He cocked his head to look at me, and my heart seized. I couldn't hang in the doorway and it'd be suspicious if I turned around and went back inside. That night the sensible voice that lives between my ears happened to be on duty. It's semiretired and tends to go on long cruises without phoning or even sending a postcard; thankfully it chimed in and urged me against standing, gape-jawed, in the doorway.

I pushed past Fleck and across the sidewalk to the curb where I paused to check traffic. Our elbows had touched as I passed. It was enough to give me a bad case of the creeps. To fight them off I focused on my old, yellow LaSalle across the street, and when the traffic cleared, I hopped the gutter and hurried across. Hopefully he'd figure me for just another working-class drunkard calling it a night.

My keys were in hand and I lingered over the driver-side

door, waiting. The night closed in and I could hear the hisses and whispering of dispossessed spirits all around me, every one competing for my attention. I had to stay focused on Fleck; once I'd dealt with Virginia I could worry over the dead throng that populated the city. When I glanced up from my key fumbling, Fleck had started down the street at a casual amble. Nobody in Fleck's line of work should be so nonchalant; it set my molars grinding.

I stowed my keys and followed Fleck from my side of Western Avenue. From my months of aching feet I knew Virginia had worked this neighborhood. Maybe the last night of her life she'd come out of Fakey's, maybe drunk and playing hide-and-seek with the moon, weaving her way from one lamppost to the next. Her ghost had moaned about meeting someone. Maybe it was a lover, a man who meant more than the quick twenty bucks she could make satisfying his carnal desires. Maybe, in a love-haze, she'd forgotten her street savvy. In that tipsy dream the stink of the factories that poisoned Manchester disappeared, the winter cold wasn't seeping into her cheap shoes, and the world became the kind of place where wolves don't lurk in the shadows. Maybe by the time she realized what was happening it was too late.

Fleck crossed the street at where Western dead-ended into Waterside Boulevard, turning left and forcing me to freeze against the front of a building to avoid being noticed. When it was safe to move, I scrambled to make up lost distance but I slipped on a polished-smooth sheet of ice. I had to concentrate just to avoid winding up facedown on the pavement. When I regained my balance, I had to make a dash for the corner. It isn't easy to run quietly in a pair of flats that were selected for the way they picked up the stripe in a dress instead of their functionality, but keeping track of my only tie to Virginia's killer trumped being heard. By the time I reached the corner the son of a bitch had disappeared.

10

The streetlights along Waterside's gentle curve cast pools of light on the empty sidewalk. Fleck could have gone into the grocery store on my side of the street, but its plate glass windows were darkened, and even with the icy sidewalk's interference I doubted Fleck could have unlocked the door and gotten inside before I reached the corner. Besides, entering the store would have meant he re-crossed the street to my side, a sure sign he was onto the fact he was being followed. If he was, losing him was the best thing that could happen. The scenario seemed improbable, and that left the building opposite me. I jogged across the street and up the dark steps where I found evidence of a fire staining the brick façade and a stout chain securing the door.

I gave the handles a yank and the chains rattled their disapproval. All my consorting with lowlifes, the favors I'd called in, all the time I'd put in, and here I stood in the cold staring at the door of a burned-out building Fleck couldn't possibly have gone into. I leaned against the banister and considered launching into one of my fabled swearing fits, the scalding, paint-peeling kind, but as I warmed to the idea, I spotted a smoldering cigarette butt lying on the sidewalk.

A narrow, garbage-choked alley ran between the burned-out building and its neighbor. Darkness hung in it thick enough to hide a marching band and all their instruments. This had to be the route Fleck took and it definitely was the worst sort of place for me to walk into. My eyes climbed the fire escapes that scaled the alley walls; their metal skeletons were silhouetted against the city's over-glow. It would have made my life a lot better to see Fleck standing in stark relief against the sullen sky. Life never did take it easy on me. My hand found the butt of the revolver I'd shoved in my coat and I started into the darkness.

I chose the wall of the burned-out building and flattened against its dirty surface. Maria at the drycleaner's was going to love me for the soot I was sponging up. I wonder which is harder to get out of a camelhair coat: soot or bloodstains? It was a question best left unanswered. I needed to focus on Fleck's whereabouts. Three steps into the alley, a couple of trashcans huddled against the building offered my first chance to take cover. Every step of the way the snow and ice seemed to crackle under my feet, echoing off the buildings to make sure everyone in a block's radius knew my location. I knelt and waited; Fleck could be hiding anywhere, biding his time and waiting for a clean shot. I promised myself I'd plan my next heroic gesture more carefully. It was reassuring to think I'd want to play the heroine again, mainly because that assumed I'd live to have the desire. All that was left was working out the logistics between now and that imagined future date.

As I debated options, a car turned onto Waterside, its headlights sweeping the alleyway and stranding me in an impromptu spotlight. I clumsily stuffed the revolver into the pocket of my coat and tried to find some way to look natural, as if there's any way to look natural crouching behind garbage cans in an alley. It seemed like a week before the car completed its turn, but the light let me see the whole alley. Aside from me and the garbage it was empty. Fleck must have gone straight through and all my caution had given him a nice head start.

By the time the headlights faded I'd exited the alley and trotted into the cinder-strewn road that serviced the backs of the buildings. A drainage ditch ran along the opposite side of the road, carrying polluted runoff out of the neighborhood and eventually to the Ohio River. Maybe the ditch was the reason for Waterside Boulevard's name. It seemed like the sort of stunt a city planner would pull: calling tenements along a storm drain "waterfront property." I spun in a circle but the road was empty in both directions. A rickety, overgrown, eight-foot chain-link fence blocked my view across the ditch, but it gave way to an opening a few paces from where I stood. On an impulse I skidded through the gap. Uneven steps led down from the road's edge to a narrow footbridge across the icy effluent that filled the ditch from bank to concrete bank.

Two people could have passed on the bridge—as long as they didn't dislike each other. On the other side of the drainage the cityscape rose in a ragged jumble of sleeping, low-rent houses. Fleck had pulled it off. There was no way I'd find him in that warren of side streets and alleys. I struck the handrail in frustration and cursed my luck. The problem was I didn't appreciate how good my luck would have been if Fleck actually had escaped.

"You following me or something?"

The words were sloppy and they carried the accent of a poor education. I spun to face a dark figure that blocked my retreat to Waterfront. With its trademark "clink," a Zippo lighter flared, illuminating Fleck's smug face. He casually placed a cigarette between his lips and touched the lighter to its tip. As he took a draw, his face turned ruddy by the light of burning tobacco. The lighter snapped closed and went back into his pocket and as it did, my revolver came out. He eyed the gun and raised his hands in a way that was too casual. Either he was used to being at gunpoint or he didn't believe I'd pull the trigger. Either wasn't good for me.

"Hey, hey baby—take it easy. A fella's got a right to ask questions when a pretty girl follows him around, don't he?"

"Just stay right there." I managed that command nicely. No trembles to be misconstrued as lilting interest. Now, if could make him drop the smug grin the evening could almost be called a success.

"All right—all right, I'm stopped."

"You're Richard Fleck, right?" It was a nonsense thing to ask because I knew the answer. I hated the fact that, even at

13

gunpoint, this bastard could make me nervous enough to ask stupid questions.

"That's me, friends call me Dickey—uh, and if you'll put that thing down I'm sure we can get a lot friendlier . . ."

That smarmy statement steadied me. No, I didn't buy the slimy smooth Johnny act and I definitely didn't think Fleck lacked the intent to do his level worst to me. The come-on felt familiar. Nothing about playing Miss Detective on Virginia's behalf felt that way until Fleck's pass at me. When it came down to it, he was pulling the same shit the grease monkeys who work for my uncle regularly try: the wolf act. Sure, most guys don't have the nerve to crack cute with a gun pointed at them. Behind the act Fleck was just another man, in this case a genuine sleaze of a man who ought to be in jail. My mouth engaged.

"Maybe you've been friendly with someone I know already?"

Fleck flinched; he was calculating. This wild broad standing up to him didn't figure into his cocky self-assessment. I'm sure he figured I ought to be cowering or flattered by now. He kept up the bravado. "Maybe. If so, I'm sure your friend told you Dickey's the real deal. Now why don't you put that—"

"You know a girl named Virginia Beal, Dickey?" His smile died. "You get friendly with her? She worked for you, right? Hustled for you?"

"I don't know no—"

"Oh come on, Dickey. Do I look stupid? Sure you know her. Maybe you even had a thing for her, maybe one night this past spring you got a little too friendly? Or maybe she was holding out on you, stealing or something like that?"

"I said I don't know no Virginia whatever her name was—"

"So maybe you don't know her, maybe you just cut her throat and dumped her body in the river just for kicks. Is that what happened, Dickey?"

"You got the wrong guy, lady."

"How about you prove that, huh? How about we go down to the precinct and have a little talk with one of the detectives? I'm sure they'll be anxious to hear how innocent you are."

Damned if the smirk didn't come back.

"You know, I bet you're a real hellcat. I like girls that talk tough. The problem is usually it's a bunch of bullshit. All show and no go." He took a step toward me and I couldn't help retreating. "Once in awhile, though, you find a wild one: a girl that gives shit instead of takes it. Which sort are you, baby?"

I barely saw Fleck's right hand coming. He slapped the gun aside and it went off, sending a bullet into the night sky. Before I could level it again he had me by the wrist and was steering the revolver away from doing me any good. Now he pressed this advantage, bulldozing me backward. The handrail caught me just above the hips, driving the wind out of my lungs, and I had to fight to avoid toppling off the bridge. Fleck was small but all that size must have been muscle and sinew; he definitely had power.

I could feel his left hand inside my coat, groping me as I struggled. "Damn." He breathed into my ear, "Most girls out here on the streets are like your friend: all skin and bone and ate up by liquor and dope. Not enough meat on them to tempt a starving dog. Not you, baby, we're gonna' have some fun—"

The first thing you learn in bad-date school is the art of the knee to the crotch and I've been out with enough creeps to give lessons. I caught him hard and square and when he doubled over I started screaming and wrenching at the gun. They tell you most perverts will run when their little games go wrong enough that the object of their attention is hurting them and making a scene. Not Fleck. Instead I caught a hard uppercut and the night exploded into sparks and ringing ears.

When my vision cleared up I'd lost the gun and Fleck had a

hand around my throat.

"You think you're something? Huh? Big tough lady gonna teach me a lesson, huh? Let me teach you a lesson—it's called how to use a gun."

He raised the revolver as he stepped backward. I think I screamed; I know I turned my head. I'm not brave so why would I want to see the end coming? There was a shockingly loud bang and my right shoulder burned like a hot knife had gone right through me. Then I went numb and the world rotated at an odd angle. For a moment I felt weightless, the wind was howling as I spun, until something akin to a cement mixer hit me in the back of the head and I sank into cold, liquid darkness.

2

I've had my share of hangovers. Fine, maybe more than my share, but let's not get judgmental. Give me a few good friends, a little spending money, and maybe a cute fellow, and by the end of the night I'll have enjoyed myself right into a full day's penance. The point is I know my hangovers and when I came to, the symptoms were worse than anything I'd experienced.

True to form, I woke up lying down, but that's where the similarity ended. Instead of nice, cool bathroom tiles to soothe my woozy head, I lay face down in the dirt. It was in my hair, in my eyes, and it stuck to my lips so persistently that I had to spit and sputter to remove it. That didn't get the taste out of my mouth. On top of the unpleasant, cotton-sucking sensation that always comes from too much high-proof entertainment, the bitter flavor of ashes filled my mouth. I lay in some kind of ditch, but not the Manchester drain I'd been crossing when I ran into Fleck. This one stood empty except for dirt, wind-worn stones, and me. The landscape rolled up from its edges in jagged hills that stood dark against a slate sky.

I tried to push myself upright at about the same moment that I remembered Fleck firing the gun. The excruciating pain I expected never came. I cautiously checked my body for the ravages of a gunshot wound and my hand came back from my right shoulder bathed in black. Not warm red blood but cold black. I sucked in a shocked breath and stumbled to my feet, still staring at my hand.

What the hell had happened? This world was utterly barren: empty of buildings and trees, devoid of anything but ash and sand whipped by a wind that seemed to moan and complain about having to circumnavigate the only obstacle in its path, me. The horizon to this nothing world was defined by an occasional flash, like distant lightning without thunder to hint at the possibility of rain.

A prolonged flicker revealed a shape moving in the distance. At first I thought it was dust caught in the wind; it was just a smudge, a shadow among shadows. The longer I looked the more it took shape and the more I became convinced it moved of its own will. I thought about running. Well, I like to believe I thought about running but in truth I probably stood there with my mouth hanging open as this blotch sailed through the air and poured itself out in front of me.

Pour is the only word that adequately describes a cloud transforming into a liquid shadow, descending, and forming into a nearly human shape. It was wrapped in a hazy blanket, pieces of which constantly sloughed off to be carried away by the wind. Where cloud didn't shroud the form, I could see snatches of what looked like bone, if the bone in question was made of smoke. The thing's cloak wrapped around its body in undulating folds until it finally formed a deep cowl. Where there should have been a face impossibly dark shadows resided.

"Melody Rush." The voice that came out of that could have been serene if it wasn't so damned cold. There was an accent, like what you might hear in a movie where Gary Cooper plays an international jewel thief.

I swallowed hard against the taste of ash that filled my mouth. "Who's asking?"

The cloud, whatever it was, didn't seem to care about my flip counter. Its voice didn't quaver; it just slowly flowed toward me. "I'm not asking. I know."

"All right, I stand corrected but I'd still like to know just who I'm talking to."

"That is immaterial. What matters is the reason we are having this conversation."

I felt emboldened. Or it might have been another of my fits of stupidity. The two feel so alike. Either way, what's the point in holding back when you're literally standing in the middle of nowhere talking to a cloud of dust?

"If you want to have this conversation you'll tell me your name. Otherwise you can blow back to . . . wherever."

That got a rise. The cloud roiled and fell back on itself. I thought I could see wispy, skeletal fingers knitting in contemplation but it might have been the poor light. When the cloud spoke again it seemed resigned to a deal it didn't particularly like.

"I am The Mort, The Great Emptiness, Thana, The Ferryman, Fate, and that which is called by ten thousand other names."

"Fine, how about one I recognize?"

The cloud oozed forward. "You know me as the Reaper of Souls, Death."

That got me. I've had men tell me a lot of things: that they were football stars, that they were executive vice presidents, that they didn't have three other girls on the side, and even more ridiculous stuff. This was the first time anyone ever claimed to be the Grim Reaper. Usually I give guys with incredible stories the boot right off but then most of them aren't ghostly wisps of smoke. There also was the little matter of me being shot to add to his credibility. I looked down at my still-stained hand.

"Your undoing was the fall and the water." He answered without me asking. "Your wound was . . . inconsequential."

I felt the wind go out of my lungs and the barren landscape swam sickeningly. "How can you talk about me dying like it's

19

just nothing? The scum who shot me gets away and I'm here, dead?"

"It is what it is, Melody Rush. It is the end. All mortals come to theirs and it is always a—"

"Shut up, just shut up, okay?" I sat down harder than I meant and a choking cloud of dust surrounded me, stinging my eyes and burning my lungs. In my mind I could still see Fleck's face; the look of hatred in his eyes came racing back. The bad guy had won; I sat for a long time contemplating that before I spoke again and if my host cared he didn't let on.

"So then this is death and everyone goes through this . . . purgatory?"

"We're not here to discuss the metaphysics of dying, Melody Rush."

"Yeah, yeah—I know, it is what it is. Could you at least do me a favor? Stop calling me 'Melody Rush,' all right? Everyone calls me Mel so you might as well too." I stood and brushed off my dress even though it didn't seem to do a bit of good. "We might as well get on with things. Where to? Heaven or hell? Did I make the cut or do I need to pay for all those Sundays I screwed off instead of going to church?"

"I do not bring down judgment."

"Right. So, we should probably get to the guy who does, instead of standing around chatting. You're a thrilling conversationalist and all, but I'm sure you've got other customers."

"That is at the root of what we need to discuss."

"Discuss? Now you want to have a discussion? You refuse to 'debate the metaphysics of dying' and go on about how you're not the guy who judges souls but now you want to have a discussion? Tell me, within the narrow confines you've placed on our relationship, what could we possibly have to discuss?"

"I will show you."

All my life my mother told me I should learn to keep my

mouth shut. I hate to say she was right but I admit at that moment it would have been nice to have heeded her advice. My companion raised an arm and the dust swirled wildly, racing around my body and stinging my bare skin as it howled angrily, and then everything fell silent.

The plain of ash was gone and when my eyes adjusted we were standing in a cold little tiled room with heavy slab tables and walls lined with metal refrigerator drawers. Light filtered in through the frosted glass window of a door on which letters spelled out "MORGUE" in reverse. The long shadows cast by the filtered light provided the perfect level of gloom for a B-grade horror flick. I could feel my personal guide lurking just over my shoulder. He probably was measuring my reaction to his little trick. I didn't plan on giving him the satisfaction of thinking he'd spooked me.

"All roads lead to the morgue. Profound but I don't know what this is supposed to prove."

"You asked what we had to discuss; the answer lies here."

He moved past me and a chill spread over my soul. It wasn't the sort of cold you can feel in your fingers and toes but kind of an inevitable doom, a despair that can't be remedied and is unavoidable. I tried to keep my gusto up, putting a hand on my hip for emphasis.

"All right, show me what you've got."

"You came here six months ago."

"Right, to see the body of Virginia Beal. Anyone could find that out by talking to the morgue attendant."

"When you looked on her, what did you see?"

"What do you mean?"

"What did you see when you looked at her body?"

I didn't like this little game. It was cruel and pointless. "I saw a girl that made some bad choices but didn't deserve to get her throat slashed for them."

A shadowy arm extended and I got a glimpse of a skeletal hand. It pointed to one of the refrigerated drawers. "Look there."

"You're not pulling some Charles Dickens trick on me, are you? You know . . . I open the drawer and see my own body and then I promise to be a good and contrite girl from here on out. Is that it?"

"Look."

I crossed the room to the drawer. Thankfully the tag on its face didn't have *my* name; instead it read "Amos, Theodore." I grabbed the handle and had to leverage all of my weight against the handle to coax the slab into motion.

A clean, white shroud covered the body like he was lying in bed trying to avoid morning light. For Theodore Amos, though, morning would never come. That thought left me feeling desperately empty. I carefully pulled back the shroud and a bloodless face stared blankly up at me. He looked depressed, as if death left him frozen in a moment of despair.

And then I heard the voice.

His pale lips never moved, the voice was just there—pleading into the chilled air.

"Can you hear me?" he called, "Please, God tell me you can hear me! Please!"

I took a step backward but I couldn't look away and as I withdrew the pleading only grew more desperate.

"No, don't go—please help me! Wait, please—"

"This is why you are here, Melody Rush. Eternity trapped inside a corpse, deaf and paralyzed. Imagine your voice echoing in the cavern of your coffin while every moment you are aware of the decay that violates and consumes you—"

"Stop it . . ." All my wit and smart-alecky retorts had left with most of my strength and the words came out as less a command and more a plea. My companion didn't listen. He hovered at the edge of Amos' drawer.

"Forever you lie in the dark. Insanity would be a blessing if it could only erase the fact that for eternity you were bound to the fetid flesh—"

"Stop it!" This time my voice echoed off the tile and when it died the only sound was Amos' pleading.

"I cannot stop it." His skeletal hand reached out to the prone body but as it drew closer his boney fingers became more insubstantial until, as if carried back by a wind, he withdrew. "It is my place to stop this—but I cannot."

"At least stop the play-by-play, then. This isn't some damned baseball game."

Death's smoky shadow lingered close to the drawer again. "You are the only one who can put an end to this abomination, Melody Rush."

"Me? Why me? I'm nobody—"

"To the dead you are somebody."

Inside his drawer, Amos had begun to sob and howl. It started eating into my consciousness. His desperation dragged me down into a spiral of despair that destroyed my ability to think until I had to blurt out, "For God sake, could you do something about him?"

Wordlessly my escort raised a shadowy arm and we were back amid the terrible winds of the plain of ash. I never knew I could feel grateful to be anyplace as dismal as that.

"You asked to be shown."

I didn't need that kind of reminder. For a brief moment I found myself wondering if the power behind those robes might be my mother. That was a horrible thought. Almost as bad as the next question I had to ask. "Shouldn't I be in a drawer right next to Theo, howling and wailing too? I mean Fleck shot me and I fell off a bridge and into a frozen creek. You said that was my undoing . . ."

"By my grace you are in between, not living, not dead."

"You'll have to forgive my saying so, but that's not exactly a satisfying answer."

"It is what—"

"I know the spiel. Why aren't you doing your job? I mean, you're supposed to be seeing the souls of the dead off to their final destinations, not leaving them trapped."

"I cannot." The shadows receded and the winds howled. "I am . . . not whole."

"Care to elaborate? 'Not whole' kind of covers a lot of ground."

"Something was taken from me. Without it I cannot fulfill my purpose."

"I see. What does that have to do with me? I'm just another soul needing ushering who's not going to get where they're going."

"You are different. You are attuned to the dead and you have a talent. A gift for finding things out."

"Whoa, you're kidding, right? You think I'm some kind of detective? There's got to be some other lost soul out there you can recruit. Maybe an actual detective, like a cop or something? Why don't you—"

"I must be made whole before the turn of the year. Should the old year expire before I am restored, I will lose dominion and what you witnessed will be the destiny for all humanity."

"But surely before—"

"None knows fate better than I, you are the one chance."

I glared at him. I'm not sure how you argue that some better qualified detective will kick before December 31, especially when you're debating Death. I hate losing arguments.

"All right, I'll help. So what now?"

The shadow oozed forward. "You must find what was stolen from me. To you it will appear to be a mask. It was taken on the first of November while I attended to the soul of a man named

Alfonzo Arnie."

The shadow stretched out toward me and before I could react a bony finger had touched my forehead. The sensation was like being pierced by an icicle and the ashen world went wobbly. Death's voice reverberated inside my head like a discordant bell.

"I renounce my claim upon you, Melody Rush. Your old life dies here but you are reborn unto a new and strange world, nonetheless, so take heed of that."

When the sound of Death's voice faded I was back in Manchester, lying half out of the icy drainage ditch, thrashing while somebody screamed at me. It took a few seconds to realize the person yelling was a cop and a few more seconds to understand he was trying to help me. He said something about an ambulance but I couldn't focus on his words of reassurance. All I could think about was how damn cold it was and, for some reason, how awful I must look. I closed my eyes and one of my mother's tirades about the importance of first impressions began to cycle through my brain. Blacking out was a relief.

3

My eyes opened to a gently folded expanse of a green hospital curtain and the sense I wasn't alone. Ever watch one of those cheap horror movies? The teenage couple is parked on lover's lane, necking, and suddenly the girl gets the feeling something's wrong. It's an ESP thing that only works just before something really horrible happens. Well, it's that way for me whenever my mother descends on my life. Lying there, I could feel her presence even without looking.

"Finally, you're awake."

Don't move, I thought, just sit still and maybe she'll think you're in a coma. God, I wish I'd learn to listen to that voice inside my head. After feeling the heat of her stare burning into the side of my head, I just had to look at her.

"You look awful!"

She tells me I look horrible and she's wearing one of those turbans that haven't been in style since Douglas Fairbanks was hot. Not to mention she's dressed in the coat she swears is ermine but looks more like a gorilla pelt poached from the city zoo. At least she was consistent—this was the kind of familial support I'm used to; if I'd gotten more I would have sworn I'd died and this was heaven's recovery room. I closed my eyes and hoped she was a side effect of the medications the hospital had given me.

"Melody, I've been sitting here by your bed for the last twenty-four hours, the least you could do is speak to me."

She'd started sniffling and even with closed eyes I could see the exaggerated dabbing-her-eyes-with-a-hanky show that was playing. No amount of medication could cause hallucinations this horrible.

"I'm all right, Mom." Maybe the docs had packed my mouth with cotton, the words felt like wool when they came out.

"All right? You call getting shot all right?"

"When it's not in any vital organs."

"Oh yes, let's make a joke!"

The show was really kicking into high gear. The next act had to be a firework show and Mom didn't disappoint. Her face reddened and she got louder.

"The police finding you half frozen in a ditch is just peachy! Oh and let's not forget they found you in the worst neighborhood in town, that just adds a little color and excitement."

"Mom—"

"This is a fine way to find a husband, Melody! I know a lot of women who met their mates by getting shot. There's Ma Barker and Bonnie Parker, I'm sure that's how she met Clyde Barrow."

"Mom, you're scaring the other patients."

"They ought to be scared! Who knows what you're going to pull next!"

We'd hit the grand finale. Have a nice evening folks, from here on out it's just the credits. She wrung her handkerchief and almost turned her back on me. Just almost; she wouldn't want the tears to be wasted.

"What was it this time, Melody? Trying to run down one of your friends' deadbeat boyfriends?"

"It wasn't any deadbeat boyfriend, Mom."

"Then what? Tell me, I'm dying to know what's worth getting shot and left for dead?"

"You remember Virginia Beal? That girl in the news—"

"Oh, Melody." More tears.

"Somebody had to find out who killed her—"

"The police, Melody. It's their job, not yours. You're a secretarial school dropout who barely holds down a job selling magazines and foot powder at Beeman's Drugs."

There was a gentle knock and the door opened slightly. "Is everything all right in here?"

The intervening voice was young, male, and belonged to a dark-haired doctor who was standing in the door with a clipboard in hand. Nice looking guy. He'd probably have been even nicer looking if I could have concentrated over the din of my mother's matchmaking machinery kicking into gear.

"Everything's fine—" I didn't get to finish; dear Mother interceded.

"Don't try to be brave, dear." She shot me a frighteningly conspiratorial look. "Just a few seconds ago she was telling me that she felt dizzy."

"I didn't—" She grabbed my hand and squeezed so hard my sentence ended with a yelp.

"See, she's suffering. Can't you take a look, please?"

The doctor walked around the bed and took my hand. His skin was soft and warm and he smelled expensive. Damn my mother.

"Where are these pains?" he asked, dark eyes studying his watch as he measured my pulse.

"At the moment in my ass."

Our eyes met and I gave him my best sweet but apologetic smile. He seemed to read the meaning behind it and he let go of my wrist, turning his attention to my mother.

"Um, Mrs. . . ."

"Rush, Edith Rush." Mom smiled and offered her hand in an all-too-royal way. "What do you think, Doctor . . ."

"James, Dr. James. It's a pleasure to meet you." He accepted

Mom's hand gracefully. "Mrs. Rush, would you mind giving me a few minutes alone with your daughter?"

"Oh, you don't have to shoo me off. I don't mind sitting here and it's not like she's got anything I haven't seen before."

I covered my eyes. Whatever crimes I committed in my former lives must have been heinous to earn this sort of karma. The doc held together though.

"It'll just be a few minutes, Mrs. Rush. I promise, after that you can have your daughter back."

My mother had been beaten back and without so much as a threat. I liked this guy! She collected her purse, mouthed "behave," and then smiled as she backed out of the room. When the door closed I was surrounded by the bliss of relative silence.

"I'm sorry, she means well. At least I think she does. I'd hate to believe that my mom's actually been *trying* to drive me insane all these years."

"Don't worry about it. Browbeating children is definitely part of the motherhood job description. Mine used to say I blew my big chance by choosing medical school over the priesthood."

"Lucky for me you chose a shingle over a priest's collar." Yeah, I actually said that. There's no graceful way to recover from letting a guy know you've been checking him out. A girl's just supposed to keep them guessing. That's the rule and once you've broken the rule you're in big trouble. I did the only thing that came to mind. I took the clumsy way out. "I mean, I think, uh, maybe . . . do you have anything to get the taste of shoe leather out of my mouth?"

He smiled. It was a good smile, genuine and not too many teeth. Guys with big, crocodile smiles either want to get a hand up your dress or they're trying to sell you something. That is, if they're not trying for both. It was hard work avoiding grinning back.

"Sorry, I'll have to call in a podiatrist to help you with that one." He thumped his clipboard on the palm of his hand. "In the meantime, how do you *really* feel, Miss Rush?"

" 'Miss Rush' makes me sound like a bitter old maid." Yeah, so maybe I was thinking of my mother when I said that. Still it was a good recovery after my initial stumble; I even tossed in a nice smile of my own. "Call me Mel, Dr. James."

"Okay, call me Mark and you've got a deal." He set his clipboard aside. "So, Mel, how do you feel . . . without coaching from your mother?"

"Sore and tired. Other than that I guess I'd say generally mediocre with possible upward trends."

"Well, in technical terms you're a lucky woman. The bullet managed to miss just about everything important." He moved from my shoulder to my head and aside from the pain of a bruised scalp, the sensation of his fingers running through my hair was wonderful. "The ice where you fell was pretty thin. A good thing; you could have wound up with a fractured skull or worse."

"There's worse than a fractured skull?"

"A lot worse, you haven't had any nausea, ringing in your ears or anything like that?"

"Just a pretty heinous headache."

"Believe it or not, that's good and I guess it means I'm pretty much done with you. The wound is patched and relatively speaking you seem no worse for wear. I guess this means my rounds are going to be a lot less interesting."

Now I needed resuscitation. I think of myself as tough, but hearing a cute guy, who's actually a doctor, say something like that turned me to butter. I'm glad I don't giggle; that would have blown the whole cool persona I was trying to project.

"Maybe I should get shot more often?"

"I think I'll sleep better if I don't feel responsible for a cute girl getting holes blown in her. How about just coming back to let me check the stitches in a few days?" He finished scribbling notes on his clipboard and tore off the page, handing it to me. "They'll set up a time at the admissions desk. Now, I better get to the rest of my patients before the head nurse sends out a search party."

I smiled at the form full of barely legible scribbling. He might as well have just given me his phone number because the way he talked made me feel like we actually had a date. I was in the middle of imagining that possibility when Mark called me back to reality. He was leaning in the doorway, his voice lowered a conspiratorial half notch.

"Oh, and you might want to know there are a couple of men waiting for you out here. Judging by the cheap suits I'd say they're police."

That did away with daydreaming. The police would want answers and my mother was out there with them—unsupervised.

4

I'm not the sort of girl who sets speed records. Look at me. I've got all the curves of a luxury model, not the sleekness of a sports car. If you want speed, I can introduce you to some of the boney beatnik chicks who hang out at The Quarter. That doesn't mean there aren't certain things that can motivate me to quickness. Like the knowledge of my mother having unfettered access to two of Pittsburgh's finest. I think I set a land-speed record for dressing with one arm in a sling. When I burst out of the recovery room I caught Mom in mid–character assassination.

". . . it's not ladylike, hanging around police stations and bars. People already are talking. God knows what else she's been up to."

What a thing to walk out of your hospital room into: your mom spilling all the shortcomings of your life to two bored-looking homicide detectives. It's a little like finding a mouse in your brassiere drawer. The initial shock is horrible but the implication of all the stuff it's been doing while you were unaware is what really gets you. To make things worse, I recognized both detectives only too well.

When I first started to hear the voices of the dead I kind of lost my bearings. It was easy to do with everyone from former friends down to my mother accusing me of being possessed, deranged, or both. With confidence in me at an all time low, rules kind of lost their potency. When nobody believes in you, why not go all the way? Why not throw out everyone's expectations? I started talking back to anyone who resembled an authority figure and I took up stealing as a pastime. Thievery wasn't a hobby I excelled at. At the age of twenty-one I wound up in front of a judge with a charge of shoplifting. That's when Don Rolland became an integral part of my life.

He'd been a friend of my mother before I ever thought about the concept of a parent *having* friends. Mom talked to Don, Don talked to the store owner, and the charges were dropped with the requirement I get counseling to prevent me from continuing on the road to serious criminal activity. My counselor was a small man in an ill-fitting suit whose long face and oversized round glasses made him look more like a librarian than a cop. Since then my relationship with Rolland had been a weathervane spinning to point out every ill wind that blew into my life.

On Mom's other side stood the newest addition to homicide and a man who could have been my brother in a previous life, Scott Gaines. We grew up together. When we were kids he played the shy, backward counterpoint to my "what the hell, I'll try anything once" extroversion. Together we were the terror of the block. Actually I was the terror; he was just kind of a bystander caught in the crossfire. Back then I never could figure what Mr. Straight Arrow wanted with me. I used to think he secretly wanted to be as bad as me, that he vicariously enjoyed my doing the things he was afraid to try. We went all the way through high school that way, me crashing and him being there to hold the dustpan when the pieces had to be swept up. He graduated from high school right into the family business of being a cop. I floundered around, quitting one thing and trying another until my life came unhinged. I guess you could say our lives finally diverged. Well, at least in terms of career choice.

Even so, Scott would do just about anything I asked. He was

the one who'd brought me a copy of Virginia Beal's file and he helped me pick out the revolver Fleck had taken away on the bridge. Maybe things hadn't changed much since high school. Except now I'd guessed why Scott was willing to follow me right off the edge of every cliff I found. He had what I fondly call a horribly insurmountable crush and, unfortunately for him, the feeling wasn't mutual. I'd thought about setting him straight; he's a good guy and there's surely some cop's wife wannabe out there just waiting for his call. Thing is, it's harder to smash someone's hopes than you might think, even for a girl who's known for smashing just about anything she lays her hands on. So I let it go on. I'd never take advantage of him so it's harmless, right?

I needed to intercede before my dear mother managed to do even more damage than she already had. I took charge and lunged into the conversation.

"Mom, I think the gentlemen are here to talk with me, not hear your opinions about my habits and hangouts."

The look she gave me could have put me back in my hospital bed if I hadn't been immunized against its deadly effects by twenty-some years of living with her. She huffily bundled herself in her mangy coat and collected her purse. "Fine, you talk to her, for what good it'll do!"

She stomped off, muscling an orderly out of the way, knocking into a man with a fistful of flowers, and generally cutting a path of destruction on her way to the elevator. Seeing Mom pushed to the very edge of her wits would have been enjoyable if it hadn't been for her personal advocate, Rolland.

"You know she's right, don't you?" His patented "don't make my day difficult" look played across his brow. "Manchester is a bad neighborhood. That souvenir you collected last night could have landed you in the morgue."

The word morgue brought to mind the wailing corpse Death

had shown me. At this moment Theodore Amos lay trapped in a dark, refrigerated drawer about three stories below where I stood. The thought made my skin crawl so I did the one thing that always made me feel better. I got sarcastic.

"Only cops and mothers would give a girl grief about being attacked and shot." I folded my coat over my sling. "Do we have to do this here? I don't much feel like arguing in public, it might be embarrassing for you."

Scott intervened. "We're just trying to help you out, Mel. Cut us a break, will you?"

"Cut you a break? What about cutting *me* a break? I'm the one who got shot!" I said loud enough to draw attention. Rolland looked uncomfortable but he deserved it almost as much as my mother.

"All right, maybe we should have this discussion somewhere a little more private." Rolland stood, pulling my car keys from his coat pocket. "I'll drive you home and we can talk on the way. How's that for a break?"

I held out a hand for the keys. "I don't need a chauffeur—"

Scott's second attempt to interject himself was cut off when Rolland raised a hand. "You've got two choices, Melody. Either I drive you home or you can come down to the station and we can take an official statement in an interview room. Which would you like?"

I was tired, and in spite of an antiseptic scrubbing I still felt like I was wearing half the scum from that drainage ditch as foundation. The thought that Rolland or one of his cop flunkies had confiscated my keys and driven the LaSalle from Western to the hospital made me uncomfortable. Cops are a little like mothers: when they're presented with an opportunity to snoop they seldom pass it up. I didn't particularly like the idea of Rolland or Scott shaking my car down for "interesting" tidbits. Still, I guess the cops driving my car to the hospital was preferable to leaving it parked in front of Fakey's where it could be stripped to the frame. With a deep sigh I relented.

Scott and Rolland rode the elevator with me down to the lobby. I've been in more talkative libraries: Scott avoided looking at me, I didn't want to look at Rolland, and Rolland idly jingled his car keys until the bell rang and the doors opened. After three floors I would have sworn enough pressure had collected to cause the three of us to shoot out of the elevator and across the lobby like corks discharged from champagne bottles. Instead Rolland silently headed for the parking lot and Scott followed me as I turned toward the main entrance.

Hospitals never have been my favorite place. There's the usual implication of sickness, something that makes everyone a little uneasy, and for me there's a second layer of general unpleasantness consisting of disembodied spirits. I guess it makes sense. I mean, if a lot of people die in a specific place it's logical their spirits would roam the hallways and hang out in the waiting rooms with their loved ones. When I told my mom I'd been chatting with ghosts, the first place she took me was the hospital. I wouldn't call the experience therapeutic.

That day a guy who looked like he'd lost a fight with a hatchet was sitting on one of the uncomfortable benches just inside the main doors, waiting for something that'd lost all importance. It might have been a bus or a cab, I couldn't be sure. The only thing I did know was he'd never make his appointment because he was dead.

I found a seat just inside the hospital's main doors and surveyed the lobby. Today the population of ghosts seemed distinctly smaller. There were no disembodied accident victims lingering around the check-in desk or mutilated ghosts hanging around the curb outside the main entrance; in fact, if I ignored the few shades repeating the meaningless rituals of their eternal existence, I could nearly pretend to be normal. The memory of

Death's tour of the morgue kept the experience from being refreshing. I thought about Amos suffering in his drawer and wondered how many other spirits were trapped inside bodies that doctors were futilely attempting to resuscitate or covered with sheets on gurneys in the hospital's maze of hallways and rooms. I was pondering the possibilities when Scott settled on the bench beside me and gave me a sidelong look.

"You scare the hell out of me sometimes, Mel."

I didn't look at him. "You're still sitting beside me so I can't scare you too bad."

"I'm sitting here because I'm worried about you. The stunt you pulled could have gotten you killed."

"People get killed crossing the street, Scott."

"Maybe, but that's not the same thing as going up to Manchester after some lowlife pimp." Peripherally, I saw him look away. "Why can't you . . ."

Oh no, I don't let people get away with starting an insulting remark and then trailing off. I turned to face him. "Why can't I what, Scott? Be like other women? Why can't I satisfy myself with an apron and husband and not worry my pretty little head over serious man stuff like getting murderers off the streets? Is that what you were going to ask?"

"Actually, I was going to ask why you can't be a little more careful."

Oops. Two shoe sole snacks in one day. I wish I could honestly claim that was some kind of personal record, but it fell far short of the mark. I put a hand on his shoulder. "I'm sorry. Blame my mother. I just spent a half hour listening to all the things she thinks are wrong with me. I guess it made me a little defensive. I really do appreciate the concern even if it doesn't seem that way sometimes."

"Eh, don't worry about it. I've got broad shoulders."

The LaSalle pulled up in front of the doors with Rolland

behind the wheel. He reached across the seat and opened the door, then sat waiting for me to emerge. Scott stood and, like the good Boy Scout he is, took my hand to help me up.

"Hey, do me a favor and remember Rolland doesn't know I gave you a copy of the Beal file." He stood and straightened his coat and we started outside. "I'd like to maintain my anonymity and job if you know what I mean."

"Got it, Mel no talk. Any further orders?"

"Just try to stay safe. At least until you have a chance to heal."

We crossed the cold expanse of sidewalk between the hospital doors and my car, and once I'd gotten inside, Scott shut me in with Rolland, then started for the squad car that had pulled up on the LaSalle's bumper. It felt wrong just being a passenger in my own car. Ask Scott and he'll tell you I don't take to a lack of control very well. Lots of men, especially older ones, feel it's their sworn duty to get behind the wheel. Normally that'd earn a guy some serious lip from me but with Rolland I know it's pointless. I did my best to relax as we pulled out of the hospital lot and made a left into traffic. About a block later the questions started.

"So, could you tell me exactly what you were doing on that footbridge last night, Melody?"

"Oh, aside from finding the man who killed Virginia Beal last spring, not much."

"Really? Care to share the identity of your suspect?"

"His name is Richard Fleck, he was Virginia's pimp and I'm pretty sure he's the one that cut her throat."

Rolland was silent for a second which meant wheels were grinding what I'd said into a digestible paste. "Pretty sure isn't the same as having evidence that will stand up in court."

"I'm sure as I can be. I mean he didn't confess or anything."

"Did this Fleck person shoot you?"

"Yes."

He glanced at me and then made a right, heading for my apartment. "I'll swear out a warrant and we'll bring him in. While I'm at it, I should have you hauled in for interfering with an ongoing investigation."

"Ongoing investigation? You know there were no leads on Virginia's killer."

"I do but the question is how do you? It wouldn't have anything to do with your buddy, Detective Gaines, would it?"

I did my best derisive snort. "Why would it have anything to do with him?"

"I might be an old bachelor but that doesn't mean I don't recognize the look that comes to a fellow's eye when a lady rouses his interest. I'm here to tell you, Scott Gaines gets that look whenever you're around."

Nice try, old man. "Whatever look you thought you saw in Scott's eyes has nothing to do with our discussion. Look, back in the summer the whole world decided that Virginia got what she deserved because she was a street walker. Why would the police department invest time and shoe leather pursuing a low-profile case like Virginia Beal at the expense of killings the police commissioner finds more politically palatable?"

He shook his head. "You've got a low opinion of me and my department."

"It has nothing to do with my opinion. I understand reality. Maybe I never sank as low as Virginia did but I got on the wrong side of public opinion just enough to know the routine. It's easier to pretend the misfits don't exist than it is to examine what they imply about the society that created them."

"Maybe, but sweeping condemnations aside, you still nearly got yourself killed and if this Fleck is Virginia Beal's killer you probably sent him so far underground we'll never find him again."

Crap. That took the wind out of me. What if Fleck skipped town or headed for Mexico? Cluing her killer in to the fact somebody had caught onto his crime was a wonderful way to help Virginia. I might as well have bought Fleck a plane ticket.

Around noon Rolland stopped at the curb in front of my uncle's garage. Yes, I said *garage*. To be specific, it's Manny's Auto and Body and the aforementioned Manny would be my uncle on my dad's side. Manny has owned and operated the garage on Locust Street since he got out of the Marines. In the service he'd run a motor pool and before that he was a high school dropout, so about the only thing in his blood is forty-weight oil. The garage is a squat building with two repair bays, a fenced lot on its north side, and a one bedroom apartment I call home upstairs.

At the sight of the squad car pulling up to the curb, mechanics began sliding from under the hulks they'd been repairing and clambering out of grease pits. Any excuse to stop working was sure to bring them out, and my arrival qualified. They collected on the sidewalk, leaning against the building and gawking. Seeing them intensified my headache. I didn't need to re-explain the last twenty-four hours to every wrench-monkey who worked for my uncle. Rolland didn't take notice of the crowd, though.

"So, you won't be going on any more jaunts to Manchester?" Rolland leaned an arm on the back of the seat and gave me a steady, serious stare. "Right?"

I ignored him, opting to give the cluster of greasy mechanics a searing glare instead.

"Melody, do we have an understanding?"

"Yeah, sure." I opened the passenger door and stepped out before he could do something stupid like congratulate me on my common sense. The day had already been bad enough without having to feign obedience.

The sight of a black-and-white pulling up behind my old Cadillac had emptied the garage of any straggling greasers. The sidewalk resembled a police lineup: a hard bunch of tattooed greasers with more than a little jail time among them standing against a wall, chewing their toothpicks, each one trying to look tougher than the guy next to him. Living above the garage was like having a half dozen hard-assed big brothers downstairs. They could be sweet but they weren't very good at it and generally they played hell with a girl's social life. They stood there, giving Rolland evil looks until Manny noticed how quiet things had gotten and emerged from his office, storming out into the daylight.

"Hey! I'm not paying you bums to hold the sidewalk down! Get back to work."

Manny sounds and looks a little like a bullfrog but damn, I love the guy. He's a bona fide saint: Manny of the Greasy Hands, the calm ark that floats above my mother's judgmental flood. Three years ago, when I reached my limit with Mom, he let me have the apartment above his garage and for half what he could have charged any other renter. The only catch was that he got to raid my fridge for lunch and sometimes dinner when he worked late. Hell, cooking three meals a day for him still would have been a bargain.

He strode out onto the sidewalk, casting a wake of grease monkeys to either side. His gaze had shifted from slacking mechanics to Rolland.

"You okay, Mel?"

Another thing I love about Uncle Manny, he's the only relative I have who gets the fact I hate being called "Melody."

"I'm fine. The good detective didn't think I was fit to drive so he was kind enough to help out."

Rolland smiled at Manny. "How's business?"

I never bought the nice cop. In my time being "counseled,"

Rolland shared his opinion of my uncle. In his eyes, Manny was no better than the guys he employed and Rolland thought they all were deviants and delinquents. Rolland thought the jobs at the garage just gave thugs money for booze, dope, and weapons.

"Business is fine. Thanks for driving the girl home, I think we can get along from here." Manny didn't hide his distain of Rolland very well. His tone was polite but the words were clipped and the underlying message said bug off. It was a sentiment I definitely got behind and one Rolland caught onto from the look on his face.

"All right." Rolland dropped the car keys in my palm. "Take care of yourself, Melody. Try to remember what I said, will you?"

"I promise." Remembering and abiding by are two different things.

Rolland climbed into the cruiser with Scott and as it pulled away from the curb, Manny relaxed momentarily before stepping into the surrogate father role he'd inhabited since Dad was killed. He looked me over and shook his head. "You got to stop doing things like this, kid. I'm gettin' too old to take this stuff."

How's that for compassion? Not so much as a "glad to see you" or "I worried myself sick" before launching into telling me how to run my life. I did say I loved him, right?

"Spare me the speech. I've already had two of them this morning."

"Mel—"

"What? Are you in competition with Mom for the biggest pain in my ass trophy? Don't you think I've been questioned enough already? Don't you think I've already heard how stupid I am and how I ought to be worrying about matching shoes and purses instead of nosing around after a murderer?"

No, he didn't deserve that. Manny can be a lout, and underneath my hurt feelings I knew it was his awkward way of showing how much he cared. The problem was, I didn't feel like enduring his clumsy attempts at tenderness. I was mad at my mother, mad at Rolland, and generally mad at the world. That was my excuse and it was a damn valid one. Unfortunately, as soon as I'd shot my mouth off I knew I'd just kicked the person who least deserved my ire. The garage fell silent. The last time I remember it being that quiet, it was closed. Some mechanics discretely watched the family conflict from behind fenders and hoods while their less couth companions stood and stared openly. I'm sure it was a sight, the big ex-Marine being taken down a peg by a five-foot-nothing woman.

Manny took a step back. "Sorry, I'll get back to work and let you be."

"Uncle Manny, I just need some rest. I'm okay, everything's okay." I hugged him, submerging myself in the comforting scent of gasoline and cigar smoke that clung to him, but he was stiff. Fixing my faux pas would take some time. I climbed the stairs to my apartment, feeling like a real heel, not least because I'd already accepted his offer to have one of his boys pull the La-Salle around to the side lot where it would be safe.

5

I woke sometime after eight o'clock and dragged myself to the kitchen to investigate the confines of my refrigerator. The prospects weren't promising. I was getting dangerously close to violating the "keep the refrigerator stocked" clause of my renter's contract. As much as I dreaded it, a visit to the grocery store loomed in the near future. Tonight, though, dinner would be Swiss with mayo on white bread.

I ate while debating the pile of smelly clothes I'd discarded when I came home from the hospital. I'd dumped everything on the kitchen floor. Nothing could be salvaged: my angora sweater was matted and bloodstained, the seat of my pencil skirt was caked with greasy muck, and the wide belt that'd tied the outfit together so well had started to come apart at the seams. Burning everything seemed to be the most humane course of action. I peered out the curtains down into the garage's fenced lot to make sure everyone had gone home. The last thing I needed was an audience when I tossed my unmentionables in the incinerator. I finished the sandwich, put the plate in the sink, and bundled everything up for the trip downstairs.

When I was a kid the incinerator had a certain cachet. Every time I took a load of garbage out for burning I felt like a secret agent disposing of the evidence of my clandestine activities. Maybe I'm still a kid or maybe burning a load of underwear and bloody clothing seems particularly salacious. Regardless of which was truer, I stoked the flames and stood bathing in the warmth of burning fashion while listening to the sounds of the city. As I stared through the veil of firelight I saw a shadow pass through the fence and enter the lot, drifting toward me. By the time the firelight died down, the figure was nearly standing by my side.

It was a woman dressed in a simple flowered dress in the muted blacks and grays of death. Her unruly hair cascaded over her pale shoulders that lay bare from the rips in the dress's bodice, and one curly lock fell in a casual, dark *S* between her plucked eyebrows. Her eyes reflected nothing—not the glow of the fire or the streetlight that stood at the corner of the lot. They stared hopelessly past the world into somewhere cold and bleak.

"Hello, Virginia." I prodded the burning lump of fabric into new life.

"Why?"

The syllable was blunted by the gaping wound in Virginia's throat. If she weren't a ghost, her dress and neck would have been bright red but, as I'd learned over the years, death robbed its victims of everything, right down to the color of their blood. A dark echo of lifeblood spread down the front of her dress and dribbled off its hem in droplets that vanished before they reached the gravel she hovered above.

I swallowed the sorrow that welled up in my throat at seeing her. "Why? I don't know. I'm doing my best to find that out for you."

As usual she ignored my response, opting to whisper another question. "Where is he?"

"I'm trying to find him, Virginia, but I need more help." I drew nearer her ghost and the air grew perceptibly colder. "Does Fleck have a hiding place that you know? Maybe somewhere he holes up when the police are looking for him?"

45

"Where is he?" she repeated, staring through me into the night.

"Please, Virginia. I'm trying to help you but I need more information."

"Why?" She began to fade, her stomach becoming a window to the empty lot behind her.

There was no point in responding to her question. Some ghosts were just shadows, some were conversationalists, and Virginia fell frustratingly between those two poles. She dropped clues but didn't give answers. She disappeared, leaving a hole in my heart and tears in my eyes. Why the hell did I think I could catch her killer? Obviously the only thing I might accomplish was making a ghost of myself. This was ridiculous; who did I think I was, the Mata Hari of the homicide set?

I kicked the incinerator door closed and it slammed with a hollow clang, loosing a cloud of sparks that spiraled up into the night sky. All the way back to the garage my mind raced between two inescapable facts: I had no way of helping Virginia and I couldn't let her down. These truths stood in stalemate with me paralyzed between them. It made my head hurt nearly as much as the bruises I got from falling off the footbridge last night, and that brought up another little obligation. I'd agreed to help Death with a little problem.

I went inside through the garage's side door. Compared to the bitter crispness of the winter air outside, the warm smell of cars in repose was welcoming. At least I had information to work with in Death's case. I had a name, Alfonzo Arnie, and the day he'd died. It wasn't much, but working with it was better than feeling helpless over Virginia until it drove me to shelter in a bourbon bottle. Working on a case with leads would be good for my soul.

I surveyed the garage; Manny was horrible for saving junk. Maybe it was growing up in the Depression. In the thirties he'd been old enough that having nothing actually left a mark, or maybe he had some sort of wiring problem upstairs. Whichever was the case, Manny kept the garage storeroom stuffed with things he just wouldn't part with. There were boxes of ratty shirts and torn pants destined to become rags, coffee cans of screws, sheets of scrap metal, and orange crates filled with newspapers. The papers were what I needed to start my investigation. I rummaged until I found the evening editions from November through December 1, and with them tucked under my arm, I headed upstairs.

Wrapped in my favorite, electric-blue kimono robe and sipping a cup of strong coffee that'd been fortified with a shot of whiskey, I settled in at the kitchen table for some research. Some people make it a point to read the obituaries. For me, seeing the dead every day kind of makes me lean toward the funnies. Who wants to read about the dead when you can chat with them in person? The obituaries were where I'd find Arnie, though, so I started on November 1 and worked my way forward. I found him in the November 10 edition. The obituary was pretty pathetic. He'd been forty-eight with no living relatives. There was no mention of a service and nothing about losing a long battle with any kind of dread illness or meeting with an untimely accident.

I turned to the crime-beat section.

The story was sandwiched between an ad for snow tires and a piece about the Fraternal Order of Police's Marching Tuba Troopers' preparations for marching in Eisenhower's inaugural parade. With typical journalistic hyperbole, the headline proclaimed "Grisly Murder Rocks Suburban Peace" above a picture of cops standing outside the door of a one-story rambler. I read on: "The idyllic little neighborhood of Sunnyvale was thrown into a state of fear Monday morning when the body of a man, throat slashed, was found in the kitchen of a one-story home at the corner of Woodford and Vine . . ." The piece went on to tell how the postman noticed a gamey aroma emanating from the house that reminded him of his days serving with the infantry during the war. He called the police and they found Arnie lying faceup on the kitchen floor in a pool of blood, his throat neatly slit. The article went on to say the investigators found no evidence of forced entry and there were no suspects. I paged through the rest of the papers without finding mention of progress on the case.

The thought of attempting to break into the murder house passed through my mind. Generally speaking, I know my limitations. Mom might disagree with that statement but it's the truth. For example, I'm fully aware it'd be pretty stupid to go trying to play cat burglar with my strong arm in a sling. Ever try to climb through a window in the dark, one-armed? It might be something fit for an episode of *I Love Lucy* but my goal in life isn't to wind up as an amusing anecdote in the police blotter. Common sense prevailed and I decided the first step would be just to drive by Arnie's house. Luckily, these bouts of rationality don't happen often and they're pretty short-lived.

It was a twenty-minute drive to Sunnyvale. Outside the confines of the city I started feeling agoraphobic; the countryside was too open and driving along at nearly midnight gave every house a sinister appearance. I'd read too many of the magazines Manny gets, the ones where a couple out for a country drive encounter a flying saucer and are taken away by creatures with bug eyes and misshapen heads. With barren fields stretching out in all directions and the darkness becoming more impenetrable by the second, the possibilities started working on me. It was a relief when my headlights illuminated the WELCOME TO SUNNY-VALE sign that stood outside the entrance to Alfonzo's old neighborhood.

I slowed the LaSalle and pulled into the neighborhood. Sunnyvale was a genuine Levittown-style hell by any definition. Every house, mailbox, and gently inclining driveway was the same and all perfectly manicured doubtlessly by happy homemakers who wore pearls and danced about doing their chores with a smile on their lips and a song in their hearts. It was the world as seen on the pages of *Devoted Housewife*, *Home Lovely*, and every other woman's magazine Beeman's drugstore carried, and in 3-D it was much worse. I tried to keep my mind on the reason I'd come to this suburban nightmare. Is it wrong that thinking about a dead man made me feel better?

Two blocks into the subdivision I caught Vine; it was yet another nondescript street lined with nondescript houses in the colors of Neapolitan ice cream. It led me down a small hill to where Woodford came in, forming a tee. There, in the corner lot, was the house. I parked the LaSalle and stepped out for a little late-night walk.

A well-kept lawn fronted the house. Hedges nestled into its foundation, anchoring flowerbeds that undulated artfully, softening the building's right angles. Obviously a lot of details about Alfonzo Arnie hadn't made the last edit of his obituary. The single tree that stood in the front lawn was ringed with scalloped clay tiles that matched those running along the walk that led up to the doorway. Two steps ascended to the front door. A pair of concrete urns flanked the steps. Doubtless they overflowed with flowers during the summer. The place looked ideal: the perfect image of the suburban dream. Near the mailbox that stood at the end of the walk was a brightly painted sign reading MCCRACKEN REAL ESTATE with an agent's name and phone number.

I could picture my mother living here. In fact, it was hard to imagine the former owner had been the victim of a bloody murder. I was mulling over that thought when an explosion of yapping jolted me back into the present.

"Heinrich!"

A dachshund strained at the end of its leash, forepaws digging at the air as it snorted and growled. The man doing the restraining was elderly and dressed in a brown overcoat. Judging from his unfastened goulashes, this was the dog's last patrol before bedtime.

"Sorry, miss." He reeled in the leash to Heinrich's disapproval. "He thinks he owns the whole neighborhood."

I smiled at the old man, praying he didn't think I looked suspicious. "I can tell. It sounds like he'd like to do me serious harm."

"That dog couldn't do serious harm to his own fleas." He nodded in the direction of Arnie's old house. "You, uh, like the place?"

"It's okay I guess. Why?"

He looked confused. "Well, you are looking at it, aren't you?"

Crap, what was I saying about not appearing suspicious? I backpedaled, trying not to get flustered by my initial gaff.

"Oh, yes. Actually I was."

"I thought so." He smiled. "We could be neighbors!"

"Maybe." I let a little flirtiness seep into my voice and draped an arm across the top of the real estate sign. "You wouldn't be able to give a girl some insight, would you?"

He shrugged. "What do you want to know?"

"Just about the house. It's been on the market for a while, hasn't it?"

"Maybe a month without any serious lookers. You'd think with all the GIs looking to start families it would have sold by now."

Maybe people didn't like the idea of starting their nuclear family in a murder house. I surveyed the darkened windows.

"Do you know anything about the former owner?"

"Not much. He worked in the yard a lot but he hardly ever even said hello. He wasn't the friendly sort." He leaned in close enough for Heinrich to start giving my shoes a serious sniffing. "Someone killed him, you know."

"You don't say!"

I tried to act startled. People expect that kind of reaction when they tell you "shocking" news. If you don't give them the start they expect, they start thinking something's wrong with you.

"Yep." He pulled the dog back. "Remember that when your husband makes an offer. Might save you two a few hundred dollars!"

"Thanks so much, I'll do just that!" The old guy had no idea who he was dealing with and that was just the way I wanted it. I glanced at my wristwatch. "Speaking of my husband, I better be off! He'll be getting off his shift at the mill soon and I don't want him coming home to an empty dinner table!"

"Well then, good luck!"

He waved as I drove away. Heinrich wasn't so cordial. He pissed on the real estate sign and gave me a snarl.

6

I chose something frilly for the occasion, a red dress with a distracting plunging neckline I hoped would make men dumb enough to answer any question put to them in the right tone. For the day I was Mrs. Lolly, wife of William M. Lolly, a big-shot with a lot of money for me to spend. A paste ring the size of a doorknob completed the costume. With one last check of my makeup, I was off to check out a murder scene.

When I pulled up in front of the house, an egg-shaped man in a bottle-green suit stood on the front step. Partially he was waiting because his name was on the real estate sign in the front lawn. I also had intentionally shown up fifteen minutes late. A girl ought to make a fellow wait, especially when he's not a love interest. By the time I rechecked my makeup in the mirror, adjusted my scarf, and collected my handbag he was standing with a hand on the car door, waiting to open it for me.

"Mrs. Lolly, I presume?"

From the smell of onions on this guy I guarantee that's all I'd ever let him presume! Still I smiled demurely; the ever-obedient wife of William Lolly was that way . . . outwardly demure.

"That's me." When I got out of the car I realized he was a full head shorter than me. The cleavage was going to be work-ing overtime. "And you must be Mr. Bussman?"

"Aw, please call me Herb." His hand went into his suit jacket after a business card, but he already was looking past me, scanning the car for the husband he'd expected to be accompanying me. I interceded, stopping him before he could voice the question.

"Willy was called away to New York." Ever notice how people with money are always getting called off to New York? At least in the movies I've seen they do. Hopefully Bussman watched the same ones. "Something about a merger or buyout. I tell you, all that business talk doesn't make a whit of sense to me."

I added a little "poor dumb me" blink for flavor and judging from Bussman's smile he liked the taste. A hint of disappointment lingered in his eyes. I'm sure in his pudgy brain a commission check had just escaped, winging its way into the sunset. Time to shoot that bird down; I needed him focused on imagined rewards, not losses.

"He said I should go ahead with the house shopping. He might be the big boss on Wall Street but, confidentially, left to his own the poor guy can't boil water! He'll just gloss over the house I recommend."

Herb's smile sharpened. It was a disturbing effect; in that green suit he kind of looked like a deranged leprechaun.

"I guess it can't hurt to show you around; this place is an amazing deal and you won't believe the closet space!"

I nodded and smiled as Herb talked but I didn't hear a word after closet space. I didn't come to hear salesman drivel; I came to see the spot where Alfonzo Arnie died.

Herb led the way to the front step, taking a moment to hold me back as a rampaging trio of preteens stormed up the sidewalk clad in cowboy hats and armed with popguns. From the outside, the house looked nearly identical to every other one on the street: charcoal-grey shingles, white aluminum siding, and those stupid fake shutters flanking every window. Herb fumbled with a jumbo key ring, never pausing his spiel. He said something about the local schools, I think, but I was concentrating on murder. He opened the door and stepped aside with a grand sweep of his hand and a bright smile.

"Ladies first!"

There was a note of poorly executed flirtation in his tone. Men like Herb pay for sex; they don't win it with wit, handsomeness, and virility. It was kind of pitiful, but only if you felt sorry about pudgy salesmen not getting lucky.

"What a gentleman!" With a flicker of a smile I stepped over the threshold into a furnished living room. "I thought the property was vacant. Did I read the listing wrong?"

I turned around to face Herb and caught his eyes darting upward. He'd been caught ogling the goods and a blush rose to his sallow cheeks.

"It . . . well, we left the furniture to show off how the place might look once you've moved in."

I surveyed the room: dark leather furniture and earth-toned throw rugs played off walls that probably never saw a picture frame. The air smelled of stale cigars and cigarettes, just like Uncle Manny's office, but that was in the back of a garage, not in the suburbs. Who did he think was moving in, the Masons?

"It could use a woman's touch."

"Oh, I don't know—your husband might like the manly, club look." He patted the back of a leather chair, probably an attempt to accent its manliness.

"He also might like paying alimony, but I doubt it." Judging by the way his hand slid back to his side, that statement threw cold water on Herb. I didn't want him getting the idea I was too submissive; it would be better if he saw me as a young, dangerous wife with an intriguing unpredictable streak. I stepped into the middle of the room and turned around in a circle. "A married couple lived here?"

"No, I think it was single man."

I knew the answer but I wanted his confirmation. It was a

gateway question that led to more information about the house's former inhabitant. "What sort of man?"

"Pardon?"

"I mean what does he do for a living?"

Herb looked flustered; doubtless there were kitchen counters, pantries, and other womanly features of the home he wanted to show off but here I was asking about the house's previous owner. "I really don't know."

Another innocent smile, this time mingled with gently massaging the back of one of the leather chairs. "Well, you are selling the house for him. Didn't you meet with him, talk to him, and ask questions?"

"We do, well, the main office does. Why don't I show you the kitchen?" Herb asked, circumventing me physically and conversationally as he crossed the room. "You'll love this, all gas and really built for modern living."

Apparently Herb's idea of "modern living" resembled a gigantic checker game. The floor was tiled in black and white squares with the white being picked up by the cabinets and appliances. Herb knew his craft; there were women who would have been transported to dreams of turkey dinners and impossibly perfect chocolate cakes at the sight of the stove and oven with their gleaming chrome and myriad dials. I've never met any of those women, but I hear they exist.

Herb opened cabinets and expounded on storage space while I made a circuit of the room. The living room smelled like a barroom but the kitchen smelled faintly of bleach. The combo didn't seem right. Halfway around the room I discovered a curiosity: though the kitchen had been scrubbed and was impeccably clean the grout around the tiles in one corner was stained. The borders of the stain traced the outline of a pool—the pool of blood Alfonzo Arnie lay in until his body had been discovered.

". . . there's a lazy Susan too, uh, Mrs. Lolly?"

I didn't turn to face him; I stared down at the stain. "What's this?"

Herb left his cabinets, taking a few steps toward me before stopping. "It looks like something was spilled. Every house is going to have a few nicks and dents if it's not custom built."

I ran my toe along the border of the stain almost expecting Arnie's ghost to stroll through the wall to give me the details of his murder. Of course, I knew he couldn't; like the poor man Death showed me in the morgue, his spirit was trapped in his corpse.

"You know, I read something about a man getting killed in this area. It might have even been in this neighborhood." Herb's smile wasn't quite as sharp when I met his eye. "Do you think it might have happened right here in this house?"

"Really, I don't think so. I mean, I don't know, I just sell houses. Besides, does it really matter? I mean you're not going to find a better house in a better neighborhood at this price, Mrs. Lolly." He recovered his salesman's smile. "Anyway, you don't go in for that superstitious stuff, do you?"

I could introduce him to a few ghosts who'd gladly clear up any questions he might have about whether they existed. Then again, if anyone else could actually see ghosts I wouldn't have spent a good part of my childhood fearing banishment to a mental institution. I did my best impression of a gossip-craving female.

"I'm not superstitious but it is interesting, isn't it? I mean I just love the whole police detective crime story thing, don't you? It's got a certain, I don't know, romance to it."

"I don't know—"

"Oh, come on, Herb. Spill!" I let a little giddiness seep into my tone. Nothing macabre, just enough to make it seem that a murder occurring in the house would bolster his chances of making the sale. "This is the house; the murder happened right here, didn't it?"

"Well, mostly we just get houses like this on auction, I mean somebody doesn't keep up their payments and the bank puts the place on the block." Herb glanced over his shoulder like he expected his boss to jump out of the Kelvinator. "Sometimes we get houses that are put on auction because the owner has, you know, passed. Some of the fellows down at the office told me that this guy who owned this house, this Arnie fellow, was found right here in this kitchen with his throat cut. So, there's your crime drama, and at no extra charge!"

"So why was he killed?"

"I wish I could tell you but, like I said, I'm just the salesman. Hey, speaking of selling points, let me show you this backyard. This being a corner lot there's lots of room to start a family." Herb caught my elbow and hauled me toward the back door in spite of my best attempts to thwart him. He opened the interior door and shoved me in front of it. "Plenty of room all right, that husband of yours can put up a slide and maybe build a nice playhouse for the kids. Do you want to take a walk around?"

He reached for the storm door but I fended off his hand. "No, really. It's kind of muddy and these are new shoes."

Herb chuckled. "I understand, still you won't find a nicer hunk of Kentucky bluegrass in this whole development."

Yeah, that's what I wanted, Kentucky bluegrass. After dealing with this guy I was going to need Kentucky bourbon and a lot of it. I stood there considering liquor on ice when I was suddenly confronted by a feline face pressed against the glass.

"Hey! Let me in!" The cat demanded as it stared up at me.

I couldn't help it; before I checked the shock I'd taken a step away from the door and a gasp had escaped my lips.

"What, what's the matter?" Herb peered out at the lawn.

I pointed at the cat.

"Lady, open the door already, it's cold out here," the creature pleaded.

"The cat?"

"Didn't you hear it?" Herb looked at me as if he was trying to decide exactly how to react but I didn't wait for him. "Didn't you hear it ask to be let in?"

"Aw, come on lady!" The cat said, pawing at the glass as if trying to get my attention.

"Ask to be . . ." Herb squinted at the cat then looked back at me. This time he wore a humor-the-crazy-lady-without-blowing-this-sale smile. "Yeah, he does seem to want in, you do want in, don't you little fellow?"

The cat growled, "C'mon buddy, knock off the goofy looks and open this freaking door, it's cold out here!"

"See . . . there, did you hear that?" I pointed at the cat as if I could have put my fingers on the words that'd come out of its mouth as evidence.

"Who wouldn't hear it? There's a tomcat in my neighborhood, sits on the fence howling and yowling all night long. It makes me crazy sometimes!" Herb laughed nervously and turned his attention to the cat. "Go on, scat! Go home! He's probably got a home somewhere around here, just looking for a free handout."

"Let me in my house, you witless moron!"

"I really think it wants in," I offered.

"Yeah, well, a swift kick will take care of—"

Herb opened the door but I intercepted him with my good arm and in the midst of the confusion the cat darted between his legs, scampering through the kitchen and out of sight.

"Aww, see what you made me do? Now I'm going to have to chase that animal down." He glanced at his wristwatch. "And I've got a two thirty."

"He just wanted in out of the cold; besides, I think he lives here." I was pleading a cat's case with a salesman? My life definitely had taken a bad turn.

"*Lived*," Herb corrected. "It might have *lived* here but not anymore." He stalked out of the room with me in pursuit. We found the cat in the bathroom, pacing.

"Where the hell is my bowl? Is he trying to starve me or something? Is this some kind of sick game?"

I seemed to be the only one who understood; apparently to my companion the meows were just, well, meows.

"Come on, buster, you've caused enough trouble for one day." Herb seized on the cat's distraction and grabbed it by the scruff of the neck.

"No water and no, hey! Ow!"

"Don't do that, you're hurting him!" I protested, blocking Herb's exit from the bathroom.

"Look Mrs. Lolly, I admire your compassion but this cat is nothing but a feral, flea-ridden menace. I should take it to the pound." He squared his shoulders, bolstered by the logic of his argument. "Now, if you'll excuse me I'll get rid of it and I can show you the master bedroom."

"Oh, ow!" the cat complained.

Herb started to push by me but I stood my ground, leaving him standing—at least what I considered—uncomfortably close. "I'll take him."

"You'll what?"

"I'll take the cat home with me."

Herb chuckled, "Don't you think you ought to check with your husband before you go dragging strays into the house?"

I had a hand on the cat's head. "Check with who?"

"Mr. Lolly, your husband?"

Damn, I almost fell out of character for a cat. I needed to toughen up. "He'll be fine, in fact he loves cats. Besides, I've seen enough and you need to get to your next appointment."

Herb handed the cat over with a suspicious look. "We haven't even looked at the master bedroom."

"It's too small." I clamped the squirming cat under one arm and started for the front door. "And there, uh, aren't enough windows."

Herb surveyed the nearly wall-sized picture window that dominated the living room as I added that last complaint. Okay, so I had to think quickly, what do you expect? I hopped down the steps and was halfway to my car by the time Herb hollered from the house's doorway.

"I've got other homes I can show you. There's a nice place out in—"

I didn't hear the rest; I'd shut the car door and dumped the cat onto the passenger seat while I dug for keys in my clutch bag.

"I sure as hell hope you're worth all this trouble," I muttered, finally fishing the keys out. I smiled at Herb, jingling them at him through the passenger-side window to deter him from coming to see if anything was wrong.

"You're catnapping me! Oh no, this is horrible! Help me! Somebody help me!" The cat jumped onto the floorboard, cowering under the dashboard as I pulled away from the curb.

"I'm not kid, er, catnapping you."

The feline peered out of its hiding place. "Wait, I understood that."

"And I understand you too." I shook my head, Jesus what was going on?

"Oh, this isn't right!" The cat drew himself up. "This isn't at *all* right!"

I turned off Woodford onto Vine, heading out of the development. "Yeah, I know the feeling. I seem to be saying that exact same thing a lot lately."

"Oh, this is no good. The stress has gotten to me. I've finally snapped. People can't talk."

"What do you mean people can't talk? *Cats* can't talk!" When I looked down at the cat it slunk further under the dash.

"This is like the end of the world or something!" The cat erupted from the floorboard, jumped the seat-back, and hit the rear window at full speed, rolling off down the rear seat and onto the floorboard behind me.

"Hey! Cut it out!"

"Gotta get out of here!"

The cat's voice sounded woozy but when he vaulted back over the seat he certainly didn't seem dazed in the least. He used my bad shoulder as a springboard, sending a wave of pain through me intense enough to make my eyes tear, and before I could do anything he'd gotten entangled in the steering wheel. The LaSalle doesn't take to an uncertain hand; being a twelve-year-old car she's wont to take any opportunity to misbehave, and sloppy handling of the wheel definitely qualifies.

Instantly we were over the curb and cutting a path through a neat hedgerow and into one of the manicured lawns, the deranged cat stuck between the spokes of a steering wheel that was bucking wildly with every bump. I stomped the brake pedal and the nose of the car dove, pitching me forward painfully. We sat in a sea of grass with the ruins of what had been hedges strewn around. The car had stopped about a dozen feet from the front door of a powder pink ranch house and I could see a shocked-looking woman staring out through the picture window at the carnage we'd wrought.

I took a deep breath and tried to speak as calmly as possible. "Listen, I don't think either one of us wants to be here when she recovers." I yanked the cat free of the wheel and thrust him back into the passenger seat forcefully enough to convey my conviction. "So sit down and shut up until we get home—got it?"

I didn't wait for an answer. I stuck the car in reverse and stomped on the gas. The LaSalle's rear end swung around violently, tires digging for traction and, in the process, covering the front of the house with sod from foundation to eaves. We jumped the sidewalk, bounded over the curb, and hit the pavement with an angry bark of whitewalls. I shoved the car into drive and mashed the accelerator, tossing pieces of greenery to either side as we headed toward town.

7

Luck finally favored me with a visit: Manny was on a parts run when I pulled into the garage's fenced lot. He might be a saint but that doesn't mean he didn't learn a rather un-saintly vocabulary while he was in the Marines. The bouquet of boxwood I pulled out of the LaSalle's grill would have earned me an earful. Thankfully he wasn't present to witness me toss them into the alley where they'd never be found. I grabbed the cat roughly and managed to haul him upstairs without drawing attention. Once the door was shut and locked I dropped him and gave him a serious glare.

"When the hell did cats start talking?"

"What do you mean when did *cats* start talking? When did *people* start talking?"

"When did people—" I held onto the counter for extra support. In the commotion I'd lost sight of just how insane it was to think a cat was talking to you. Much less talking back to *it!*

"The fall must have done some serious damage to my mind."

I headed for the closet and the twenty-three volume medical reference set Mom had given me for my twenty-first birthday. "I'm having hallucinations, the doctor missed something."

"Why did you catnap me? I demand to be taken home, now!" the cat growled.

Just ignore it; playing along probably will make it worse. I thought for a moment. Or will *refusing* to play along make it worse? Crap!

"Take me home!"

The cat's demands made it impossible to think about whether I should be looking up hallucinations or concussions. I sat on the floor with my hands over my ears, trying to squeeze this whole experience out of existence, and then something Death said recycled through my brain: ". . . a new and strange world." I eyed the cat.

"I don't like that look." He backed away, ears flattening and tail furling.

"Maybe you *can* talk. Maybe that's just the way things are now." I stood. Towering over the feline was a wonderful antidote to the spiraling-out-of-control sensation I'd been experiencing. "Let's just let go the explanations of why either of us can talk. The whole conversation's getting us nowhere. Instead I'll settle for your telling me why you were trying to get into Alfonzo Arnie's house?"

"*My* house." The cat's ears still were flattened and he was squatted and ready to bolt, but apparently he wasn't frightened enough to resist correcting me. "By rights *I* should be asking you what you were doing around *my* house."

"You're Arnie's cat?"

The cat's tail switched in a way that said I'd violated some unknown social rule of cats. I'm okay with breaking a few taboos. Society expects a lot of things from me on which, frankly, I don't intend delivering. I step on social norms so often I barely notice the glares and muttered insults anymore.

"Listen, let's get something straight, lady." The cat assumed a regal pose. "Nobody owns me, I'm my own cat. Understand?"

"Sure, I understand. Since we're dwelling on social niceties, you can stop calling me 'lady.' I've got a name."

I didn't know cats could snort derisively. Apparently it's just one more thing I'd missed because my feline houseguest did just that.

"A name? Oh come on, people don't have names."

"We have names."

"Well, the names that *we* give you." He sniffed the air. "And, since I can tell no cat's claimed you, obviously you don't have a name."

"I've got a name!" I usually reserve that sort of emphasis for mashers but this . . . cat really had me irked. "From here on call me Mel, got it?"

He looked unimpressed. "Whatever you want. Doesn't matter to me."

"Good, I think. And what should I call you?"

"Voetsek."

He had to be making that up. I mean, Voetsek? What kind of a name is Voetsek? It sounds like what happens when you eat too much cotton candy before getting on a roller coaster: you get Voetsek. Of course what kind of name *is* normal for a talking cat?

"That's kind of a mouthful. How about Voe?"

"Yeah, sure, whatever. Listen, Mel, since we're on a first-name basis and all, do you think you could dig up something for me to eat?"

"To eat?" I looked around the apartment; Manny had stuck a note about groceries to the refrigerator door and I still hadn't gotten to the store. "I don't have any cat food."

"What about salmon or tuna? I like kidney too. Do you have kidney?"

"What's this look like, a butcher shop?" I opened the fridge; Mother Hubbard's cupboard was better stocked except for the fact I had a box of baking soda. "I've got steak sauce, half an onion, and cheese."

"This is pathetic. How do you live?" I looked down. Voe was sitting between my feet in a perfect cat pose, eyeing the interior of my refrigerator. "Maybe you should run out to get something?

I can wait."

"Maybe you should run out and catch a mouse."

He stared up at me. "I thought we agreed to be nice to each other. Or maybe this is some definition of 'nice' I don't know?"

I grabbed the wedge of cheese from the refrigerator and got a knife from the silverware drawer. "I am being nice. I'm sharing what I have. Here, we'll suffer together."

I cut a slice of cheese for Voe and crumbled it on a saucer, setting it on the floor for him before cutting a slice for myself. It was an odd feeling, watching Voe eating cheese crumbs. He was scrawny: his ribs showed through a silver tabby coat that was dirty at the edges. The world had been rough on him without Arnie's protection. The world is tough on the powerless. It's worse for an animal. How many times have you walked by a hungry stray on the street? How many crushed animal corpses have you seen lying by the roadside? I know: I can't say either. It's like life hardens us to the plights of anyone or anything we deem less important than ourselves. That makes it easier to ignore the carnage as the world grinds them under. For me, the sedative had worn off and I couldn't stay numb. And it had to happen right when I faced telling Voe his life had been violently and irrevocably changed. I steeled myself.

"Voe?"

He didn't react, just kept eating.

"I need to tell you the reason I was in your house today."

He looked up in the nonchalant way only a cat can pull off. Maybe he wouldn't even blink when I delivered the news about Arnie. I wondered what would be the natural reaction for a cat.

"You see Alfonzo, well, he's not coming back."

For a moment I wasn't sure whether he'd heard me. He just assessed me with his pale green eyes. When he did speak it was with a cool, dismissive tone.

"Why do you insist on keeping up this charade? It's really

unbecoming and it insults both our . . . well, at least *my* intelligence."

"Hey, what happened to nice?"

He swished his tail and went back to his saucer. "I get cranky when I'm hungry. Go on."

"Look, how long have you lived with Alfonzo?"

"What's an Alfonzo?"

"The man who—" I stopped myself. Who knew if saying Alfonzo owned the house would be as big a faux pas as saying someone owned Voe? I definitely wasn't in the mood for the debate. "The man you *shared* the house with."

"Long enough. You know I don't feel like being questioned by my catnapper so if you'll excuse me—"

He started to walk away but I knew he wasn't going far; my place isn't that big and cats, even talking ones, don't have opposable thumbs to operate doorknobs.

"Voe, has Alfonzo ever just run off and left you? Ever just put you out and not come back?"

The cat stopped. "No, but he's a human and humans aren't very smart, so anything's possible."

"What about your bowls? Do you think he'd get rid of them like he didn't plan on you coming back again?"

Voe sat down. "No."

"I'm sorry to be the one who has to tell you, but Alfonzo Arnie is dead."

"Dead? What do you mean, dead?"

"You know, the opposite of alive? It's like—"

"I *know* what dead *means*." He snapped. "What makes you think he's dead?"

"Voe, I know he's dead."

"Oh, and I'm supposed to take the word of the person who snatched me from my home? For all I know you could be the one who locked me outside!"

"Voe, the house is being sold by the bank. With nobody alive to make the payments they're trying to recoup their money."

"Whoa, slow down! I don't know what all that stuff you said means but it sounds a little like you were there to *take* my house. I don't think I need to point out how that wouldn't convince me I ought to trust you?"

"I wasn't actually going to buy the place. I was just pretending, so I could find some clues." I let out a desperate sigh. "I don't know how to make you believe me."

I hopped down from the counter and crossed the kitchen to the door that opened to the stairs that led down to the fenced lot. I put my hand on the doorknob. I had to take the chance.

"If this was some kind of kidnapping scheme I wouldn't do this." I opened the door and stepped aside. "If you want you can leave. I won't stop you. I hope this will show you that you can trust me but if it doesn't at least you'll be free."

He took a step toward the door, keeping an eye on me. I held my breath and stayed still. If he decided I wasn't trustworthy he'd be gone along with my chances of getting any more information about the night Arnie died. For a moment he stared at me, and then he sat. The air was filled with the worst howl I ever heard; it was ragged, mournful, and desperate and between its sorrowful notes were short, sobbed sentences. As if he'd only just that instant realized his world had come adrift—big-time!

"What am I supposed to do now? Who's gonna feed me? Where am I gonna sleep?"

It was hard not to think of him as a person: a poor, pathetic person who'd just lost someone he'd depended on. It was a feeling I recognized from personal experience.

"I promise you I'll find whoever is responsible for his death."

"What does it matter? He's still dead. You can't change that." He sniffed and moaned. "You know, you kind of get attached, even to a human, and then, one day, they're just gone."

Obviously the inter-species gap would take a while to breach. I did my best to be magnanimous. We shared the bond of loss. Okay, I'd lost a father and for Voe it was something more akin to a cherished pet but pain is pain.

"Yeah, I know. I understand." I fought off the memory of my dad that came to mind and gently pushed the door closed. This wasn't about exorcising my personal demons. Besides, Voe was so wrapped up in his own grief that he probably wouldn't hear a thing I said. My role was sympathetic ear and that meant nodding and making comforting sounds at the right moments. I leaned against the doorframe and listened.

"Seems like just yesterday when everything was normal. The big lug was letting me out. If I only knew I wasn't going to see him again . . ." He trailed off, sniffling.

There are moments when I suddenly realize I've been really dense. I don't share that with just everyone and if anyone goes spreading it around I'll call them a liar. Just the same, this was one of those moments. I stood by the door, listening to Voe, and suddenly I realized something I hadn't even considered.

"He put you out and then just never let you back in?"

Voe sniffled but apparently it didn't dampen his sense of pride. "He *let* me out. Nobody puts me anywhere."

"You're missing the point." I drew a deep breath; learning cat etiquette was going to be tough. "Okay, so he *let* you out and when you came back home he just never responded? He never came to the door to let you in again?"

"Right, so?"

"So what night was that? What was the date?"

"Date?"

"Yes, what was the date of the night he didn't let you back inside the house?"

"What, exactly, is a 'date'?"

"You're kidding, right?" The look he shot me answered the

question. I didn't wait for the verbal abuse. "It's a way of measuring time. There are twelve months in a year and . . . oh, now I'm trying to explain the calendar to a cat! How about this, how long were you outside before today?"

Voe seemed to think. "Forty, maybe forty-one nights?"

"Today's the tenth of December. That works out perfectly, Arnie was killed on the first of November. That means you were the last one to see him alive!"

"Thanks for that painful reminder. Don't you think I've already suffered enough?"

"Voe, just bear with me. Did you see anything weird that night? Like strange people coming to the house or something?"

"People were always coming and going. Nothing strange about that."

"What about that last night? Maybe there was someone new?"

Voe seemed to mull the question over, his tail swishing side to side. "There were two men. He let them in as I went out for my evening stroll."

"Do you know their names?"

"I did mention that you're the first person I've ever been able to understand and that before tonight I didn't even know humans had names, right?"

"Damn it!" I started pacing. "So, no names, that's fine; did you recognize them?"

"Maybe, I mean yes, well, I recognized one of them."

"Describe them. Start with the one you recognized and tell me everything. Catching Alfonzo's killer depends on you remembering every detail about that night."

Voe joined me in pacing.

"Okay, the one I recognized was young with dark hair and brown eyes. I always called him Laundry Basket."

I stopped and fixed Voe with a confused stare. "Laundry Basket?"

"Yeah."

"Why the hell do you call him Laundry Basket?"

"Because he smelled like a laundry basket."

There was a certain soundness to that kind of reasoning. I already could think—in feline terms—of names for certain people in my life: Ass Pain leapt to mind. "All right. I'm not sure how that's going to help but at least I understand. What about the second guy?"

"He was old with long white hair and a beard. I never saw him before that night." He looked at me expectantly. "Do you know them?"

"Oh sure. Probably have their phone numbers somewhere around here." I leaned against the counter. "You see, there are a whole lot of people in the country, and right now we're looking for the distinguished pair consisting of a young guy who smells like laundry and a guy who's just—"

"Old. Right, I'm sorry." Voe sat, his ears drooping.

"Maybe there's something else? Alfonzo's throat was slashed; did you hear a scuffle or yelling after these two men went into the house?"

"No."

"What do you mean no? You had to hear a struggle or maybe an argument?"

"I was doing something."

"Doing something? You said you were outside the house when they went inside."

"I didn't *stay* outside the house. I went over the fence to visit Jezebel."

"Jezebel?"

"Yeah, she's this hot little Persian. She's got the cutest whiskers and you ought to see her tail!"

"God, men! Even when they're cats they're only interested in one thing!" I started pacing again. "So you step outside, these two guys go into the house, and then you go to, visit, Jezebel."

"Yeah. So . . . ?"

"And you didn't hear anything?"

"I was occupied!"

"Right, occupied. Don't go into detail, I get the idea. When you came back you couldn't get into the house and that's it? After that you just roughed it until you met me?"

"Pretty much."

"Wonderful." I massaged my aching head. "That leaves us nowhere."

"Well, there was the other man." Voe said tentatively.

"What other man?"

"When I came back over the fence there was this guy leaving the house."

"Damn it, Voe! Do you think you could have shared that with me when we started this conversation?" I yelled, causing Voe to shrink away. "Anything weird about him? Maybe he smelled like pickles or something?"

"What are pickles?"

"Just answer the damn question!"

"No, I mean I'd seen him around the house before and he looked mad, kind of like you do now. But that's all."

This was hopeless. I couldn't even ask what time these mysterious men had come and gone. I mean if Voe didn't get the concept of a calendar, time surely wouldn't be any more familiar. Besides, ever see a cat wearing a watch? Hell, even the descriptions of the people involved were practically useless.

"I don't suppose you know if Alfonzo had any enemies?"

"I'm not sure, I mean why would he have enemies when all he ever did was sit around the house, squawking with other men? Well, that and digging in his favorite hole."

I stopped rubbing my temples.

"His what?"

"His favorite hole. I figured it was some kind of human thing. Don't you all dig holes?"

"Where is this hole?"

"It's in the backyard behind the bushes, why? Is that important?"

I didn't answer; I had a hole to find—just as soon as I'd found someplace to buy cat food.

8

The cat food was the easy part. But once I'd got it, taken it home, and watched Voe launch himself into dinner as if he was a Labrador retriever instead of a cat, I found myself with time on my hands and no wish to spend it watching a cat—talking or otherwise—grooming himself and sleeping off his gluttony.

I killed the rest of the evening at the Teepee. It's a popular teen hangout with good malts and killer onion rings. As a bonus, watching high school boys pretending to be James Dean always makes me laugh and I definitely needed a little levity. When the sun went down and the crowd thinned out, I paid my bill, saddled up the LaSalle, and headed for the suburbs.

By the time I parked on Vine, Sunnyvale had turned into a suburban cemetery. A few hours ago it'd been alive. The neighborhood around the garage always had something going on. When the respectable businesses closed up, the bars opened, bringing in a new cast to populate the stage. I checked the street before looking at my watch; the luminescent dial said one o'clock and the place looked absolutely embalmed. Considering my situation, it wasn't exactly the most comforting comparison but it made sneaking around a lot easier.

I dashed across the lawn, flattened against Arnie's house, and crept along the foundation until I reached the gate that led into the backyard. It was the one feature I'd noticed before Voe plastered his face to the storm door; now it was going to serve me well. I shifted the flashlight to my right hand, the weight reminding me why I'd been using my left, and opened the gate. Now Arnie's apparent fascination with gardening worked in my favor; though they were bare of leaves, the bushes around the lawn's perimeter shielded me from view. Getting hauled down to the station on a prowling charge didn't exactly sound like fun. A night with the drunks and hookers in lockup would be memorable, but not nearly as unforgettable as the lectures I'd get from Rolland and my mother.

I followed the fencerow, scanning the ground as I walked. According to Voe, there'd be a hole behind one of the bushes. Hopefully whatever Arnie had buried would provide a clue to why he'd been murdered and give me a lead on Death's case. I crossed my fingers. If I didn't parlay my information into something that pointed to a killer, this case could easily turn as cold as Virginia's. The last thing my bruised ego needed was two unsolvable mysteries.

As I drew near the corner of the lot I heard a car coming down Vine. I doused the flashlight and dropped to my knees, shrinking back against the tangle of branches and praying they'd hide me. A black car rolled down the street, slowing near the corner. I held my breath and tried to be still while it crept by my car. After what felt like a century, it picked up speed and rounded the corner onto Woodford, disappearing from view. I stayed crouched in the dark until the sound of the car's engine died away.

The fence intersected a shared span that divided two identical, square parcels of land. Now I could see across the neighbor's empty expanse of snow-covered grass. Things were getting interesting. The windows of the house were dark, but that didn't mean I wasn't being watched. Someone could be standing behind any of them wiping the sleep from their eyes and wondering if they'd really seen someone with a flashlight lurking around the old Arnie place. I needed to find whatever

Alfonzo treasured so much he buried it in his yard to keep it safe.

Near the second corner post my foot sank into a low spot in the lawn. Wet snow squeezed in around my ankles. I'd managed to ruin a perfectly good pair of flats, but at least I'd located Alfonzo's favorite hole. I knelt on the ground and set my flashlight aside. Not wanting to raise suspicion, the digging would have to be done in the dark and with the added disadvantage of not having a right hand. With my left hand I dug in the pocket of my coat, coming out with a big serving spoon.

I don't own a shovel, an arrangement I'm perfectly comfortable with. The only sort of gardening I want to do involves a shopping basket in the produce section. For the sake of finding Arnie's killer, though, I made an exception. I pushed the sleeves of my coat up as high as possible and gripped the spoon awkwardly in my left hand. Winter had been warmer than usual this year; we hadn't had a long enough bout of cold to freeze the ground solid, which made digging easier and messier. After a few enthusiastic stabs the spoon cut into the ground and I came up with a wet clod.

After thirty or forty spoonfuls, I had an elbow-deep hole. Trying to stay clean was pointless. Cold mud soaked my coat and sweater sleeves and squished between my fingers—making this the second outfit I'd ruined in one week. At this rate I'd have a new wardrobe before spring and for all the wrong reasons. I wiped my forehead, hoping I hadn't just applied a really bad mud mask, and tried to check the time. Unfortunately my watch's glow had long since died away. I took another dig at the ground and struck something hard, metal, and hollow. I grabbed my flashlight out of the snow and leaned over the hole to see what I'd unearthed. The wavering pool of light revealed the familiar square shape of an ammunition box. Manny uses one like it to hide his girlie magazines back at the garage, the ones he denies owning. I reached into the hole and grabbed a handle and, after a few tugs, dragged the box out of the hole and clear of the excavated piles of dirt.

A leather-bound book sat inside but it wasn't the most interesting part of the contents. Beneath it was cash: lovely bundles of bills bound with rubber bands. The box held more money than I'd seen in my life and all of it buried in a suburban yard. I snapped the box closed, kicked the dirt back into the hole without really caring whether it was obvious someone had been doing a job on the lawn, and headed back to my car.

I sat the ammo box on the roof while I unlocked the door. Thousands of dollars buried in a flowerbed didn't jibe with what I'd seen. Arnie lived in a Sunnyvale, single-story rambler. Nobody with real money lived in the suburbs; they had big houses in Shadyside far from the working-class rabble. Arnie had to be rich; I didn't know anyone who could afford to bury the kind of money that was inside the box I'd excavated. Hell, I didn't know anyone whose yearly salary was much more than what Arnie had buried. The way I figured, Arnie was either a post-Depression paranoid or crooked, and my bets rode on crooked.

Headlights stifled my internal debate about Arnie's ill-gotten gains. They came from a car parked just beyond the intersection of Woodford and Vine. The engine revved and tires squealed as it lunged toward me. I hardly had time to throw myself onto the LaSalle's hood. The car barely missed and ricocheted off the curb before roaring down the street.

I rolled back to my feet, shoulder screaming for the abuse it had taken during the dive. The car barreled a half block down Vine before turning into a side street. I didn't plan on giving him another shot at mowing me down in the street. I grabbed the ammo box and jumped into my car, spinning tires as I made a U-turn at the intersection of Woodford and Vine, and headed back toward town.

My new friend wasn't deterred by my attempted escape. He caught me as I turned out of Sunnyvale and onto the main road. By *caught* I mean rear-ended. My head snapped backward and I fishtailed as the impact propelled me across the road. I had to cut the wheel hard to avoid winding up in the ditch. The LaSalle's tires flung gravel until they contacted concrete, then it leaped into the left-hand lane and headed for the city. The escape was short lived. In seconds my mystery date reintroduced himself, slamming into my right rear quarter panel. I pushed the gas pedal to the floor, accelerating away from him as his bumper grated against my poor car.

The open spaces between town and the suburbs had a new, palpable terror. Creeps from outer space vanish in the light of logic but crazed drivers bent on running you off the road, they thrive on a good strip of deserted back-road. The LaSalle's engine screamed but my pursuer's headlights raced up on my rear bumper and the impact jerked my head backward a second time. Whatever he was driving had too much horsepower to overcome. I wasn't going to outrun him.

We vaulted over a rise in the road. The momentary sensation of weightlessness added to my panic but it did force my pursuer to back off. I didn't have a gun; I'd lost the one I got from the pawn shop when Fleck attacked me. If this creep succeeded in putting me in a ditch, the only weapon I had was the muddy spoon I'd used to dig up Arnie's stash.

The money put another terrible spin on this situation. What if my pursuer wasn't just a motorized nutcase? What if he was Arnie's killer? The pieces fit together so nicely. If Arnie had been killed in a botched robbery the killer probably wanted what I found: a box full of cash! I remembered the black sedan that passed the house while I was prowling around the backyard. Maybe the same car that was trying to run me off the road now.

He'd pulled around the block, parked, waited until I found the loot, and then tried to run me down in the street.

I pulled the wheel hard and swerved back into the right lane, cutting my pursuer off before he could ram me again. He dropped back, probably contemplating the angle of his next attack. We were coming up on a narrow bridge and I could see the stripes painted on its rusty supports reflecting my headlights. This was my chance . . . maybe my only one.

The headlights in my mirror drew closer and as they did I switched back into the left lane and took my foot off the gas. I might as well have stepped on the brake; a black sedan jetted alongside my LaSalle. For a second we were door to door and staring at each other. Judging from his profile my attacker was a short man. He wore a porkpie hat, pushed back on his head. He probably was wondering why this woman was so hard to run off the road. Women were supposed to be the weaker sex, after all.

I didn't wait for him to figure out the answer. I put all my weight into the wheel and slammed into the side of his car, sending it lurching toward the ditch. I jumped on the brakes. The impact wasn't enough to send him over, but I didn't need to knock him off the road. My plan was to bump him into the rapidly ending emergency lane and it worked horrifically well. He hit the bridge abutment at full speed. The rear end of the sedan leaped off the ground and came down again with so much force the back axle snapped.

The night got quiet. A dislodged wheel wobbled drunkenly across the road before disappearing off the edge of the road and into the darkness. Over the low rumble of the Caddy's engine, I could hear steam escaping from under the sedan's smashed hood. It billowed out into my headlights, clouding the night with antifreeze-scented fog. I took a pad out of the glove compartment and scribbled down the sedan's plate number before letting off the brake. The Caddy crept forward, idling past the wreckage. Through the smoke and steam I saw what might have been a body leaning against the steering wheel. My pursuer might be dead but I didn't have the nerve to check. I stepped on the gas and left the crash in my rearview mirror as I headed for town.

9

Cops appreciate hierarchy. Everything about the police department is based on rank and time on the force. The guys with
seniority and rank pulled day shift and didn't work weekends or
holidays. Guys without, like Scott, well—their lives pretty much
stank. That's how I knew he'd be getting off work about four in
the morning which gave me time to stop at a bar and use the
restroom to clean some of the mud off myself. I got strange
looks but I've gotten worse.

I loitered, parking across the street from the precinct, until I
saw Scott emerge and then I swung around and cut him off at
the curb. The look on his face was priceless. Almost funny
enough to make me forget the game of tag I'd just played on
the road from Sunnyvale. His eyes got big and he took a half
step backwards, only relaxing when he realized who'd cut him
off. I put the car in park and wrestled the door open with one
arm, stepping out onto the deserted street.

"Hey, a little help for an old friend would be nice," I chided,
slamming the door and heading toward the curb.

"What the hell happened to your car?"

That was the first time I actually got to see the damage. I
looked at the rear end and all I could manage was a strangled,
"Oh crap."

"Were you in a wreck? Are you okay?" Scott asked, joining
me behind the car as I knelt to run my hand over the crumpled
fender and marred bumper.

"Oh crap," I repeated.

"You didn't leave the scene of an accident, did you? Mel, you know that's illegal. Mel?"

I didn't pay attention; the fit Manny was going to throw was playing out inside my head. There'd be the inevitable reminder that fixing an old car like mine wasn't exactly cheap. He'd rail about how hard it'd be to find parts, and he'd bellow that he didn't keep the LaSalle running just so I could tear it up. Then he'd soften and emote over how I'd wind up dead if I didn't get some common sense. Doubtless he'd reinforce that fact by revisiting how my impulsive foolishness had already gotten me shot. He might even add that every time I did something stupid, he got it from my mother, absolutely the best way to wring sympathy from me.

I can handle angry: yelling, fist pounding, and foot stomping really aren't so bad. I can suffer through anything so long as I know I'm right—and I usually am. The thing that gets me doesn't even require a word. After Manny blows through his anger and fear he'll look at me with eyes that glint a little in the garage's fluorescent light, then he'll shake his head and walk away. In that moment I'll remember how much disappointing Manny is like failing my dad. And even though Dad's been gone for ten years it'll be like a kick in the stomach.

"Mel!" I jerked out of early penance and realized Scott was giving me the street cop stare-down. "What's wrong with you? Are you drunk?"

"I'm not drunk." I stood and smoothed my skirt. "You know I only get drunk on the weekends."

"Then how about explaining the whole swearing and drifting off routine? I've seen a lot of drunks in my time and I've got to tell you, you're doing a pretty good impression."

"You know me better than that, Scott. I'm not *that* kind of drunk. I'm a happy drunk. Now, if I'd started singing—"

"Cut the jokes and tell me what happened to the car."

I glanced from Scott's fierce look to the creased fender. "Some moron in a black sedan tried to get overly friendly, which is why I came to see you."

"Great. Well, let's go see the desk sergeant. He can get the forms—"

"I don't want to file an accident report. I just want you to check the license number for me."

A look of horror crossed Scott's face. Deviating from police protocol seemed to have that kind of effect on him. My asking for favors does too, which means I've had time to learn a few good remedies. Tonight it would be the old *yanking the Band-Aid off quickly* approach.

"Come on, I just want you to look up a license plate number. It's not like I'm asking you to help me pull a bank heist!"

"Why don't you just let me file a report, Mel? A uniform can find the guy who hit you."

"I don't want to turn the guy in, just exchange insurance information. Besides, if we go fill out some form you know somehow it's going to wind up on Rolland's desk and that means he'll call my mom." It was a dirty trick; I admit it. I needed the name of that sedan's driver, though, and Scott was being difficult. What else could I do?

"Don't bullshit me, Mel."

"Whoah! You're hanging around the guys in Vice too much!" I reached over and pinched his cheek. "The little Scottie I grew up with couldn't say 'shoot' without blushing. Soon you'll be bad as me and then you'll make the bad guys cry."

He pulled away. "Cut it out, Mel."

"It's kind of thrilling to hear you talk dirty. Say it one more time for me."

"Mel."

"Come on. You know you want to."

"Mel."

"I'll say it with you, just whisper it. *Bullshit.* Come on, I won't tell anyone, it'll be our guilty secret."

Scott let out an exasperated breath, and as he did the corner of his mouth tugged upward slightly. His resolve had faltered. I had him. "Promise me this isn't another halfwit scheme that's going to get you shot."

"I promise. This one is definitely full witted."

He shook his head. "I don't know why I hang around with you."

"Because I'm cute and rumor has it I remind you of the fun you could be having if you'd just loosen up a little." A cold wind blew through the streets and I turned my collar up around my chin. "Maybe we can discuss my sanity and shortcomings somewhere a little warmer? How about I buy you a cup down at The Quarter? I'll even drive you home afterwards. It'll save you the bus fare."

I opened the passenger-side door while he gave me one more skeptical look. "Come on, I don't buy every guy coffee. Usually I make *them* pay; you ought to feel honored."

"Coffee and a ride home in exchange for risking my job? I'm going to have to up my prices."

"You wouldn't dare charge me," I said with a smile, holding the door as he started to step into the car. Instead of getting in, he paused on the curb.

"What's this?"

I'd forgotten about the ammo box and when I spotted it, Scott nearly had hold of the handle. The jolt nearly made me spit my heart out on the pavement.

"Ah, let me get that out of your way."

"What is it?"

"Nothing . . . er . . . road flares and that sort of thing. You know how my uncle's always on me about being prepared in case the car breaks down. I'll just put them in the trunk."

"Here." He tried to intercept me. "Let me carry them, you've got an arm in a sling."

"No!" The words came out way too urgent. I tried to shoulder Scott aside but there was no way I was going to fight him off with one arm. He grabbed the handles and lifted the box out of the floorboard before I could stop him. "I mean don't put yourself out. It's light."

"You're acting weirder than normal tonight, Mel." He gave the box a look. "This thing is filthy; what do you do, bury your road flares to keep them fresh or something?"

I grabbed the handle and jerked the box away from him. "Are you making fun of me?"

"No, I just—"

"Oh, I get it. Just because I'm a woman you don't think I'm capable of taking care of myself! Packing my own road flares is just more than my pretty little empty head can handle, is it?" I crowded Scott until he threw up his hands in surrender.

"Hey, I didn't mean anything. I just wanted to help."

"You can help by having a seat while I put the box in the trunk."

He muttered and got into the car. I knew he only bought about half my bluff, but for now it worked. I locked Alfonzo's stash in my trunk and brushed the dirt off my hands, satisfied at preventing my only solid evidence from being confiscated before I'd gotten a change to examine it closely.

Matthieu's French Quarter was a coffeehouse on the corner of Mission and Fifth that regulars, like me, knew simply as "The Quarter." It was a suitably dreary hangout for the city's beatnik population, complete with dark booths and Thursday night poetry readings. It was one of my favorite places in the world: I could disappear into the smoke and shadows and scour off the day's disappointment with strong coffee and cynical verse. The clientele kept to themselves, a plus, and the guy behind the counter, Marko, was a good looking gypsy of a man with a neatly trimmed goatee and a sly wit, a double plus.

I nodded to Marko and headed to my favorite spot, a booth in the back with a unique geography that allowed me to watch a poet on stage, Marko brewing espresso, or the door, depending on the needs of the moment. I'd spread the photos of Virginia's murder on that same table without the intrusion of a single interloper. Things seemed so much simpler then, back when I was chasing a psychopathic killer and not working to restore the power of death personified.

"So." Scott frowned and brushed off his seat before settling in. "Are you planning on telling me how your car *actually* got mangled? I mean if it's going to cost me my job I deserve to at least have the truth, don't you think?"

I fought to remove my coat with one arm, feeling Scott's eyes on me the entire time as he tried to decide if I was daring him to help, or daring him not to. "Like I said, some jerk ran into me. I need to find out who he is."

"In court they make you swear to tell the *whole* truth."

I smiled. "I guess I should be glad you're cross-examining me in a coffeehouse booth instead of the witness stand, huh?"

"I guess so." He kept looking at my sling. "In the hospital I worried about you but with Rolland there the entire time I didn't think I should let on."

"I understand. You did the right thing."

"Yeah, the right thing." He gathered his strength and fixed me in a gaze that told me one day he was going to make one hell of a father. "My help already got you shot once. I want you to swear you're not going to do anything stupid if I run this license plate for you."

What a thing to ask! I'm known for my stupidity. In fact,

aside from recklessness, stupidity is what I do best. Now Mr. Conservative wants me to become cautious and thoughtful? Where's the fun in that?

"I'll do my best." I pulled the scrap of paper I'd scribbled the license plate number on from my purse and handed it to him. "I really appreciate you doing this for me."

He took the paper and that goofy "aw gosh" look filled his face for a moment. "I'll call it in tomorrow after the day shift's gone home. Maybe we could talk about what I find out over dinner?"

This is where my rationalizations about my relationship with Scott get weak and I start to feel guilty. Like I said before, Scott's good-looking in a kind of kid brother way. Kid brother is the only way to describe how I feel about him. When you've played stickball with a guy, teased him about his Cub Scout uniform, and run through an uncapped fire hydrant by his side, everything about him becomes play. I loved him. I'd do just about anything for him. I just didn't feel the spark of romance for Scott, not even a little. We sat there: him waiting for an answer and me trying to find a suitable one until the situation was taken out of my hands. Marko arrived and put a cup of coffee in front of me.

"Fruit of the java vine for the lady." He cast a wary eye in Scott's direction.

"Just black coffee."

"Sumatran or Brazilian and need I ask about the roast?"

Normally I adore Marko's sense of humor. He's sarcastic and doesn't apologize for that fact, something we have in common. I delight in hearing him scorch some square who's earned his ire or rail against the conventions of the establishment. But razor wit isn't so thrilling when being used to fillet an old friend. If this was a knife fight, Scott had shown up unarmed. I did my Good Samaritan bit and interceded.

"Just give him the house blend."

Marko smirked. "Dishwater for the cat in the bad suit."

Scott frowned and watched Marko return to the bar. "Why do you come to this place, Mel?"

"I like the atmosphere."

"You could get the same atmosphere hanging around the unemployment office. All this place does is attract drifters and no-accounts. Hell, for all you know Communist sympathizers conduct their membership drives from the storeroom."

"Oh, ease up, Scott! Look around you, these people aren't Communists. They're odd alright, but they're artists, poets, and freethinkers. You know, some of the greatest minds of our century came from the fringes of society. Maybe it's just in the way you look at it?"

"I look at it from the vantage point of a guy who's cuffed a hundred guys like coffee-boy on everything from felony possession to manslaughter."

Marko returned and put a cup in front of Scott. "Careful with this stuff, Jackson. Compared to the crap they sell at A&P this is seriously atomic juice."

Scott drew a deep breath and stared down into his coffee cup. "You know, I think I'm going to call it a night, Mel. I'll call you tomorrow."

He slid out of the booth and eyed Marko before heading for the door. I didn't try to stop him. What was the point? This was supposed to be a treat, a way of thanking him for doing me a favor. You didn't force someone to accept your thanks. Making him endure more sarcasm, well, that wouldn't be much of a treat for either of us.

10

I stumbled into my kitchen trying to hold the door open with one foot while wrestling a mud-caked ammo box left-handed. Through the entire ordeal, Voe reclined on the table, passively taking in the scene with what I interpreted as amusement. I thought about throwing a dirt clod at him but I'd only miss and wind up scrubbing it off the wall.

"Found it," I panted as I leaned against the kitchen counter to catch my breath. Right after that I realized how much mud I was wearing and started swearing.

"That's the same box the old boy used to bury in the backyard." He stood and stretched and then jumped down to pace around the box. "Right where I told you it'd be, wasn't it? Did you bring anything for dessert?"

I'd started undressing and building a new pile of horribly soiled clothes, and was able to ignore his last remark. "Yeah, it was buried behind a hydrangea bush. Damn, I think I have mud in my ear."

"So, what's inside?" Voe asked.

I tossed my skirt and blouse into a heap and kicked my shoes off on top of the mound. Still in my underwear I retrieved some of the papers I'd brought up from the storeroom and spread them to protect the kitchen table from dirt. I hefted the box and turned out its contents. Bundles of money covered the tabletop, flowing in an avalanche that sent bills tumbling onto the floor.

"Something a lot of people would kill over."

Voe sniffed at the cash. "What is it?"

"Money, you use it to buy stuff. Trust me; this has something to do with Arnie's murder." I surveyed the cash, thinking about the day's adventure. "By the way, you don't know somebody who drives a big black car, do you?"

If a cat could shrug, Voe did. "No. Why?"

"I had an encounter with a rude guy driving one. He tried to run me off the road after I found this box. That means I've got something somebody wants so bad he's willing to commit murder."

I pulled the book from the pile and thumbed through its pages. It was a ledger. Manny used one like it to keep track of the garage's accounts. Unlike Manny's ledger, though, this one was filled with obviously fake names and numbers that didn't seem to have anything to do with debits and deposits. I set it aside for later and turned my attention to the cash. It took a half hour to count. In the end I counted ten thousand dollars in ones, fives, and tens. The bills were well-worn, tired money, probably obtained from hardworking hands. But why had the people who'd earned it turned it over to Alfonzo Arnie and what had he provided in return?

"Your friend was into something bad, Voe."

"Why do you say that?"

"Nobody buries this kind of cash in a hole. Well, unless they need to hide it." Sitting in a kitchen, looking at a pile of bundled bills, I wondered if this was what it'd be like to be a gun moll.

Voe pawed at the pile. "Can you tell who killed Arnie from all this?"

I let out a slow breath. "No."

"Then, what do we do now?"

"I don't know." I picked up a bundle and fanned through the bills. "I'll find out who the guy in the car was tomorrow. This box is the key and as long as we've got it, we've got leverage. The important thing is to keep that control."

"How do you plan on doing that?"

"For starters I'm going to stash this until I can figure things out. Unfortunately that means slipping into something a little less comfortable."

I pulled on my muddy clothes again. The clammy feeling of damp cloth started me imagining the hot bath and warm bed that waited at the end of this long day. With the ammo box in hand, I stepped outside. Below me the security light mounted on the side of the garage buzzed, illuminating the lot and the few battered cars parked there awaiting repair. I descended the stairs and used my key to enter the garage through the side door.

Just outside Manny's office stood a deep sink where the mechanics washed up at the end of their shifts. I dumped the box's contents on the oil-stained floor and washed the mud away with hot water and Lava soap. Once the dirt was gone, I dried the box with a rag and returned its contents with the exception of the ledger and two bundles of money. Hey, after what I'd been through I deserved a tip. Before snapping the latches, I tossed in a pair of pistons that'd been sitting on Manny's workbench for almost six months. I'd need the weight for my plan to work.

The next step was grease. I opened a big can of axle grease, dipped my hand in, and pulled out a fistful. The grease didn't feel that much different than cold cream. Well, that's what I told myself to avoid thinking about being wrist-deep in sticky, disgusting, smelly goop. I applied handfuls of grease until the box was completely coated in a thick layer. It resembled the worse cake ever conceived: grease and tin with a cash surprise in the middle. I grabbed the box by a slimy handle and hauled it outside.

Manny keeps fifty-gallon drums for collecting old motor oil in the lot beside the garage. After an oil change, the mechanic empties the collection pan into one of the barrels. I don't know exactly what happens when a barrel gets full. Heck, I can't say I ever really cared. All I know is they stay by the garage for months at a time and that meant they'd serve my purpose.

I took my greased box to a half-filled barrel and, as carefully as I could, lowered it into the inky depths. It was a strange sensation, my arm being submerged in oil but the layer of grease preventing it from actually touching me. It was almost like the oil didn't exist, like it was an illusion and if I paid attention I'd see the magician manipulating me from behind the curtain. I leaned over the barrel's lip and reached until the ammo box rested on the bottom. The weight of the pistons kept it there when I released the handle. If there was any doubt about the oil being real, it was dispelled when my hand came out trailing black goo.

I returned to the mechanic's sink and scrubbed myself with hand cleaner. When I emerged from the garage again, I smelled like a chemical plant. As I climbed the stairs, fatigue began to set in. My back ached, my neck was sore, and my eyes felt like they were covered with a fine film of grit. I stopped at the top of the stairs and leaned on the railing; the stars had started fading and dawn couldn't be too far off.

I undressed in the kitchen for the second time, piled my clothing, and then nearly tripped over the mound. After giving the miscreant clothing a kick to teach it a lesson, I dragged myself through the living room and into the bedroom. There were a thousand things I should do: a hundred strokes of the brush for silky hair, scrubbing my makeup off for a glowing complexion, and taking the bath I'd longed for just touched on the top of the list. Instead I changed into comfortable pajamas and fell into bed. For a few moments I stared through my bedroom window at the sky. It was tinged pink; dawn wasn't far away and with it would come new trials and frustrations. Voe jumped up onto the windowsill, composed himself, and sat with his tail neatly wrapped around his haunches as he watched the world through the glass. I closed my eyes and drifted off into a dreamless sleep.

11

Seven in the morning is a terrible time and having an argument with your favorite uncle doesn't do a damned thing to make it better. It went like I expected: lots of fury and in the end I felt like a genuine, grade-A ass. I thought about getting more sleep but my recriminations and the sounds of the new day intruded. I finally gave up. I showered, dressed, tried to cover the dark circles under my eyes, and headed out hoping that refilling the refrigerator might help heal the rift between my uncle and me.

I stepped through the gate and onto the sidewalk. The suburbanites in Sunnyvale might have lawns and carports but the tradeoff is they can't accomplish all the little things they need to do on foot. Even on a chilly December morning it's nice to stroll down the street to pick up your groceries or drop off your cleaning, window-shopping along the way. It's that much nicer when your car's been turned to a multi-ton paperweight and your favorite uncle doesn't want to speak to you. Quietly disappearing without having to borrow a car was very therapeutic.

Ten blocks from the garage the neighborhood takes a steep decline. Pleasant shops turn into rundown stores and the gutters gradually fill with garbage. It's the northern border of poverty, an area my uncle's generation callously refers to as "the slums." As I walked the houses became shabbier, the cars rustier, and rapidly I became the only white person on the street who wasn't twirling a baton while walking a beat. God, if Manny knew where I'd gone he'd have a major conniption. My ignorance of the color barrier was just another symptom of my rebellious and flawed brain. Maybe I did despise society enough to purposely flaunt its expectations. I certainly had a history that supported that accusation. Then again, maybe I'd been an outcast long enough to appreciate that society's opinion usually wasn't worth a steaming pile of crap.

I stepped into the pawnshop at the corner of Williston Avenue with one purpose in mind, replacing the gun Fleck had taken.

"Good morning, Morris," I said, passing the watches and rings and heading toward the back of the shop where pistols coiled in lit, glass cases like snakes in a reptile house.

I heard Morris before I saw him. He's a man of size, probably 260 pounds and built like he rolled off a Detroit assembly line. He's dark skinned and wears his hair close cropped. With the shirt, suspenders, and tie he wears, Morris looks more like a Southern Baptist preacher than a purveyor of goods that are hocked, hot, or both.

"Miss Rush." He paused, his eyes going from me to the guns and back again. "You looking for another pistol?"

Morris's tone was as courteous as always, but in the way he said "another" I detected a note of what I could only interpret as either disbelief or concern. I ignored it and leaned on the glass, taking in the display. What was I going to do, admit that someone had taken the last gun from me and shot me with it?

"You got anything that I could put in my purse? The .38 was kind of bulky."

"I don't know." Keys jingled and Morris grunted under his own weight as he stooped to unlock the cabinet. His big hands danced under the fluorescent lights of the cabinet as he pulled out the velvet trays that contained the collection of pistols. He placed them atop the case in front of me but his eyes never left my face.

"Who are you planning on shooting?"

I snorted. "I didn't say I was *planning* on shooting *anyone,* Morris."

"Whatever you say, Miss Rush." He folded his arms in an "I know better than that but I'm not getting involved" stance which suited me just fine.

The tray contained a pair of .38s, their shrouded hammers designed not to catch on clothing which had been the reason I'd bought one the first time I'd gone shopping for a gun. I picked one up with my left hand and its weight felt oppressive. It would be a real pain to hold leveled on a target for any length of time.

"What happened to your arm?" Morris broke his silence along with his self-professed policy of non-involvement in the lives of his customers. It was cause to glance up from the weapons.

"Nothing." He didn't look convinced. "I fell, all right?"

"Doesn't look like any fall I'm familiar with."

His tone was thick with the kind of sarcasm I'm supposed to dish out. I didn't look up from weighting pistols.

"I thought you had a policy about not getting mixed up in your customers' lives."

He'd told me that when I bought my first .38. In fact, if Scott hadn't been with me, I don't think he would have sold me the gun at all. That probably would have been a wise decision on his part. A black man selling a white woman a pistol screamed trouble. The only thing that screamed louder would have been refusing to sell the same gun to the same woman when she, obviously, had friends in the police department. Poor Morris had gotten caught in a terrible conundrum; whichever way he turned he'd arrive in a bad spot. I returned the .38 I'd been weighing to its tray and promised myself I'd let him out of his trap—after I had a new weapon.

I glanced at him as I picked up a small box from the tray. "Any word on the street about a pimp named Richard Fleck? He's a rat-faced white guy who works the Manchester area."

"Like you said, I don't mess in people's business. Maybe you ought to adopt the same policy?"

"Can't, I'm a chronic busybody." I opened the box, inside was a compact nickel-plated automatic with a pearl handle. I let out a low whistle and looked at myself reflected in its mirror finish. It almost was a gun and jewelry at the same time. "I like this."

"It's a .25-caliber automatic, seven-round clip. I'll toss in an extra clip if you pay cash."

"I'm good for the money, Morris."

"Another policy of mine is no credit. It's on the sign right in the front window."

"I'm hurt . . . you don't trust me?"

"No ma'am, I'm not saying that. It don't matter to me if you're a priest or my brother-in-law, no credit."

Owing to Arnie's bad luck I had the cash. It wasn't like he'd miss the money and spending a crook's earnings on setting things right had a very pleasant irony. I opened my purse and pulled out my wallet. "Throw in a box of shells and we've got a deal."

Morris' eyes lit up at the sight of me counting off bills. I smiled as I handed them over. "If you do hear anything about Fleck and you find a loophole in your policy manual, I'd be grateful if you let me know. You can leave a message for me at Manny's garage."

With gun in purse, I stepped out onto the street feeling like I actually had traction on Death's case. When Scott ran down the plate of my anonymous friend in the black sedan I'd have a name to put with the evidence I'd dug up in Arnie's backyard and hopefully the sum of those two clues would be a link back to Death's missing mask. If the thought of easy money shook Morris up enough, I might catch Fleck on the side. Now, if I could handle Manny's bruised feelings, restock the fridge, and cook the casserole I'd promised Mom for Christmas dinner, life would be just peachy. I headed back for the garage taking a route that led by the Mill Street Market.

Cooking and the languages spoken on the remote islands of the South Pacific have one thing in common: I don't know anything about either. I make a mean grilled cheese, if by "mean" you're talking about burned, but beyond that my culinary skills can best be described as nonexistent. Mom's reminders that my failings in the kitchen are, doubtlessly, partially to blame for my being single have become as much a part of the holiday tradition as stockings hung by the fire and Bing Crosby records playing on the phonograph. To placate her, or at least shut her up, I had bought a couple of cookbooks. Nothing gourmet, they're geared toward the girl on the go, which I've decided is a euphemism for the girl who's an idiot in the kitchen. My favorite is *Casserole Fun!* with the jaunty exclamation point implying they mean fun in a way that's slightly psychopathic. It's always entertaining to see the look of terror on Mom's face when I pull the foil off the cream and cheese monstrosity that will be marring her "traditional family Christmas." Knowing she wouldn't dare complain for fear of killing what she misconstrues as my nascent interest in the culinary arts is even more fun. This year I was bringing Hawaiian Three-Bean Poi Joy.

I stepped out of the cold and into the warmth of the little market where I've done my grocery shopping since I moved in above the garage. Mill Street Market has a comfortably worn feeling. The linoleum floors are stained, the shelves are uneven, and the vegetables are arrayed in the crates they were packed in when they came off the truck. Mom took me to one of the new supermarkets that are becoming the rage. All the cauliflower was wrapped in plastic and stacked in a refrigerated bin. It looked too science fiction for my taste.

While inspecting cans of soup I caught sight of what appeared to be a dwarf dressed in a shawl and feathered hat. Margaret Beeman, so far as I know, is the oldest living creature on the earth. In her time she's seen dinosaurs, cavemen, and the stock market crash and she's outlasted all of them. Margaret is the proprietor of Beeman's Drugs and my boss. You'd think a woman approaching ninety would have the common decency to have bad eyesight. Not Mrs. Beeman; she could spot a pin lying on the floor at fifty paces and I take up a lot more space than a pin.

"Melody, my dear thing." She was shuffling in my direction, clutch purse clasped to her bosom and a concerned look adding to her extensive collection of wrinkles. "I heard the terrible news; are you all right?"

"I'm fine, Mrs. Beeman."

"You don't look fine, dear. You look peaked. Why are you out roaming the streets in the cold instead of at home, resting?"

"The doctor said I was fine. Really, I'm just a little sore."

"A little sore is too much time digging a garden, Melody, not being accosted by some horrid criminal." She clasped my hand; hers was small and cool. "Be honest, dear. How do you feel?"

My mom could learn a lot about guilting from Mrs. Beeman. I'm just lucky the two of them have never conspired against me. I definitely needed to take a different angle of attack if I was going to get out of this aisle with my dignity.

"You're right, I am tired." Feigning agreement is the first step to escaping one of these traps. Trust me, I know. Next comes playing on your audience's sympathies. "It's just that Christmas is on the way and I promised I'd make my mother something special for the family dinner."

The concern turned into a gentle smile and she patted the back of my hand appreciatively. "You're such a good daughter. I wish there were more young people like you nowadays. Thinking of your mother and when you're in such poor health."

"You know me; I'd do anything for my dear mom. It just wouldn't be Christmas without seeing the look on her face when she sees my contribution to the family dinner."

It wasn't *really* a lie. Well, not all of it. I did look forward to seeing the expression on Mom's face.

She gave my hand one last pat. "Well, I won't keep you from your shopping. Try to get a little rest."

"I'll do my best."

She started to shuffle away and then paused. "Oh, Melody? When do you think you'll feel like returning to work?"

"I don't know. Whenever the doctor says it's okay. Why?"

"Well, you know I always take the train to Miami to spend Christmas with my sister. I just wondered if I should telephone to cancel our plans."

Ah yes, there's a hint of normality. Tradition at the drugstore was for Mrs. Beeman to catch a train to Florida every Christmas where she stayed with her sister through New Year's Day. That meant I tended the store from Christmas Eve through New Year's Eve.

"Don't worry, Mrs. Beeman. I'm sure I'll be back by then."

"I don't want to rush you."

"You're not rushing me. I promise I'll be more than ready to get out of the apartment and back to work."

"Well, if you're sure."

She smiled and I felt good for my good deed. Yeah, Mom definitely could learn a thing or two from that frail old woman. I waved and watched her shuffle off into the market's recesses. Actually, I enjoyed store-sitting, especially since it meant a vacation from the boss. No matter whether you like the person you work for or not, it's always nice to run wild once in awhile. I took a quick inventory of my shopping basket: lima, navy, and kidney beans, as well as a can of cream of mushroom soup and a bag of shredded coconut.

Now all I needed was cat food. It was becoming only too obvious I could *never* have enough cat food on hand.

12

Scott's call came from his desk in homicide. I could tell by the background noise: clattering typewriters and male voices. The other thing that made it apparent was the way he hushed his words. Obviously he felt like he was peddling company secrets or betraying a sacred trust. I probably should have felt bad for putting him in that situation but I didn't. The electricity of having another clue to the identity of Arnie's killer and locating Death's mask overrode my sense of right and wrong.

"You picked a real winner, Mel. That sedan you tangled with belongs to a guy named Vince Morello—originally of East St. Louis."

I grabbed a pencil but couldn't find any paper so I had to use one of the ten dollar bills I'd taken from Arnie's stash. "Morello, great. What's his address?"

"Usually the state pen."

I let out a frustrated sigh and leaned against the counter.

"Yeah, I got it. He's a bad man and I should be afraid. You're a gentleman for making sure I understand exactly what sort of danger I'm getting myself into. Now, do you have a *local* address, Sir Galahad?"

"The latest one on file is Nineteen and a Half West Fillmore."

It was a good thing this was a phone conversation. I don't think I would have kept the evidence of my visceral reaction from showing in my face. The neighborhood around West Fillmore is kind of like ground zero at Nagasaki after the bomb dropped. The evidence of civilization is spotty at best. I'm not the kind of girl who's afraid to do just about anything, but driving by Fillmore and seeing the rotting husks of houses and the skeletons of stripped cars definitely dissuaded me from any ideas of a long-term visit. I tried to maintain a level tone. After all, I'm just asking questions so I can trade insurance information and get my car fixed. Right? Still I couldn't help being flip. If I hadn't Scott would have gotten suspicious.

"Great place, I hear people get combat pay for living there."

"Tell me about it. I make a run a week to Fillmore and not to solicit for the Policeman's Ball. I guess people like Morello aren't put off by a little urban blight and blood in the gutters. Maybe it cuts down on his morning commute."

"Thanks, Scott." I hesitated, trying to figure the best way to get my next probing question answered. "So, what did Morello spend time in jail for? Is he that bad of a driver?"

The question made me feel kind of sick, but playing dumb will get you more than you might think.

"People usually don't go to state prison for moving violations, Mel."

"So what did he do?"

Papers shuffled. "He's been in for bookmaking, running illegal card games, money laundering, and assault. Apparently he's multitalented."

"I see. He's a real choirboy. This is where you tell me to forget looking for this guy and leave it to the police, isn't it?"

No, there was no way I'd lay off Morello but stroking Scott's ego and playing up to his parental side didn't hurt even if it was a bluff.

"I'd be in favor of you dropping the idea of confronting anyone willing to hit-and-run regardless of whether it's Morello or a priest."

With Scott's need to give sage advice satisfied, I could move on to plumbing Morello's past. If I wanted to chase him down, and I did, I wanted to know as much about what might happen when I caught him as possible. The approach still had to be subtle, though. I laughed, doing my best to sound nervous.

"It's kind of scary though, I mean a gang kingpin like Morello rear-ends my car. Should I plan on going into some kind of federal protection program or something?"

"He's not really what I'd call a kingpin, Mel. He hangs with the wrong crowd all right but I seriously doubt that he was ever on Capone's Christmas card list. If you've changed your mind we still can write the accident up and a uniform can roust Morello."

I hated to crush the budding hope that had taken root in Scott's voice but it had to be done.

"Thanks for the offer, but I think I'll take the path of least resistance. Manny said the damage wasn't as bad as it looked." If I repeated what Manny actually said Scott's head would have exploded. "Sorry I made you do all that work for nothing."

"Don't worry about it; I'm just glad to hear you're not pulling some boneheaded stunt."

Yeah, that's me. The one who *doesn't* pull boneheaded stunts! I managed to hold back my laughter by redirecting my attention toward something that had been bothering me.

"While I'm apologizing for things I owe you one for last night. I should have picked someplace besides The Quarter. I guess I'm just comfortable there."

"As long as we've known each other, I would think you'd be comfortable talking to me in a bus station."

He was right. We'd lived through good and bad times together for over twenty years. God, it's a mistake to start measuring friendships in decades. It detracts from your appreciation by making you feel old.

"Maybe it was the accident. Home turf just felt good." Yeah, or maybe it was the fear Scott might finally get up the nerve to try to kiss me. "I'm just sorry Marko gave you a hard time."

"Marko, so that's his name."

Uh-oh. "I don't like the way you said that, Scott."

"What? What way did I say it?"

"The same way you used to say 'Barkley Cline' before he mysteriously dumped me and moved off to Dubuque."

"Oh yeah, I wonder how old Barkley's doing. Last I heard he'd taken up pig farming."

There was a hint of satisfaction in Scott's voice and it troubled me. It's probably the same feeling people get the first time their cat drops a dead bird on the doormat. It's hard to look at Mittens in the same way when you know she's a calculating killer. Inside I knew Scott had put my relationship with Barkley out of its misery, doomed though it may have been, but I didn't need the body exhumed and autopsied.

"Yeah, thanks for your support."

Obviously he caught onto my acidic tone, probably because I didn't try to hide it.

"He was a jerk, Mel. Do you know what he used to do? He used to go around spreading all sorts of rumors . . . about you. I did you a favor by chasing that clod off."

"I can protect my own honor, Scott."

He snorted. "You don't have to tell *me* that!"

"Yeah, well try to remember it when you get the urge to intercede between Marko and me, huh? We're just *friends* and I'll be the one to decide whether that changes regardless if it's for the better or worse. Got it?"

"Got it."

His confirmation was a little more playful than I would have liked but I couldn't stay mad. Barkley and I had been over for years and Scott had a point, the man *was* a jerk.

"Just the same, thanks for caring."

"My pleasure. If you want to make it up to me, though, you can come to Christmas dinner at my parents' house. Mom always cooks enough turkey for a battalion."

Wow. There are dates and then there are dates that are one step away from a flat-out proposal. This one fell firmly into the category of the latter. Luckily I had a genuine out.

"Scott, you know what my mom would do if I skipped family Christmas. There'd be cries of treason, burning effigies, and an impromptu lynching to cap off the evening. You'll excuse my saying, but that isn't exactly my idea of the holiday spirit."

Scott chuckled. "Yeah, I see your point. How about a late dinner on the Friday after Christmas? Oh, and if you say no I'm going to start thinking you've lost all interest in your old pal from high school."

God, Scott, you're killing me here! Pitting proof of friendship against showing I don't want to be his girlfriend definitely constituted poor sportsmanship. But what could I do?

"Where should I meet you?"

"Oh no, I'll do the driving. You have a history of vehicular incidents. I pulled graveyard shift that night so I'll swing by around seven thirty and we can cruise up to the Twelfth Street Bistro."

Graveyard shift meant he'd have to leave dinner and head directly to work. It also made this rendezvous feel a lot more like palling around than courtship. Apparently, I do get lucky from time to time.

"All right, you've got a deal."

"Good, I'll see you then."

I returned the phone to its cradle and leaned against the kitchen counter, thinking about Scott. Friday I had to tell him to stop chasing me. The whole thing made me sad. I might be standing on the cusp of our friendship's end. I prayed he was the same kid that bounced back from life's blows, the one I'd known in school. The only thing I could be sure of was that I'd find out on December 26.

13

It'd taken all morning to convince Manny I could be trusted with a loaner car to drive to the hospital. Even when he gave in, I could tell it was mostly so I'd leave him alone. His revenge, though, was setting me up with a '39 Pontiac Deluxe that looked like it'd been a part of the first wave into Berlin. Put a couple of screaming ankle-biters in the backseat and I'd willingly shoot myself. I said a silent prayer Mark wasn't standing in the lobby, looking at the smoking heap that'd just pulled into the hospital parking lot. Then I doubled that prayer and turned the motor off.

A salvo of backfires rang through the early afternoon air announcing my arrival and sending an elderly man scurrying for cover. I tried to remain coy, stowing my keys and pulling out my compact while the car's motor continued to knock and chug. Among the sputters and pings I swear I could hear Manny's vindictive laughter. He'd pay, but at the moment I had to focus on other things. I dabbed powder across my cheekbones and nose and then touched up my lips.

As I crossed the parking lot, my brain ran through my first meeting with Mark. What if I'd been too forward? Did he think I was too much of a flirt? Did he think I was some kind of cheap floozy for flirting so much? I must have looked awful that day: hair matted and smelling like God knows what. But then he'd flirted back, hadn't he? Or had he? I reached the lobby before resolving that particular question.

There were even fewer ghosts in the waiting room than the day after I'd been shot and I knew it wasn't because the death rate had gone down. I took a seat near the statue of Sister McAuley that decorated the hospital lobby. I remembered the statue from my first visit to Mercy Hospital: she'd seemed radiant and kind in a world that had turned scary, and the sad look of her downturned face had touched something inside me. There had also been the little girl's ghost to pique my interest; the Sister stared down on the little girl's ghost who played a never-ending game of hopscotch. My mother had brought me to the hospital hoping that her daughter's stories of talking to the dead could be cured with the right combination of pills. Instead, my time there taught me to harness my fright. Watching the little girl skip across the marbled floor, occasionally stopping to pick up an invisible marker before continuing her game, became a refuge from my mother's desperation and the probing questions of doctors.

Years had passed, but the girl still played her game—with only one difference. This time I didn't need to hide from my mother or doctors. It was the voices of trapped souls I wanted to evade. The lingering evidence of my encounter with Death, aside from talking cats, was the ability to hear the voices of those who'd died but couldn't leave their bodies. Where ghosts were sad and wistful, these new voices terrified me. They wailed and keened in an all-too-alive way. Hearing them left me feeling breathless, like the weight of their pain could crush the air out of my lungs, leaving me to suffocate. Even the repetitiveness of the little girl's game couldn't salve the welling sense of panic. I headed for the front desk hoping mind-numbing bureaucracy might help.

By the time I finished checking in, I'd become so distracted I barely remembered my name let alone my social security number, insurance information, address, and the answers to the ten dozen other idiotic questions that populated the hospital forms. From my dazed looks, inability to focus, and the cold sweat I'd broken into, I'm sure the nun working the desk thought she was signing in an addict. It was a blessing when a nurse showed up and ushered me into an examination room.

I changed into the world's least comfortable gown and had a seat on the exam table. At least the voices of the trapped weren't as loud in the examination room; I distracted myself by concocting inhumane purposes for the room's collection of medical instruments. It wasn't a comforting way of passing the time, but listening to the pleading voices that encroached on my brain from the morgue downstairs wasn't any *more* comforting. After about ten minutes of my game there was a knock at the door and a familiar face looked in on me.

"Is everyone decent in here?"

Mark's bright smile contrasted strikingly against his perfect tan, a good combination.

"Hey! I didn't expect to see you again!" Yes, I had an appointment with him. It's awful when my brain turns tail and hides in the face of pressure.

"I couldn't pass up another chance to see the girl who swan-dives off bridges into frozen ditches."

"Don't forget the bullet."

"Ah, yes—the bullet." He had an easy laugh, not forced or a place holder while he thought up a witty retort, just genuine. He closed the door and flipped through the paperwork the nurse had left. "Speaking of bullets, mind if I take a look at that shoulder?"

"Kinda why I'm here."

He eased the gown down my shoulder and started to remove the bandage from the wound. His hands were soft and warm and for the first time since high school I felt a flush of giddy shyness.

"Someone did nice work here. I hope you left the fellow who sewed you up a big tip."

"I think I forgot. It was a hectic day, you know, with getting shot, falling off a bridge, and all."

"You know I meant to ask how a cute girl wound up in the emergency room with a bullet in her shoulder." He hesitated, "Uh, that is if it's not too personal."

I glanced at my bare shoulder and then into his brown eyes. "If this gets much more personal I'll expect a ring."

I think he blushed, I'm not sure. He swiveled his stool to get gauze awfully quick. I have that effect on men—at least the ones that aren't aware I'm prone to do or say anything at any time with little or no provocation. Mark was new to the Mel experience so I tried to ease his embarrassment.

"It's not too personal; actually I'm surprised my mother didn't tell you my entire history of miscreant behavior. See, I have a habit of not doing the respectable thing. I go getting involved where good girls shouldn't."

He returned with a roll of bandages. "Really? Do tell!"

"Well, about eight months ago the police found the body of a girl floating in the Monongahela River." He stopped bandaging as I kept talking. "Maybe you read about it in the paper?"

Mark didn't look up. "Maybe, eight months is a long time."

"Yeah, that seems to be everyone's attitude. Her name was Virginia Beal and she was a hooker down around Manchester. Well, until somebody slit her throat and dumped her body in the river."

His eyes flickered up to meet mine and then, just as quickly, went back to my shoulder. "That's awful. The police are handling it, though, right?"

"Not really. I mean, not well enough." What was I going to say? Tell him that I'd been visited by her ghost who convinced me I should interject myself into an ongoing police investigation

111

with total disregard for personal safety? Absolutely not, I don't like the regular hospital and definitely have no desire to see the inside of a *mental* one. I finally let out an exasperated sigh. "To be honest I don't know if they're really even looking for her killer."

Mark shook his head and grunted what sounded like disapproval before returning to dressing my wound. His hands danced around my upper arm rhythmically as he layered gauze strips to hold the bandage pad in place.

"You should have faith in the system. They probably have detectives working on the case right now."

"You watch too many cop movies, Mark."

He smiled and tore off a piece of adhesive tape to secure his work. "Were you and this Virginia friends?"

"Never met her in my life." Well, technically I hadn't in *her* life. Just another thing I couldn't explain without being fitted for a blouse with tie-in-the-back sleeves.

"I guess that's good."

The comment seemed both genuine and callous. "Good?"

"I mean in a general sense." This time I saw him blush. "Streetwalkers live dangerous lives. I mean they consort with the wrong sort of people, get mixed up in drugs, and that doesn't even start to address the diseases they're exposed to. Syphilis, gonorrhea—"

"Uh, you can stop anytime. If you don't mind I'd like to have an appetite when lunch time gets here."

"Sorry, I guess the public health part of my job interceded there."

"Well, you don't need to worry. I just felt like someone should be looking out for her, regardless if she was a prostitute."

"I admire your altruism." He pulled up the shoulder of the gown and stood, probing my bruised scalp. In spite of the twinges of pain and the cold, medical setting, having his fingers run through my hair felt intimate and romantic. "Still no double vision, persistent headaches, or any of that fun stuff?"

"Nope."

"Good. So, have you made any progress towards finding the poor girl's killer?"

"I managed to find her pimp, a real jerk."

He stopped examining the bump on the back of my head. It smarted to have his fingers lingering on the spot where my skull impacted the ice.

"That sounds risky."

"It did get me shot," I quipped.

"It concerns me that you're putting yourself in that kind of a situation over someone you don't even know. You could have been killed."

Great, the guy I've been infatuated with reads from the same script as Mom and Rolland! This could turn out to be the shortest whirlwind romance on record. "You're not telling me there aren't any causes worth risking your life over, are you?"

"On the contrary, there definitely are good reasons to risk your life. But my job's *saving* lives and although I appreciate your conviction, I wouldn't condone anything that gets you shot, tossed off a bridge, and necessitates your resuscitation at the crime scene. Maybe it's a crazy doctor thing." He tossed the gauze roll back into the drawer. "Just consider it free medical advice."

The smile on his face eased my mind. He was stating principle, not lecturing. I guess I wouldn't want a doctor who was in favor of me getting shot.

"Point taken."

For a second he stood there, arms folded over his chest and his gaze unfocused. He more looked through than at me, like he was trying to read his next step from notes on the wall behind me. After a few moments he took a seat beside me, sitting right next to me like this was the park instead of an examination room.

"Mel . . . you did say you preferred 'Mel,' right?"

"I've been known to sock people over the distinction."

He reached into his pocket and pulled out a small spiral notepad. "You know there's the whole doctor-patient thing about professionalism. We're supposed to treat our patients like they're nothing more than a file full of symptoms instead of real, interesting human beings we'd like to know better." He pulled a pen from his coat pocket and placed it and the pad on the table between us before standing. "Whenever you're ready you can check out with the nurse at the desk."

I changed back into my clothes, staring at the pad as I pulled on my shoes. My big chance had materialized. Mark was a man with a job—no, a profession—and enough money to make any girl he wanted happy for a very long time. Things like this don't happen to me. I attract broke losers. I opened the pad and wrote my number down, checked three times to make sure it was right, and then headed toward the desk without hearing a single pleading voice. The happy beating of my heart drowned them out.

114

14

My family isn't religious. The only occasions in my childhood when I can remember being inside a church were weddings, funerals, and the time I told my mother I'd been conversing with the dead. When the doctors at Mercy Hospital suggested Mom look into sending me to a state institution to look into my "problem," she turned to religion. Apparently she figured if a Catholic priest can perform an exorcism, handling a twenty-one year old who chats with the deceased ought to be a snap. She wound up being disappointed and I wound up with a new friend.

While Mom pleaded her case with the priest, I roamed the cathedral. The fluted pillars and vaulted ceiling of the nave gave me the uncomfortable feeling I was standing in the belly of some monstrous animal, so I wandered outside. The massive building surrounded a quiet cloister garden where birds twittered and butterflies danced among the flowers. That's where I met Johnny G.

Johnny was the first ghost who interacted with me. Before that day there'd been a lot of mumbling, groaning, growling, thumping, bumping, hollering, and even some swearing, but nothing that made sense. I saw apparitions, like the girl playing hopscotch at the hospital, but either they didn't see me or didn't care. Maybe most ghosts aren't capable of seeing the living and the ones who can are like me—outcasts. Or maybe the blame lay with me. It's possible I had to acquire some experience before any of the ghosts thought I'd be worth their time. All I know is it felt both scary and kind of wonderful when Johnny strolled up and said hello. Things haven't been the same since that day. Like that night so many years ago, I needed a friend.

Tonight light filtered out of the cathedral in colored motes that shown on the snowy garden. The color was amplified by the blue purity of moonlight that filled the spaces manmade light couldn't reach. Trees slumbered around the still fountain and a slight breeze stirred their snow-frosted boughs, shaking loose sparkling flakes that swirled and disappeared into the night air. I turned my collar up, leaned against one of the carved pillars that supported the arcade that surrounded the garden, and then I reached into my pocket for the necessary implements for summoning Johnny G.

Lucky Strike came first. Why Johnny couldn't smoke menthols or at least filters was beyond me, but he set the terms of engagement a long time ago. When a fellow's dead I guess the least you can do is buy his favorite brand.

The lid of my Zippo clinked as I flicked it open. I had to protect its guttering flame with one hand as I drew life into the cigarette. The air was filled with the fragrance of naphtha and burning tobacco as the tip burned brightly. I did my best to hold in the lung-searing smoke like a big girl but it fought my efforts until I gave up. An eye-watering cloud erupted from my lungs as I coughed and choked. My vision had barely cleared when Johnny's baritone voice filled the arcade.

"Lucky Strike—best damn smokes in the world."

A gray shade stepped out of one of the neighboring pillars, drawing in the semblance of a deep, appreciative whiff of the smoke that lingered in the air as it took definite shape. In life Johnny hadn't been an attractive man and death had done nothing to improve his looks. He had a prodigious paunch and was balding in the least graceful way possible. His nose was long and downwardly sloped, coming to an Airedale-like point. Above

116

---

this proboscis, bushy eyebrows crowded down until they'd nearly made his small eyes disappear. At least three chins squatted under his heavy jowls, forming a quivering ceiling over his outdated tie. A funny thing about ghosts; every one I've met has a fixed wardrobe. I'm not sure whether what they wear is determined at the moment of death, burial, or by something more arbitrary, but it's enough to make me check the mirror twice every time I go outside. Johnny got lucky; he'd drawn a simple striped shirt, suspenders, and a perpetually crooked tie.

"Hey there girly, haven't seen you for awhile!" His face folded deeply as he smiled. "How's tricks?"

"Not so good, Johnny. Actually, I hoped you could help me with something."

"Anything for a pretty girl."

He eyed the burning cigarette that dangled between my fingers, a cue for me to take another drag. I choked a billowing cloud right through his shadowy face but he didn't seem to mind. I left the cigarette hanging between my lips and reached inside my coat for the ledger.

"I wondered if you could tell me anything about this."

"It's a book."

"Of course it's a book. I know it's a book. Do you think I'd be standing out here in the cold just to hear that?" I opened to a random page and presented it again. "Can you tell me what all this garbage means?"

Johnny squinted. "Hey, hey! When did you go into the bookmaking business, kiddo?"

"Bookmaking. So this does have something to do with gambling."

It wasn't really a question but Johnny took it that way. He leaned in and traced one of the columns with a pudgy, ghostly finger.

"Sure does. The ponies, if old Johnny boy isn't off the mark, and when it comes to the ponies he never is. You been hanging around the track, little girl?"

"No, not really." I turned the book around and held it so that the light from the cathedral tinted the pages in a wash of rose. "So, can you tell who's been placing the bets?"

"Nah, every bookie uses a code. The betters will be listed by nickname, something that only the bookie and his closest associates will understand. It's protection in case the cops bust the operation. Hard to get people to testify if you don't know who they are."

"Great. Just wonderful."

I snapped the book closed. The sound bounced off the cloister garden walls until the snow smothered it. No names meant no leads. I'd hoped Johnny would read off a handful of names that I could look up in the phonebook. I stared at the worn cover of the ledger for a few seconds considering my options.

"Johnny, can you tell me something about the bookmaking business?"

"You're not thinking of starting your own book, are you? I mean unless things have changed since my time the bookie's life ain't for the faint of heart. I don't want you getting in no trouble."

"I promise I'm not starting my own gambling ring. I just want to know how it works."

"Here, sit." Johnny nodded toward one of the benches that looked out on the garden. I brushed the snow aside and settled in as Johnny took a seat by my side. "There's three parts of bookmaking: collecting the bets, dealing with security, and running the bank. See, you got guys out there taking bets, they work bars and street corners taking in money and keeping track of who's betting on what."

"Right. Same as the tellers at a horse track."

Johnny's heavy brows arched pitifully. "I thought you said

you ain't been hanging around the track."

"I haven't."

He looked wistful. "God, I miss the track. Hearing the sound of the hooves and the smell of the racing form—"

It felt bad to interrupt his reminiscence but I had places to go and crooks to catch.

"I saw it in an old movie, Johnny. The Marx Brothers, I think. I hate to tell you this, but I've never actually been to a horse track."

"Never?"

"Not even once."

He clucked disapprovingly. "They don't teach kids nothing these days. If you were my kid I would have taken you to the track as soon as you were old enough to hold a racing form. You gotta start young if you're gonna get somewhere in life, you remember that, kiddo."

I laughed in spite of the cold. "I promise, I won't forget, Johnny. So, we were at dealing with security?"

"Oh, sorry—I forgot myself." He leaned in, lowering his balding head and knitting his brows. "So, you got the bet collecting bit and with all that money you got to have some muscle to make sure things run right. You need a couple real hammers, reliable guys that like to hurt people but not so much that they scare the clientele."

That description seemed to fit with someone I'd encountered on a lonely road. Well, except the not scaring the clientele part. Morello sounded like the kind of guy who'd give any right-minded person the willies for six weeks. Thankfully it'd been a long time since anyone implied I might be in my right mind.

"Okay, so we've got the money coming in and the guy who'll break legs to keep it safe. What about the banker?"

"That smoke's getting kind of lonely."

I followed Johnny's eyes to the cigarette that was slowly burning down toward my knuckles. I flicked the ash off and drew another drag. Johnny smiled ecstatically.

"The guys working the streets bring the money back to the banker. Usually he stays out of sight, nice and quiet so that the cops, or anyone else who's got a mind to make some cash, don't snatch the bank."

"The bank—I'm guessing that's the stash of money the bookie and his cohorts have collected?"

"Exactly. The bank is the money to pay off winners, if there are any. What's left gets divided up."

"So the banker probably would try to pass himself off as someone respectable?"

"Yeah, but not someone so respectable that he draws attention to himself."

That answered a lot of questions. Morello had a history of running illegal gambling rings so it wasn't hard to imagine he was involved in another one. Our little encounter happened in Arnie's neighborhood so I didn't need to be convinced the two of them were connected. Arnie had to be the banker, which made the ten thousand dollars worth of broken dreams buried in his suburban lawn the bank.

"So, what would happen if the banker got killed?"

"I thought you just wanted to know how the business ran."

"It's a hypothetical question."

It didn't look like Johnny bought my answer but I puffed the cigarette again and the nicotine elixir seemed to erase his concerns.

"I guess it depends. Most bookies aren't exactly trusting. I imagine there'd be a lot of mad people."

"People who wasted their hard-earned paychecks on bets that aren't going to pay off?"

"Maybe there'll be a few pissed gamblers. The ones I'm thinking about are the bone-breakers who'll be out their protection money."

"Wait, protection money? I thought you said the bookie has enforcers who get a cut of the bank."

"Yeah, but every bookie pays tribute."

"Crap. The Mob?"

He looked at me like I was stupid. "Of course, and watch your mouth, this is a church."

I ignored his protest. He'd taught me to shoot craps in this very garden. If that didn't rain brimstone down on both of us, a little potty mouth wouldn't go over any worse.

"What if the protection money didn't get paid because the bookie was killed before he could pay?"

Johnny shrugged. "Someone has to pay. These guys don't give extensions due to personal hardships if you get my meaning."

"I'd kiss you if I could, Johnny." I stood and straightened my coat.

"I'd accept. Uh, you did bring something else for me?"

"Sorry, I almost forgot."

The second necessary part of summoning Johnny, the part that made sure he'd come back when I called again, was a cheap bottle of booze. His brand was Gail's Select Kettle and it came in bottles that ranged all the way up to a gallon. A small flask was concealable, fit into my pathetic budget, and provided more than enough booze for the occasion. I screwed the cap off and the smell of high-proof alcohol tinged with notes of paint thinner assaulted my nose. Johnny looked on, smiling, as I poured the bottle around the base of his column.

"Hey, you got some time? Save some of that stuff and we'll sit and reminisce for awhile."

I poured the rest of the bottle down the front of the column. " 'Fraid I can't tonight, Johnny. I got some errands to run."

"Aw, that's too bad. Well, maybe next time?"

I tucked the empty bottle back inside my coat. "I'll save some time on my calendar."

"You're a good kid. You take care and don't be such a stranger."

"I won't, I promise."

I watched the old-timer fade into the evening murk, then flicked the cigarette butt into a snow bank and headed for the car. Not bad for an evening's work. I had Arnie and Morello linked; now I just had to tie them to my client, a goal that I had no idea how to achieve. It's a shame when a sense of accomplishment collapses under its own weight.

15

Taking care of the drugstore on the morning of Christmas Eve was wonderfully dull. A couple of the firemen from the station across the street came in for smokes, there were a few harried dads looking for film or flashbulbs, but for the most part I sat behind the counter thinking about Arnie and Morello. Occasionally Mark would waltz into my mind and we'd go on a wild fantasy excursion that involved a beach, cold cocktails, and applying tanning butter to his warm, bronzed shoulders. Mostly, though, I thought about murder. At noon Manny pulled up in front of the store and beeped his horn. I shut the lights off.

We drove out past the suburbs and into the country where Manny had promised a second shooting lesson. This time it'd be how to shoot left-handed since my right arm still hurt and wobbled pitifully when I strained it for any length of time. He wasn't happy I'd gone and bought another pistol, but considering what we euphemistically referred to as "the sedan incident," he agreed I'd be better off with a little protection. We followed the highway over the river, beyond the suburban sprawl that'd developed around the city, and then exited onto a rough country road. A few miles from the highway stood an orchard. The rows of bare apple trees had been invaded by briars and scraggly mulberries. Eventually, it would look like a stand of forest, all evidence of man's influence erased by nature's persistence. Manny parked his Buick on the weedy shoulder and we clambered out of the car. A rotting, three-rail fence separated the road from the first row of trees.

Manny opened the cavernous trunk and pulled out a stained cardboard box that contained the day's supply of targets: empty oil cans. He waded through the weeds and balanced three empty oil cans on a span of fence rail that hadn't collapsed. He returned, holding out a hand for my gun.

"Let me try it first."

"That doesn't seem fair. It's my gun, after all," I teased, handing the weapon over.

"Life isn't fair, so get used to it." He took the pistol and looked it over before ejecting the clip. "Besides, you're on my turf now so I'm making the rules for a change."

I smirked at his false bravado. Today he made the rules but by saying so he'd admitted that every other day he didn't.

"The bullets slide from the top, you push down and in." He demonstrated, loading the clip up with seven shells.

"Yeah, I figured that much. I noticed there's no bead."

He slipped the clip into the gun, a smile playing across his face. "You didn't call it 'that aim-y thing.' "

"I know how to listen." The last time we did this he'd gotten a kick out of my names for unknown gun parts. This time I didn't plan on playing the part of comic relief. "So, what gives with the sight?"

"This gun's for close quarters. You just point and fire." He ran his finger along a groove in the top of the pistol. "Just put what you want to shoot in this valley. Safety's the lever on the side; you'll have to pull the action back to chamber a round."

He worked the action and then pointed the pistol at the cans. In his hands it looked tiny but the bang was impressive; not as loud as the .38 but enough to make me jump. The cans didn't seem nearly as impressed.

"Nice," I quipped. "You do plan on shooting *at* the cans eventually, don't you?"

He didn't respond, just drew down and rattled off the remaining six rounds. The last one clipped its target sending a wounded can tumbling into the briars.

"When the action stays back you're empty." He displayed the pistol to show what he meant, then passed it over to let me reload. "*If* you ever have to use this thing you're going to want to be really close."

"What, you doubt my shooting?" I started refilling the clip. "You said I was a natural when you taught me to shoot the thirty-eight."

"That was right-handed." He leaned against the hood of his car, watching me reload. "Mel, I'm worried about you."

"We're not starting this again, are we?" I snapped the clip home. "I explained what happened with the car."

"Yeah, yeah I know. But I'm not talking about the car or even getting shot. I'm talking about how much you remind me of your dad."

I stopped feeding bullets into the clip and stared at Manny.

"You two are just alike, bullheaded and full of ideas. He never could sit back and let things go."

"Funny, I remember him always worrying and telling me to be careful."

"That was his father act. Growing up he was voted 'most likely to fall on his own sword.' He never met an underdog he didn't like." Manny drew a deep breath. "That's why he volunteered after Pearl. Forty-eight years old and flying fighter planes with the kids, tells me he's gonna go shoot down some Nazis."

The last time I saw my dad he'd been dressed in his uniform, standing under the rotunda at Union Station, and bound for New York and then England. I remember how the old man suddenly looked young with his hair shorn and that silly hat pulled down over his ears. Mom had tried to act brave though her lip quivered as the train chugged out of the station. I watched the rail cars pass and hoped I'd see Dad's face through one of the windows. I never did, no matter how I tried. That much hadn't changed; to this day I've never seen my dad's ghost either.

"I just remember how strange it was to see him in uniform. All my life Dad was this guy in a tweed suit who drew pictures of buildings for a living. Then, one day, he's this impossibly tall guy in a neat kaki uniform with a pair of wings on his hat."

"He looked good in that uniform," Manny mused absently.

"Yeah, he did." I pulled back the action and let go, then I leveled the gun on the cans. "He sure did."

The first round sent shards of wood spraying off a fence post but the second found its mark. The .25 was so short it didn't feel like a gun at all. Instead it was like pointing my finger at a target. After a clip I was pretty proficient. By the time we left, I could put seven shells in seven targets without a miss. We headed back to town around two, the smell of gunpowder mixing with the scent of my casserole as Manny drove. When we'd passed the suburbs I took the opportunity to enlist Manny as an unwitting accomplice in solving Death's case.

"Hey, do you think we could take a different route to Mom's house?"

"How different? You know how she is about being on time."

"It's not too far out of the way. A friend wants me to check out a house and I promised I would. I forgot until just now."

"I don't know, where is this house?"

"Nineteen and a Half West Fillmore Street."

Manny looked away from the road just long enough to frown at me. "West Fillmore?"

"I know it's a bad neighborhood but I promised."

"Jeeze, Mel. That's not really on the way to your mom's place."

"Please?"

126

He kept muttering but after a few turns I knew I'd gotten my way. Though Manny didn't know it, we were about to pay a visit to the owner of a certain black sedan.

Back when Rutherford B. Hayes sat in the White House, West Fillmore Street must have been something to behold. From one end to the other, the street was lined with two- and three-story Victorian houses. In their day they'd been painted pastel hues that set off the gingerbread brackets adorning every eave. Back then each house reached skyward, throwing up ostentatious peaks and turrets in an attempt to outdo its neighbor. I could imagine horse-drawn carriages carrying smartly dressed couples downtown for dinner and the symphony. But those days were gone and urban blight had taken a toll on the good old days. The neighborhood's wealthy had sold out to slumlords, leaving their grand houses to be subdivided into squalid little apartments. The bright paint jobs and bric-a-brac had decayed, leaving ghostly echoes of pride long dashed into ruin.

"Stop here." I patted Manny on the shoulder as we neared our destination. The last thing I wanted was to roll up in front of Morello's place. It'd ruin the surprise.

"This is one hell of a neighborhood." Manny peered out of the window with the look of a tourist who'd taken a wrong turn and accidentally crossed into East Germany. "Why the heck would anyone want to move into a neighborhood like this?"

"Good question." Like Scott suggested, probably for easy proximity to their customers. I didn't plan on sharing Scott's opinions with Manny.

"What is this friend of yours? Some kind of roller-derby queen or something? I was in better neighborhoods during the war."

"I thought you ran a motor pool in San Diego during the war."

He gave me a sour look. "Don't backtalk your elders. There are plenty of bad neighborhoods in San Diego; maybe just as many as in Berlin."

I smothered a laugh; considering Uncle Manny my "elder" was like calling a trash collector a "government official."

"This friend is pretty tough."

Manny nosed in front of me, leaning across the passenger seat to peer out my window. "I'd hate to meet her in an alley."

"Uncle Manny."

"What? I'm just saying."

I grabbed the door handle and stepped out on the curb before Manny could protest. "Stay here, I'm just going to walk by the house."

"I don't think—"

I slammed his complaint in the door and started down the uneven sidewalk. The houses were built on steeply sloping lots that met a battered retaining wall at the edge of the sidewalk. I imagined the glorious gardens that must have fronted every house, their blooms spilling down to perfume the passerby's evening stroll. Now the lawns were rank with weeds and litter. I checked off addresses until I reached my destination. The building had been painted the color of mustard and the remains of a once-grand porch embraced its corpse. The home had been split into a double. Number 19 stood boarded up with sheets of plywood and 19½ looked vacant. Torn blinds closed off every street-facing window and no light leaked out through the tears. I went around the bombed-out side of the building, ducking under a scrawny tree that leaned against the peeling siding.

The back of the lot was chaos. Nineteen's back door had been kicked in to reveal that a fire had been its undoing. Its charred guts were strewn across the lot: burned boards, broken glass, and the blackened remains of a refrigerator lying on its side against a scraggly oak. Trash sheltered in every nook the burned remains offered, making it hard to walk without twisting an ankle or tripping. I hugged the building, doing my best to move stealthily until I reached the back of Morello's place. The back door had a window and was up just enough to offer a view of the kitchen. I shaded my eyes and peeped through the dirty panes into Morello's life.

Inside the house was as dismal as it was outside. Peeling wallpaper revealed cracked plaster. The room was bare of decoration unless you counted the light bulb that hung from the ceiling. The only evidence of habitation was an ashtray sitting on the kitchen table in front of a single, straight-backed chair. I reached for the doorknob but a piercing sound stopped me.

"Psst!"

I turned to see Manny, his head poked around the corner of the house. He didn't look pleased.

"What do you think you're doing?"

I shrank away from the door and hissed back at him. "I'm checking the house out. Go back to the car."

"I'm sick of waiting. Let's get out of here," he replied, this time a little louder.

"I'm almost done."

He was louder still. "Come on, Mel."

I had a choice: stay and wait until Manny got loud enough to alert Morello to the fact he had a couple of prowlers or go away without getting any more information. Crap.

"Fine." I stepped away from the door and caught Manny's arm as I rounded the corner headed for the car. As we drove away, I kept my eyes on the house. Maybe the accident at the bridge had been fatal. When I got back to the garage I'd have to check the obituaries and police blotter.

16

The aroma of Christmas dinner wafted across Mom's front lawn and greeted me as Manny opened the car door. For all of her shortcomings, and they are numerous, Mom was the best cook I'd ever known. The testimony to her skill with a ladle haunts me whenever I try on a bathing suit. Manny put a hand on my shoulder as I started to step out of the car. His grip was firm and he added one of his famous cautionary squeezes to let me know he was about to bless me with some sage advice. I braced myself.

"Mel, it's Christmas."

I handed him the casserole, forcing him to release his grip. "The calendar agrees with you."

"Try to be nice to your mom, huh? Maybe you could declare a truce for the sake of the season?"

"I could, but she won't. A one-sided truce is the same as surrender. Didn't they teach you that in the Marines?"

"Mel, please."

I took a deep breath of ham-scented air. Mom was standing in the front door, watching us. "I'll do it for you. If she starts her usual shark act you're going to owe me big-time."

I pushed past him and started up the walk as Mom opened the storm door. "I'd started to think you two weren't going to show up."

"You said be here at four o'clock," Manny replied, but the casserole prevented him checking his wristwatch and left him vulnerable to Mom's verbal thrust.

"It's a quarter past." Exasperation tinged her voice. To Mom a minute late was as good as an hour late. The principle mattered a lot more than the substance. "I hope the dressing hasn't dried out too much from sitting in the oven. There isn't anything in the world less edible than dried-out dressing."

She greeted me in the doorway with a hug and a kiss on the forehead. "How are you, dear? Is the shoulder any better?"

"I'm fine, Mom."

Her attention returned to Manny who'd just reached the top step.

"That's a miracle considering your uncle's had you out in the cold and damp." She took the dish Manny carried. "You shouldn't be riding around in that rusty old junker. I bet the heat doesn't even work."

"Junker? You have no idea what you're talking about! That car is solid. Do you know how many miles I've put on that car? Almost a hundred thousand, and it runs perfectly! Mark my words, in fifty years everyone's going to be driving Buicks and the other car companies will go under because they can't compete!"

Manny was preaching the gospel of Buick, but with the exception of me the congregation had left the chapel. Mom had departed for the kitchen carrying my casserole. She called back instructions for Manny with a casualness meant to show his automotive fervor was wasted in her household.

"Make yourself useful and take your niece's coat to the bedroom, Manny. Oh, and bring the presents in too, the tree looks bare without any packages."

"The truce didn't hold for long," I chided, smirking as Manny took my coat.

Manny headed for the hallway and I went to the kitchen. Mom stood over my contribution to the dinner and the look on her face was akin to someone who's preparing for a mouthful of penicillin. Grim resolve would be the best description, I think. Over the years my cooking has become infamous. It's good to be known for something. That way you know you won't be forgotten.

"Go ahead, Mom, open it."

She glanced at me with a pained smile gracing her face but her eyes were drawn back to the foil. I think she expected to see movement.

"I don't want it to get cold."

"Don't worry; the cookbook said it was just as good at room temperature."

I could see her swallow the bile that doubtless was rising in her throat. Cautiously she gripped the corner of the foil, steadied herself, and pulled. She opened one eye and then the other, reapplied her fake smile, and tried to find something encouraging to say.

"Oh, it looks—are those raisins?"

I took a seat in one of the chairs around the kitchen table. "They could be raisins or maybe kidney beans, the two look alike once you add the coconut milk."

The way Mom drew back you would have thought I'd said it was unhatched cockroaches. "Oh, it has kidney beans and raisins? How very interesting."

She was being polite and that wasn't fighting fair. I wanted the same mom who'd dressed me down in front of Scott and Rolland, not this friendly imposter. I meant to push her today, just to get even in my own, small way.

"Why don't you taste it?"

"I couldn't, I wouldn't want to ruin the beautiful . . ." She gestured but no words came.

"Crust?"

I got up and retrieved a spoon from the silverware drawer,

then sidled up beside her and pushed it into her hand.

"Don't worry; it's just the three of us. No need to put on airs."

The spoon hovered over the dimpled surface of the casserole. Mom's lip quivered and her hand was unsteady. I had her stuck between two extremes: either she maintained the mirage of the perfect mom and took a big bite of a dish she knew would be disgusting or she rebuffed me and accepted the Rush family holiday in all its dysfunctional glory. I held my breath as her hand moved downward. Uncle Manny had to spoil everything.

"Edith, where's the eggnog?"

Mom withdrew the spoon and turned away from her coconut and condensed soup nemesis. I'm surprised she didn't let out an audible sigh of relief.

"Oh! I almost forgot the eggnog! I'm sorry, dear. Why don't you put this in the oven to warm while I take care of your uncle."

She disappeared before I could mount a counteroffensive. Another holiday, another defeat. One of these years she'd actually have to eat my cooking and then I'd have revenge for all the cod liver oil she shoved down my throat as a child. For now, though, I shook my head, took the casserole to the oven, and then wandered into the family room.

The tree looked splendid; a flawless representation of the holiday Mom was trying to create. It was plump and crowded with ornaments, garland, strung popcorn, lights, and topped by a golden star that twinkled slightly in the dimmed room. From having lived with Mom, I knew Thanksgiving dinner had hardly been cleared away when she started decorating for Christmas. The planning might have started in August. The aura of desperation it shed was oppressive. Since we lost Dad every Christmas got progressively more complex. Layers of tinsel couldn't staunch the emotional bleeding. I had to get out of the room before my mood lost its natural buoyancy.

The hallway just off the living room leads to what used to be my bedroom. It sits across from Mom's room and down from the bathroom. Since Dad's death, that hall has been a gauntlet. Then as now, there are no ghosts, no lurking specters waiting to assail me with their sorrow. There are no knife- or gun-wielding thugs poised in the shadows, waiting for their opportunity to pounce. Fact is, it's way safer than my everyday life. That's part of the reason I dread and feel compelled by the space. Maybe when you're surrounded by the dead and their killers, they become a comforting feature of a familiar landscape and their absence becomes its own tension. There are other reasons I dread that hallway, though—and they're a lot less comfortable to think about.

The first door on the left, right next to what used to be my bedroom and just across from the tiny bathroom, leads into a small, windowless room. I stopped in the doorway and leaned against its frame as casually as I could manage. The place hadn't changed. The drafting table still sat in its corner with a goosenecked light arching over a cup of pens to hover above an expanse of blank paper. The tall stool Dad used to perch atop while he labored over the floor plan of some new school or office building still sat with its back casually facing the doorway. If he were sitting at his desk, we'd be looking at each other. Everything stayed the way Dad left it. Dust gathered and the drawings he'd tacked to the walls had yellowed, but the room remained unchanged, holding its breath and waiting.

"I still think I hear him sometimes."

Mom caught me in a bout of nostalgia. I didn't realize she was standing behind me until she spoke. She put a hand on my back and joined me in the doorway.

"I remember hearing Dad whistling when he worked late. It used to come right through the wall." I smiled at the memory, the sound drifted into my mind. "What was the name of that tune?"

"Three O'clock in the Morning." She drew a deep, unsteady breath and then started to sing.

> *"It's three o'clock in the morning*
> *We've danced the whole night through*
> *And daylight soon will be dawning*
> *Just one more waltz with you*
> *That melody so entrancing*
> *Seems to be made for us two*
> *I could just keep on dancing*
> *forever dear with you."*

I'd forgotten Mom's singing voice. It was far from perfect but there was a loveliness in it that I remembered from a time before everything derailed. I picked up the second verse.

> *"There goes the three o'clock chime, chiming, rhyming*
> *My heart keeps beating in time*
> *Sounds like an old sweet love tune*
> *Say that there soon will be a honeymoon."*

The hallway grew awkwardly quiet until Mom felt compelled to break the tension. "I don't know why he liked that silly old song so much."

"Maybe someone sang it to him when he was a kid?" I suggested, and for a moment the hallway fell silent again.

"I miss him," Mom said sadly.

"Me too, Mom."

"Do you ever . . ." Mom's voice quivered on the edge of the question, nearly tipping over but not quite.

"Do I ever what, Mom?"

"Nothing." She put on her brave smile. God, I hated the

brave smile. "Wash your hands; I'm not sure how long I can keep your uncle out of the rolls."

I didn't move. I knew what she wanted to know. She wanted to ask if I'd ever seen Dad's ghost, if he'd ever visited me. There were days I thought she assumed I got with Dad's ghost for regular wild parties without telling her. In actuality Dad wasn't one of the hundreds of ghosts I'd met. Knowing that might have eased her misgivings, but she wouldn't ask and that meant I wouldn't tell. The potential cost of broaching the subject wasn't worth paying. So we stood for a moment, eyes locked.

"Well, go on, dinner's getting cold!"

She turned and left me in the doorway. In a moment I heard her berating Manny for fingering the ham. I sighed, took one last look at Dad's office, and went to wash up.

17

Dinner at Mom's house pretty much flowed in the traditional way if you discounted our time together in the hallway. There was a wonderful ham with equally wonderful sides of mashed potatoes, green beans, carrots, hot rolls, and three types of pie. Compared to the Norman Rockwell spread Mom set out, my casserole looked like something Martian invaders would unleash to wreak havoc on an unsuspecting Earth. We opened presents, drank eggnog, and Manny retold his stories of all the horrible things I did as a child. I guess comedy is good; I'd rather not be its subject, though. After eating way too much I left burdened down with enough leftovers to keep my fridge stocked for a month; oh, and my untouched casserole.

It was past ten thirty when we pulled away from Mom's house. My full day conspired with the heavy food and soon the motion of the car had me dozing. My eyes fluttered closed and my casual contemplation of the events of my life melted into dreams. Manny and Mom got into a food fight, flinging steaming hunks of my casserole at each other while Voe sat on my shoulder telling me that Morello and Alfonzo were outside and that they wanted their money back. In the dream I could hear them pounding: angry fists beating on the front door. When my eyes opened, Manny had parked the car and stood outside tapping on the passenger-side window.

The lot outside the garage was nothing like the snug interior of the car. The wind carried stinging snowflakes that bit my ears and bare cheeks, but with my good arm burdened down with the larder Mom sent home and a casserole, there wasn't a lot I could do about the situation.

"Looks like the boys are still here."

Manny was looking at the partially rehabilitated Model A that sat by the building. It belonged to Drew, one of the greasers who worked at the garage. Manny started toward the side door.

"I wonder what they're working on."

Restrained by my sling, I one-shoulder-shrugged.

"Maybe they're stealing the fixtures?"

Now he shot me a dirty look. He's learned a lot by hanging around me!

"You've been hanging around that prison guard–wannabe Rolland."

He was right; I shouldn't be casting aspersions on the guys around the garage. Sure, they deserve it on occasion, but the kind of assumption I just made could have come right out of Rolland's mouth. I hate it when he's right. I hate it more when I'm wrong.

"Sorry, I guess I'm just tired and cranky."

"Don't worry about it." Manny's voice contained a note of triumph but he didn't lord over me. "You might be able to pawn that—thing—you cooked off on Drew."

"Really?" I frowned at the casserole. "You think?"

Manny shrugged. "Eh, once I saw him eat a MoonPie that got dropped in a pan full of oil."

I gave another half-shrug. "Huh, if that's the case we might as well try!"

I followed Manny into the garage to find Drew manning a hoist, lowering an engine into a hotrod in the making. He stopped when we walked in, turning his round face in our direction.

"Heya, Mel."

He smiled. It was a broad, dumb smile that fit Drew perfectly. He was a six-foot-tall high school dropout and he weighed maybe 260 pounds. He reminded me of a professional wrestler: big, muscular arms and a potato-like body. He had the temperament too. Drew might be slow to anger but once he'd been pushed past his limit nobody could talk him down. Rumor around the repair bays was that he'd once beat a Ford to death with a tire iron when he couldn't get the carburetor to work. I liked Drew but I felt sorry for the Ford.

Manny pulled his hat off and approached the car.

"You working on Bob's junker?"

As Manny got near the front bumper, Bob slid out from under the car.

"She's no junker!"

Bob's voice fit perfectly: nasal and whiny. Everything about him made me queasy. He had the physique of a pipe cleaner, so skinny it looked like his pompadour might land him on his nose. He pulled himself from under the car and looked me over. I think it's the way his right eye doesn't quite track the left that creeps me out the most. I put the casserole on top of a rolling toolbox to stave off the willies.

"I thought you two might like some leftovers."

"Hey, what's that?"

Drew locked the hoist in place and came over as I peeled the foil off the dish.

"It's Hawaiian Three-Bean Poi Joy casserole." Suddenly the silliness of that name was embarrassing. Funny, when I was using it against Mom it felt so rhythmic coming off my tongue. "I, uh, found it in a cookbook."

Drew didn't wait for me to finish the explanation. His fingers were in the dish and he'd scooped out a dripping mass. I think I could have said it was barbequed lizard spleen and it wouldn't have slowed him down. I shot Manny a look and he simply shook his head. Bob didn't dig in. Instead he stood back, wiping his hands on a rag.

"So, about eight o'clock we're pulling the block out of the car and this guy calls." He stuffed the rag in his back pocket.

"Someone need a jump start?" Manny was inspecting the engine.

"That's what I figured at first." Drew chimed in. He was chewing and talking at the same time; it was kind of like watching the lions being fed at the zoo.

"Yeah," Bob continued, "but this was a personal call. Some guy looking for Melly."

If I hated being called Melody, I hated being called Melly even more. I tried not to give him the pleasure of knowing it bugged me and stuck to the important question. "Who was it?"

Bob patted his pockets, finally pulling a slip of dirty paper from the breast pocket. He shook the folds out. "Some guy named Mark. Hey, this a boyfriend, Melly? Don't ya think you should let us check this guy out before you go getting all smoochy?"

If you ever wonder what baboons sound like when a fit of hilarity overtakes them I can describe it perfectly. It'd exactly match the whooping, hollering, and guffawing that came from Bob and Drew, at least up to the point when I snatched the paper from Bob's hand, jabbed a finger into his chest, and burned into him with an angry stare.

"Who I go out with isn't any of your business." I headed for the door. "And if you call me 'Melly' one more time I'll break your scrawny ass in half."

Bob was on the receiving end of the hooting when I slammed the door. Like I said before, they're like big brothers—irritating, insulting, meddling big brothers. Occasionally you have to put your siblings in their place. When I left the garage, excitement sent my heart floating against my ribcage. I dashed upstairs, taking two steps at a time. When I reached my kitchen I locked the door and unfolded the note.

Mark's number and message were recorded in Bob's bad handwriting. The note said "Call as soon as you can."

I knew he'd call, I mean he'd asked for my number in a kind of surreptitious way, so obviously he was going to call. I didn't expect the request for me to call him as soon as possible. What did that mean? There had to be some underlying meaning, some secret guy thing I should decipher before I grabbed the phone and started dialing. But what was it?

I was leaning on my elbows, contemplating that question, when Voe wandered into the kitchen.

"My water's all icky. There's food in it," he announced, barely checking a bored yawn.

"That's good. Mark called!"

Voe settled, wrapped his tail around his haunches, and stared with his nostrils flaring. "What's that smell?"

I picked the note off the counter and walked under the light where I could see it better. As if lighting was the problem in decoding the meaning of his message.

"I should wait, if I call him tonight it'll seem like I'm desperate."

"It smells like ham. Did you bring me some?"

I started pacing. "But he *says* call as soon as I get a chance and if I wait he might think I'm blowing him off. I don't want him to think that."

"What about the ham?"

"Still, I don't want him to think I'm easy."

"Did I mention I want some ham?"

I snatched the receiver from its cradle and started dialing.

"Hey, I'm starving here!" Voe squalled.

"Huh, what are you talking about?"

Before Voe finished whining Mark picked up.

"Hi there, uh, I mean, merry Christmas!" Damn, so much for playing coy.

"Well, merry Christmas to you too. I hope I didn't interrupt the holiday festivities."

"No, not at all. But I thought I gave you my number, not the garage number."

"I tried your number but nobody answered. I called the operator and the address came back to a place called Manny's Garage. So I called, left a message, and here we are." He paused. "I hope I didn't cause any problems."

Not if you discounted the brand new possibility for embarrassment: his leaving a message with a dimwit mechanic.

"It's okay. Uh, the guy you talked to didn't make any sort of comments, did he?"

"No. I didn't get you in trouble or anything, did I?"

"Not at all." Bob's life had been spared and the moron didn't even know how close he'd come to death. "I never get in trouble, you should know that."

He chuckled and the comic eye roll came right through the phone. I love guys with expressive voices.

"So," he started, "what's going on at the Rush household?"

"Nothing really. I'm just feeding the cat and washing out a few things."

"Wow, how do you bear the excitement? It makes me wonder what do you do to celebrate New Year's? Laundry?"

Mark had a sense of humor, another reason to like him. "Something like that."

The line fell silent. I sat, twirling the phone cord around one finger feeling the urge to talk but for once I was unsure what to say. It was something when a guy could bring out the side of me that was capable of bashfulness. On the other end of the phone, I could hear Mark move and I wondered if he was feeling the same thing, the strange momentum that kept us orbiting this moment in time. Finally, I cleared my throat just to hear a human sound, the tension seemed to collapse under its own weight and he spoke.

"Mel, I wondered. What would you think about getting together for dinner? Maybe this Friday?"

The moment I'd waited for. Now, if I could just manage that casual cool attitude I'd pictured myself having when this moment arrived. Unfortunately, my sense of what I'd like and the reality of what happens often are so far apart. My voice seemed to boom over the receiver.

"That sounds wonderful!" Crap, I might as well go all the way now. "I'd love to."

"Great, I'll pick you up at six."

"Six," I repeated, living in the warmth of the idea. Six sounded wonderful. There couldn't be a better time than six.

"So, I guess I'll see you then?"

"Sure, six o'clock." Could I repeat that one more time just in case he didn't think I had some major problem? "I'll talk to you then."

"Yeah, I'll talk to you then. Bye."

I listened until the dial tone came. It was a high school thing to do but it made me feel like he was still with me, at least until I had to admit otherwise. I replaced the receiver, feeling giddy and light headed as I turned toward my living room—only to be stopped by the looming, black smudge of a figure that stood between me and my destination. The reaction was involuntary, shrill, and it took almost a minute for my heart to stop hammering in my chest.

"Jesus! What are *you* doing here?"

Death hung in the air like smoke, present only in the most technical of terms. He didn't apologize for scaring the hell out of me. Maybe that sort of reaction was so common he didn't think it warranted an apology.

"Melody Rush, our time grows short."

"*What?* You're telling me you just invaded my private space and scared me witless just so you could check up on me? Do you know I almost peed myself?"

He didn't seem impressed. "I am here to remind you of the urgency of your task."

"I *know* it's urgent. I'm getting close. I just need to get a little more information." I leaned against the counter while my heart rate slowed to something that approximated normal. "I think a guy named Vince Morello has something to do with Alfonzo Arnie's killing. The problem is I'm not sure how to make the link and I have no idea where he's gone."

"In six days no amount of information will matter."

"Right, I understand we've got a *dead*line." If he noticed the pun he didn't react. I nodded to the refrigerator. "Do you, uh, want a beer or something."

There was a pause. "No."

"Could you drink one if I got it for you?"

"This isn't a social visit. I'm not here to—"

"You can stop there; I'm done with the distant, unknowable arbiter of fate bit." I opened the refrigerator and grabbed a bottle of beer for myself. "You hired me; you're going to answer some questions. So, have a seat and let's chat."

After another chilly interval, Death glided across the floor to one of my kitchen chairs. He was too insubstantial to sit in it. He and the chair simply occupied the same space at the same time. I took that as acquiescing and took the seat across from my haze of a client.

"Explain the cat to me."

"What cat?"

I leaned over the back of my chair toward the living room. "Hey, Voe, I've got some ham for you."

"It's about time you—" The feline trotted into the kitchen and froze, fur standing on end and wide eyes fixed on Death. "What the hell are you doing with *that* in our house?"

"Wow, look at that. I guess I'm *not* the only one who can see Death." I popped the top off my bottle of beer. "Question one: why can I hear Voe talk when no other human being can?"

"I warned you that you no longer were part of the normal world, Melody Rush. You now are an inhabitant of a different realm, one that extends beyond the borders of the natural and supernatural."

"Are you saying I'm some kind of zombie or something like that?"

"Do not be foolish."

Death's response actually had a hint of emotion. Indignation if I didn't miss my guess. I think I liked it better when he had no personality whatsoever.

"Okay, so I'm between the 'natural and supernatural world' and that's why I can hear Voe talking? Does this mean I'm going to have conversations with every chipmunk and squirrel I meet?"

"Not all animals can talk," Voe answered from just inside the living room, which seemed to be as close to Death as he was comfortable with getting. "Some of us are connected; others are just dumb animals. Dogs, for instance."

That explained why the dachshund I ran into didn't give me a lecture in German but it fell way short of being sufficient.

"Whoa, connected?"

"Part of the mystery."

"You're going to have to do better than that."

"Some beasts carry darkness deep in their souls," Death said, his voice sliding across the table like a draft.

I wasn't sure I wanted to know which animals had this dark connection. It was bad enough to know I'd taken one of them as a roommate. If there were animals roaming the world that were able to see Death and, presumably, other unnatural beings, that opened another possibility.

"Are there other people like me?"

"There are others."

"How many—and where?"

Death's form faltered slightly. "No more questions, Melody Rush. Find the mask before the last stroke of midnight on the last day of this year or all is lost."

I watched Death's form become more insubstantial until all that remained was the scent of ash floating on the air.

Voe shivered. "I hate that guy. Everything about him is way wrong."

Voe sauntered away leaving me to drink my beer and consider Death's words and the rapidly expiring year. I needed to find Morello and to do that I needed to know what he looked like. That meant conning Scott into letting me see Morello's mug shot tomorrow. Tonight, though, it was a bubble bath, a beer or two, and a good night's sleep.

18

When she returned from her holiday, Mrs. Beeman would expect certain things: that the store had been properly cleaned; "properly" meaning all the display cases polished, the floors swept, and the Christmas stuff put in storage. I'm not sure whether she believed it was bad luck to display a plastic Santa after New Year's Eve or if she just found it depressing, but I knew I'd rather meet her expectations than face the consequences.

I pulled up in front of the drugstore and parked my loaner station wagon at the curb. The luxury of my boss being in Florida was that I could handle these chores over the span of her vacation rather than having her personally supervise the process. Another benefit was that I could close the store to take a break whenever I wanted. That was my plan for the afternoon, because Scott would be at his desk. I sat in the car, waiting for it to finish its ritual convulsions, and when it finally fell silent I hopped out. Across the street the firemen were having a snowball fight, ranging up and down the sidewalk and yelling like boys. I smiled at their antics as I headed for the storefront. There's something attractive about virile man-children at play. I had one hand on the door handle when someone pressed into the entryway close behind me. Something ominously hard jabbed me in the back. Remember that saying, "speak of the devil and he will appear"? Apparently it works for homicidal hoodlums too.

"Just go inside and everything will be all right." His voice was low and his commands terse.

"You must be Morello," I replied, stiffening my back against the gun.

"And you must be deaf; I said get inside the building now."

I figured it was better to listen than to get shot standing in a doorway, so I obeyed. Morello shoved me inside and shut the door behind us. He grabbed my bad arm and pushed me headlong into a counter, sending racks of cosmetics tumbling and candy scattering across the tile floor. The pain of having my injured shoulder wrenched brought tears to my eyes. He didn't give me time to recover, pulling me around to face him.

Since the last time we met the porkpie hat had disappeared. In its place were bandages and two black eyes. His nose had been broken and his lip split. The wreck had done so much damage it would have been hard to connect his battered face with any mug shot Scott could have provided. That didn't really matter, though; what did was the mean-looking pistol he had trained on me. You'd think a gun would make me behave, but sometimes I can't help myself.

"Say, that's some bump you got there."

My mouth earned me a jab with the barrel of the gun.

"Shut your smart mouth!" When he yelled spit rained down across my face. "I want my money and I want it now."

"You mean Alfonzo's money."

"I mean *my* money. Now, either I walk out of here with it or only one of us will walk out of here. You tell me which it's gonna be." He cocked the gun to show his seriousness.

"Can I point out one thing without you beating me to a pulp?" I didn't wait for an answer; I didn't really care what he had to say. "If you kill me you'll never get a cent of that money and unless I miss my guess there are some pretty tough characters who will be very disappointed if they don't get paid."

My observation seemed to befuddle Morello. Obviously, he'd made me out as some kind of crook who'd stolen the bank and the concept that I'd be using it to bargain for something else didn't fit into that assumption. I pulled my hand free and straightened my coat.

"You want your money and I want information. I think we should be able to come to some kind of arrangement."

He didn't lower the pistol but those blackened eyes showed interest. "Keep talking."

"Don't worry, that's what I do best." The joke was lost on him, I should have known better. I nodded to the Carmex and Life Savers that littered the drugstore floor. "Mind if I clean this up? My boss won't be happy if she comes back to a trashed store."

"Stop screwing around and ask your questions, lady."

I picked up the rack and started collecting candy from the floor. "You and Alfonzo were running a book out of his house in Sunnyvale. You handled the protection and collection while he handled the bank and kept the books, right?"

"Yeah, so?"

"So on November first you went to Alfonzo's house and killed him, why did you do that?"

Morello snorted. "You got the wrong guy. I didn't kill Alfie. We had a good deal running, why would I ruin that?"

"I don't know. Maybe he was dipping into the till or maybe you two just had a falling out." I set the candy back on the counter.

"You're cracked, lady. I didn't kill anyone, or at least I haven't yet."

I eyed the gun. "Yeah, let's work on keeping it that way. Explain something to me, you were at Alfonzo's house the night of the first, right?"

"I went to his house lots of nights. I had to drop off the

149

money and betting slips."

"So, if you didn't kill him what happened?"

"I don't see what this has got to do with me and my money."

"It's got to do with the fact that to *get* your money you need to *answer* my questions." I nodded to the loops of garland that hung across the counter front. "I need to take these down."

"So take them down already."

I started taking greenery down, hoping my asking permission made him feel more in control and less like putting a slug in me for asking too many questions. If he was comfortable I figured he might talk more freely. It was a theory; whether it was a good one remained to be determined.

"Tell me about that night," I asked, looping garland around my bad arm as I worked my way down the counter.

"When I got to the house Alfie already was dead. Somebody slit his throat and left him laying there in the middle of his kitchen floor."

"So if you weren't robbing the place why did you ransack the house?"

"I think you put it best when you said certain people expect to get paid. To keep them happy I needed that money."

"You didn't know where Alfonzo kept the bank." The arrangement between Alfonzo and Vince was becoming clear. "Insurance?"

"You catch on quick. If somebody leaned on me I couldn't give up the money. To keep Alfie honest, I had all the connections and I knew the right people, so he couldn't run the book without me." He smiled and with his battered face it looked painful. "A little racier than the drugstore business, huh?"

"Maybe a little."

I moved to the door and that prompted a reaction. "Hold it."

I nodded to the plastic Santa face in the door. "Just cleaning up. You've got the pistol."

"Just take it easy," he advised, relaxing a little.

I smiled and pulled the decoration down. Outside the firemen were really at it. If I could just get some help from them I might be able to evict Morello without getting shot. I casually slid the door sign from CLOSED to OPEN in hopes it'd be noticed, and then returned to the counter.

"Tell me something; when you found Alfonzo did you notice anything strange?"

"Aside from my business associate lying dead in a pool of his own blood? No."

"You didn't see anyone lurking around the house?" I couldn't exactly ask if he'd seen the Grim Reaper hiding in a closet, could I?

"Nobody was in the house. I turned the place upside down looking for the bank and if someone had been there I would have found them."

"You probably would have." He had to be lying. He had to have killed Alfonzo and been too stupid to have asked where the bank was hidden. The problem was, if he'd been that stupid it was hard to believe he'd been cunning enough to have stolen Death's mask or to have even had a reason to steal it. Something was missing and I wasn't going to find it with Morello's gun pointed at me.

There was a knock on the door and both of us jumped. A face was pressed against the drugstore's door, a big moon face with plastered wet hair and a red nose.

"Who's that?" Morello looked like a cornered dog and he definitely was ready to bite.

"It's just one of the firemen from across the street. They come here all the time."

"Tell him the store's closed."

"You seem to be under the impression you're in charge just because you've got the gun. It doesn't always work that way,

Morello." I smiled; the look on his face told me he sensed the power had shifted and there wasn't a damned thing he could do to regain control. "If you ever want to see your money again you'll listen and do exactly what I tell you."

"And what is that?" he growled.

"Once the seasonal festivities are over, I'm going to pay a visit to the firetrap on West Fillmore you call home. When I show up I'm going to have a lot of questions and I expect you to answer all of them. If you help me, I'll help you by telling you where to find your money."

I walked to the door, praying Morello wouldn't shoot me in the back. It was a relief when my fingers touched the lock. I opened the door and the inrush of cold air felt better than the nicest spring day.

"Hey there, Willie, what do you need?"

"I thought you were closed but then I saw the sign." He glanced at Morello. "Howdy."

"Willie, this is Vince Morello. Vince came in to get some bandages for his nose."

Willie squinted at Morello. "Whoa, I guess so! You look like you ran into a tree face first!"

"We were in the middle of something," Morello snapped.

"Actually, I think we're done. I've got your address, I'll be in touch when we have more to discuss."

The look Morello gave me was nearly as good as a bullet. "A week, you got a week."

"More than enough time." I smiled. "Try not to have any more accidents in the meantime."

He headed out the door, eyes fixed on me as he pushed by Willie. I waved as he went, just to prod him before turning my attention to the paying clientele.

"What can I do for you, Willie?"

He held up a dripping pack of cigarettes. "The guys filled my pockets with snow."

I smiled as Morello disappeared around the corner. "This pack's on the house, Willie."

19

It's a known fact that most women ask for fashion advice, even when we're pretty darn sure we don't need it. Maybe our mothers beat such a sense of self doubt into us that we spend the rest of our life trying to get rid of it or maybe we just want someone to admire our accomplishments with a "you look amazing, I sure wish I had the figure to wear that." Whichever is the truth, I can tell you the worst source of affirmation is a cat. The evening of my date with Mark I put on my favorite black satin dress, the one with the sequined bodice that displays my assets while downplaying my shortcomings. The fit is perfect: snug where it ought to be without creating an embarrassing scene. The deal-of-the-season red spike heels weren't so kind. I had to wrestle my feet into them, risking breaking an ankle the entire time. Finally I had the shoes on and I held onto the dresser for balance as Voe watched from the foot of my bed.

"Explain why you wear them again," he asked with an unpleasant smug tone in his voice.

"Because of the way they make me look." I had the left shoe fastened and switched to the right.

"And just how do they make you look?"

"Taller and thinner."

"Ah, I see." He yawned and reclined. "Personally, I think sleek and low to the ground is a lot more attractive."

"Yeah, personally low to the ground is the sort of thing I'm trying to avoid." I stood in triumph, looking at myself in the mirror. "See, taller and thinner, just like I said. What do you think?"

"I think you're going to break your neck."

"Oh come off it, Voe. Cats are supposed to be Casanovas, where's your sense of romance?"

"I've got romance. I'm just not into masochism. Besides, you ought to be working on Alfonzo's case instead of carousing. Your shadowy friend wants answers and I wouldn't disappoint him."

I went to my jewelry box to pick out a rhinestone bracelet. His protest brought up something I'd been meaning to discuss.

"This darkness in your soul thing, what's it like?"

"What do you mean?"

"What should I expect now that things are 'different' for me?"

"Aside from seeing Death?" Voe seemed to consider the question for a second. "You're going to get to understand why every cat thinks human beings are just barely brighter than the average squirrel."

That made me laugh. "Wonderful. So, I, I gather there isn't anything dumber than a squirrel."

"Do you really want to know?"

Something in the way he said that told me I did but it also told me I should be afraid to ask. I opted for the safe route for once. "In comparison to cats, I guess people really bumble around the planet."

"Pretty much. You're not that bad though. You're trainable; that's a big plus."

"So, any advice you'd like to pass on to this naive girl before she goes out into the dark old world again?"

"For the time being, my only advice is not to disappoint Death. Frankly, you shouldn't be wasting time toying around with this man, you should be working."

"Oh, really? I'm getting this sage advice from the one who has a kitten on the side that he describes as having 'one fine tail'?" For the first time since I picked him up I had the chance to needle Voe and I damn well meant to take advantage of the opportunity. "It's just one evening, one little go-round on the nice side of town with a fine-looking fellow who can afford to show me what a good time is about. Surely you're not implying a single night will blow my chances of tracking down Alfonzo's killer."

Voe swished his tail frenetically. "I don't know."

"I promise I'll work all the harder tomorrow. Morello is the killer, I'm sure of it. I'll negotiate with him to trade Alfonzo's money for the mask. Once Death's problems are solved, I'll turn Morello over to the cops and everything will be set." I chucked him under the chin. "See, I'm on the case even when I'm not."

"Fine, have your night on the town." Voe hopped down and followed me to the coat closet. "Tell me, what's your plan?"

"Weren't you listening? I just told you the plan."

"Not *that* plan. The plan for handling this—man—you're going out with."

"I don't think I've got a *plan*. I figured we'd have a little fun, eat dinner, and have a few drinks."

Voe looked more disgusted than usual. "People really don't get it, do they? I mean do you think this Doctor whatever doesn't have a plan? I know whenever I go for a little moonlight mischief I've got one. Your date may be an ignorant human but I doubt he'll be any different."

"If I'm lucky he's got one! The fun comes in foiling it until I'm good and ready for him to succeed." I pulled on a red coat that matched the shoes and complemented the dress. "Now, I think I'll wait downstairs outside of the advice zone. Don't wait up."

I stepped out onto the stoop and took a deep breath of cold air. It was early enough that the sun hadn't quite sunk past the horizon and the city seemed to be on fire. It was glorious, but with anticipation of the evening ahead tinting the world in hues of rose, everything seemed glorious. I held the banister to counter my high heels and made my way downstairs where I could watch for Mark. Every date I'd had since I moved into the garage had to pull up to the repair bay where they beeped their horns like truckers fetching a load. The downside to my living arrangement was the high fence that protected the lot also precluded fellows knocking on my door with roses and candy in hand. I promised myself as soon as finances allowed, I would move to some apartment building where my standards barred admittance, not the safety of a bunch of cars waiting to be fixed. I let myself into the garage with my key and headed for the bay doors to check for Mark.

The gloom of the garage always soothed me. It was a safe place filled with the smells of Manny's cheap cigars and motor oil. That scent reminded me that the winnowing commentary of my mother and the scrutiny of the world were far away. After closing, Manny's garage existed in a neat envelope, safe from the world's inconveniences and intrusions. Well, from the intrusions of the *living* world. As I stood, looking out at the empty street, a chill slithered over my body. I knew exactly what that feeling meant.

I found her by a stack of tires near the washroom. Against the filth of the garage, Virginia looked as if she'd been carved out of moonlight: a shivering luminescent girl hovering just above the dirty floor. The saddened air that circulated around her still smelled of cigars and oil but the feeling of safety had been replaced with sorrow. Her dark eyes regarded me, questioning.

"I haven't forgotten, Virginia. I promise, as soon as I finish what I'm working on I'll find Fleck. I won't give up until I find him."

She stared vacantly. Her head was tilted enough to show off the gash that'd ended her life. Her pale lips parted but the air seemed too cold to allow speech.

"I wish you would tell me something I could use to find Fleck, Virginia. I want to help you so bad."

A car horn intruded on the moment and Virginia's eyes reacted to the sound. It was shocking to witness. All these months she'd hovered and pleaded for someone she wouldn't name; she'd spoken to me but never reacted to the world. Not once before tonight. Her form shimmered and dimmed, disappearing into the murk of the garage. By the time Mark beeped his horn again she was gone. The mystery of Virginia's behavior would have to wait. I hurried to the curb where Mark waited.

I stopped outside the garage door, admiring the car while Mark walked around to open my door. It was small, sporty, and the color of a bright new apple. Nothing like the monstrosities the boys around the garage played with.

"I don't think I've ever seen a car like this one before."

"It's a Jaguar. I liked the color and it goes over well at the club."

His smile said the modesty was false; the car was a point of pride and it probably cost more than everything in my apartment. Some guys are too well trained to boast outright. They like to approach bragging at an oblique angle. I played along.

"This must be some club. You sure you want to take me there?"

"Absolutely."

He held my hand as I eased into the car's black leather seats. Sitting in it felt like wearing a good glove: the fit was tight but perfect and I knew it looked good. I glanced up at my little apartment and saw Voe's silhouette in the window. I gave him a wave as Mark slid in behind the wheel.

"I was wondering, do you like to dance?"

Even if I didn't I wouldn't have admitted it.

"A little, just socially."

"Great, the club has a really decent band on Friday nights. The music's a little stodgy but if you're game we can take a few laps around the floor."

He pulled away from the curb and made a U-turn, heading out of the neighborhood. Maybe we would have a dance or two. The night was filled with possibilities.

20

A sign mounted on the high, wrought iron fence outside the drive that led to the club bore the name IDYLWOOD GOLF AND HUNT CLUB in majestic gold script. A less grandiose, meaner placard mounted just below stated PRIVATE PROPERTY. The implication was clear: the ordained and moneyed were welcome while the poor riffraff should turn around before they found themselves in trouble. My instincts told me I belonged to the unwelcome class; even in Mark's company I'd be a pretender. The second thoughts about this date had started and I hadn't even seen the club.

We turned into the drive; on both sides lay acres of rolling woodland sequestered behind a stout fence. A gatehouse protected the only way into this Shangri-la of excess. If the fence and signage didn't reinforce the club's exclusivity, the presence of guards let you know that if you had to ask what lay beyond the gates you didn't belong. A uniformed man in a patrolman-like cap approached the car. His saunter said wannabe cop and he stooped to look into the car, giving Mark a nod and smile and me a skeptical once-over.

"Good evening, Dr. James."

"Evening, Hal."

The guard made a note on his clipboard and signaled to his partner in the gatehouse. The gates crept open and soon the Jaguar was jaunting up the curving cobbled road that led into the property's recesses. Through the woods, I caught an occasional glimpse of the club's lights. They shimmered with an almost celestial quality in the night air. I got a strange feeling in my gut, like I was experiencing the same kind of nervous wonder Dracula's victims did as they were led to his remote Transylvanian castle by strange footmen. Mark seemed to sense my unease.

"You'll like the Club Room. It can be a little formal, but the food's marvelous."

"Something to look forward to."

"I'm sure I can make up for anything dinner lacks."

"Really? Do you always self-promote?"

"Sorry, it's a nervous habit. Then again, I *am* a stunning conversationalist."

His eyes sparkled mischievously, catching the dashboard lights in a way that made them seem to burn with an inner fire. Bringing a commoner to the club broke all the rules, both of us knew that, but he was enjoying his little rebellion. I hoped it felt as thrilling when the evening ended.

We rounded a final turn and the drive ended in a cobbled courtyard. The clubhouse rose out of the landscape: its roof like the prow of a ship breaking through a wave, its soaring eaves wore a draping of snow that resembled the froth of a stormy sea. A wall of glass extended from the roofline to the ground, letting the soft light of the interior mingle artfully with the strategically placed spotlights in the courtyard. Specimen trees and architectural features stood starkly highlighted in the hard lights. They testified to what the architect had deemed "important." My dad used to draw plans for buildings like this. He called them pure or high-minded; to me they just looked cold.

As soon as the car stopped, a black man in a red coat and cap approached and opened my door, offering a gloved hand to help me exit. I stood, straightening my coat while Mark performed all perfunctory rituals of reinforcing social demarcations. He was polite and warm, which is better than most rich people treat those who serve them, but just beneath the conversation I sensed a modicum of disdain. I thought about the fondness I felt for Morris back in the pawn shop and Mark's interaction became too uncomfortable to watch. I bundled myself against the cold and turned away from the clubhouse.

The artificial halo of light that surrounded the club was brash but short-lived. Within a few yards of the courtyard, night regained her rightful hold on the countryside and the shadow of the surrounding woods loomed up into the nighttime sky. In the darkness, I could feel restless spirits circling. Mark's club intruded on their territory, but their protest was invisible to everyone but me. The rich and powerful partied while the departed picketed safely out of sight: death imitated life. As I contemplated the irony, the spice of Mark's cologne wafted around my shoulders, letting me know he was coming a moment before he spoke.

"Let's get in out of the cold. I didn't ask you out so you could catch pneumonia!" He offered an arm and I took it.

We stepped in from the cold and passed through an atrium lobby behind the great glass front of the building. The room paid homage to the ultramodern, paneled so that it seemed carved out of a solid block of blond wood. Another man, this one in a white jacket with a black bowtie, took our coats and ushered them away into the recesses of the club coatroom. Mark hooked his arm in mine and led the way toward a set of double doors as I stared upward, admiring the high ceiling.

The Club Room, as Mark called it, was a staid space that looked too masculine to be a restaurant. The contrast to the atrium was so striking it took my eyes a second to adjust. The dark paneling and the deep red carpets conspired with muted light to make the space intimate. Where the atrium was cavern-

162

ous and echoing, the Club Room seemed to absorb sound, reducing everything to a hush. Pictures of foxes dressed as jockeys and golf paraphernalia decorated the walls and just inside the entry a glass case displayed a collection of tournament trophies. We wound through the tables to a candlelit booth near the back of the room. The crisp white tablecloth contained more varieties of forks, knives, and spoons than I knew existed. By the time I settled, Mark was giving me his increasingly familiar, sly smile.

"What?" I asked defensively, stowing my clutch and trying to avoid eye contact.

"This place really isn't you, is it?"

"No, it's wonderful. Really, I do this kind of thing all the time." I met his eyes and couldn't maintain the charade without cracking. "Okay, it's a little alien."

"Don't worry. We'll get through it together." He leaned forward. "Don't let on but I'd usually rather be in some little Italian place, having a slice of pizza.

"So, pardon my asking, why didn't you take me to one of those Italian places instead of here?"

"I don't know. I thought you might want something special."

"I appreciate the thought, Mark, but I'm no social maven."

He nodded. "And I appreciate that, it's refreshing. When you decide you want to impress you wind up making a lot of sacrifices."

He sounded resigned, like his membership in this highbrow club was a burden he longed to cast off. I looked around the room, taking in the decoration and the host of attendants.

"Pardon my saying this, but I think most of the country is trying to get a shot at making this kind of sacrifice."

"They don't understand what it really costs." He sat back in his chair. "It's like being chloroformed. After you've been smothered with questions about your lineage, connections, and bank account you start to lose consciousness. If you're not really careful, you start to believe the club's standards actually are the yardstick you should be measured by."

"At least you don't have to worry about the rent," I offered. "You'll never get tossed out on the street."

"Oh, you can be tossed out."

There was something in the way he said that. Maybe money changes things; I really had no way of knowing. Even the bonanza I excavated from Arnie's yard couldn't buy the sort of company Mark ran with. It probably didn't even qualify me to hang out with the kitchen staff. I did recognize the change in his lighthearted demeanor, though. Changing the subject seemed like a wise course so I picked up the menu.

"Um, I hate to complain but my menu isn't in English."

His smile returned and the space between us warmed. "It's in French."

"Ah, I see. Well, you're going to have to help me. The only French foods I know are French fries and French dressing."

"I tell you what; if you trust me I can order for both of us."

I folded my menu. "I don't know, this is our first date. Is that wise?"

He placed a hand over his heart. "On my honor as a gentleman I promise, I won't order anything you'll regret eating."

"All right, I'm in your hands."

I couldn't have pronounced the dishes Mark ordered. The meal started with a tiny salad followed by a bowl of soup after which the waiter brought an entree of Chicken-de-something-or-other with roasted vegetables. Everything tasted wonderful, even if the portions were so small I'd have to raid the refrigerator when I got home. What the food lacked in volume, the wine and after-dinner cocktails made up for in potency. Through the course of dinner we drank two glasses of wine apiece, then, with the plates cleared and the crumbs swept away, we lingered and talked. The light of the candle lent Mark's face a soft glow; it made him look like a dime romance novel hero—or maybe that was the alcohol.

"I never got to ask how your Christmas went." I stirred my Collins. "What's the holiday like around the James estate?"

"Quiet."

"You don't really think I'm going to settle for that sort of answer. Regardless of what you've been told, girls don't really like men of mystery."

"Okay, what do you want to know?"

"Do you spend your holiday with family?"

"Dad's been gone for fifteen years now, Mom for eight."

Great, the evening had just started and I'd already killed the romance. "Sorry, I shouldn't have pried."

"It's fine. My parents and I had a—cool—relationship at best." He contemplated the ice in his glass. "Dad made his fortune when I was just a kid. If you were a doctor, you'd probably recognize his name: Spencer James. He invented a couple of surgical clamps, big important doctor stuff."

"That sounds like something to be proud of."

"It is. My mom must have reminded me of that about a million times. After Dad died it got worse. Everything little Mark did was weighed against the example of the late, great Spencer James." Bitterness had crept into Mark's voice. "Unfortunately nobody could ever really live up to the example of dear old Dad."

The topic of family should be added to politics and religion when it comes to things you shouldn't discuss in polite company. There's really no adequate response to hearing that your date's childhood was crushed by unfeeling parents. I did my best, even if the words felt utterly inadequate coming out of my mouth.

"I'm sorry, Mark."

Mark shook his head. "No, I'm the one who should be apologizing. I shouldn't let a few bad memories ruin our evening. Let's change the subject. How are you getting on with that police case you told me about? Any progress?"

Who would think murder could be a *more* comfortable topic of discussion than childhood memories? I grabbed onto the topic like it was a life preserver.

"Not really. I did get to meet a first-class criminal, though."

"Sounds like an adventure. Is he the pimp you mentioned?"

"No, this guy's named Vince Morello. He's a tough one, scared the hell out of me at the drugstore yesterday." I chuckled, "Not exactly a visit from Santa, huh?"

"Yeah, I guess not. So, was he involved in the murder?"

"No—well at least not Virginia's murder." I sipped my drink. "This is kind of another case I've adopted."

He raised his eyebrows. "Now you're looking into *two* murders? You sure live an interesting life."

"Yeah, you could call it that. Morbid would be another word."

"I guess! So, what's this new guy into?"

"Gambling. He worked with a bookie that showed up dead back in November." I watched Mark as he took a long, slow drink. "Save your warnings, I know what you're going to say. I realize that I shouldn't be mixing with that sort of element."

"Actually, I was going to say you're about the most fascinating woman I've ever met."

I gave him the get-serious look. "Fascinating because I do crazy things that get me in trouble?"

"Fascinating because you're fearless." He set his glass down. "I mean, I'd be terrified if I ran into this—what was his name again?"

"Morello, Vince Morello."

"I'd be terrified but to you . . . ." He stood and offered his hand. "I admire you and I'd like to ask you to dance. Care to accompany me to the ballroom?"

I blanched as we stepped through a pair of double doors and into the ballroom. I'd been to big dancehalls that weren't as fancy as what Mark's club had to offer. Velvet curtains draped the walls and potted palms stood in the corners, softening the space and giving it a royal feeling. Tables were lined up in three tiers around the edges of the room, leaving its center free for dancing. A band was playing at the opposite end from where we entered, well-dressed men who looked like they were into the concept of the music but lacked the vigor to give it life.

I took in the crowd as we made our crossing. This place could have been the waiting room for the funeral parlor; aside from Mark there wasn't a single man under the age of seventy. There were, on the other hand, at least two dozen twenty-something women around the room. Pretty young things who sipped drinks, laughed playfully, slipped gracefully across the dance floor, and every last one of them was accompanied by a man who could only, politely, be described as elderly. Every one of these women wore dresses that probably cost more than I made in a year—and the jewelry! There were enough diamonds, rubies, and pearls in that room to fund a sultanate. Mark caught me ogling the hardware and as I settled into my chair he was shaking his head.

"I'd like to say every match is made in heaven but, as you can see, some are crafted at Cartier."

"Judging from the number of carats in this room I'd say it's not so much a sealed deal as a rental-renewal proposition." I swiveled to gape at a diamond and ruby monstrosity as it passed. "Does the queen of England know someone's been in her toy box?"

"Seems like the richer they are the harder they try to claw onto the good old days." He sighed. "At least it'll be a few years before either of us has to cope with thoughts of our own mortality."

If he only knew I'd already faced my mortality and the bony bugger had me on retainer. I contented myself with not answering the question. His next statement caught me unprepared.

"If you don't mind mashed toes I do a decent foxtrot."

"Huh?"

"I'm asking if you'd like to dance."

"Dance?" I glanced at the mix of spike heels and orthopedic loafers on the floor. "I don't know, I usually don't dance to this sort of music."

"Ah, if I can do it I'm sure you can. Besides, the fellow takes blame for any mistakes we make, so if I back you into a circuit judge I'll get the summons."

He held out a hand and my heart thrilled in spite of the lingering terror over our imminent dancing debut. In a moment we were on the floor and Mark was looking into my eyes.

"Just relax and let me drive. It's just like walking, nothing to it."

I swallowed hard and we started moving. If you don't know anything about dancing let me tell you its a lot easier when you can actually see where you're going. This whole let the man lead thing, well, even though I like a strong fellow I'd rather have my hands on the wheel. Still, for the first couple measures we seemed to float; his hands were soft but his strength came through and it felt good to be in his arms. It felt more than good; it felt like a dream.

"So, do you like being a part of this club?" I hoped running my mouth would make me feel better about being stranded on the dance floor with the upper crust.

"It's not about whether I like being a member or not. My dad was one so I am, it's what you do when you want to be 'connected' as he called it."

"Sounds like you were joining the Mob."

"It's not that exciting." He surveyed the floor and from my backward-facing position I got a good look at his disgusted expression. "Everyone in this room inherited their position in life. They didn't earn it, maybe their father or their father's father did but not a single one of them came by the power they feel so entitled to honestly."

"And you put yourself in that category?"

"You know what they say about the proverbial shoe, don't you?"

"You graduated medical school; your father didn't do it for you. I can't see how you can say you became a doctor because of your father's influence." A noticeable flash of guilty despair ran through Mark's eyes as he met mine. "Uh, you did graduate, didn't you?"

"Yes, I graduated through hard work and sacrifice. Getting accepted into medical school, well, let's just say the name didn't hurt."

"Aren't you being a little hard on yourself? So maybe your dad's name got you a break or two, you're the one who made the most of the opportunities."

"There's a difference between making a career of your opportunities and making the most of your life. I very well could wind up just like these people."

"I believe in you."

The despair vanished to be replaced by a sheepish smile. "You might be the first person who ever told me that."

"I'll go farther than that. I'm sure you'll do something absolutely unforgettable."

He chuckled. "With that sort of support how could I go wrong?"

We were in the middle of beaming at each other goofily when something bumped into me. Lost in the moment Mark had backed me into a waiter carrying a tray of highballs. The glorious feeling dissipated and our dreamy moment devolved into a scene from a nightmare. You know, like the one where you're wandering around in public naked except for a sign that says KICK ME. The waiter let out a sharp yelp and there was a smash followed by the collective gasp of everyone in the room. I stood, back turned to the carnage, as ice cubes and speared pieces of lime skittered between my feet and spiraled out onto the dance floor. When I turned the first thing I saw was a couple at one of the floor-side tables wearing their round of drinks. My mouth hung open.

"I'm so sorry!" Mark interceded. "My fault, I wasn't watching where I was leading."

The man sputtered but Mark didn't wait for his composure to return. He patted the stunned waiter on the shoulder as he was hauling me off the floor. "Please put this table on my tab. I hope you'll forgive my idiocy."

By the time I found my voice, Mark had hauled me off the dance floor, through a side door, and onto the veranda. He was snickering into his hand. I couldn't see the humor.

"Mark, please tell me that wasn't one of the circuit judges you told me about?"

"Actually he's a district attorney." Mark peeped through the window; the band was starting up again.

"Oh Mark."

"Don't worry; he'll probably be going to Washington after the election. It's good to have enemies in high places."

I reached for the door handle. "Someone like that could ruin your career, Mark! I'm going to tell him it's my fault—"

Mark caught my arm. "No, it's okay. It's more than okay, it's really great."

The moonlight reflected in his dark eyes in a way that made me smile in spite of having dumped a night's drinks right in a

DA's lap. "You're actually getting a kick out of this, aren't you?"

"A genuine thrill."

This was more my element. "So, do you have a particular vendetta against district attorneys or is it authority figures in general?"

"Call me antiestablishment."

"That's an odd one coming from a doctor who frequents an exclusive social club. I was under the impression doctors were reserved and cautious."

"You've got me mixed up with the people in there." He nodded toward the ballroom. "They might be satisfied with candlelight but I want a bonfire."

"Ah, a revolutionary." I gave him my best smirk. "Stick with me, given time we can flambé an entire branch of the judiciary."

"Tell me when and you've got a date."

He moved closer and I felt the moment's gravity pull me forward but I resisted. I wanted to give in. I wanted to fall into his arms and to taste his lips, but not on a first date. I'm not against wild abandon, but girls who let passion rule over brains wind up broken and abandoned. I pivoted away from his advance, redirecting him into a close cuddle. Then I rubbed my shoulders briskly.

"Speaking of fires, it's a little cold out here."

He nodded and I felt the moment's passion wane.

"Yeah, it's a little chilly. I'll brave the fury of the coat check. Meet you out front?"

"Don't be late."

I walked around the veranda toward the front of the building, cursing my good sense all the way. Would one kiss have been such a bad thing? This was 1952 not 1852; it wasn't like I'd earn a scarlet letter for a little harmless necking in the moonlight. Then again, I've heard that alcoholics claim they can stop whenever they want. Once we'd started kissing, it would have been hard to break the momentum because a large part of me definitely wouldn't want to. I climbed the steps that led to the courtyard and shortly after I stepped onto the importantly lit foyer, Mark emerged with my coat draped over his arm.

We drove back to the garage to the tune of the Jaguar's engine and Rosemary Clooney. I glanced at Mark a couple times, trying to judge whether my snub had done permanent damage. His face remained impassive and his eyes focused on the road. About a block away from home I made a decision: if he tried to kiss me goodnight, I would let him. I wasn't giving in to anything serious, no long passionate lip-locks, just a simple goodnight peck. Afterwards, I could feign innocence and fall back on the protection of my womanly reputation, scurrying upstairs while trying not to giggle like a high school kid. If things got uncomfortable or he was too pushy, I'd just give him a swift knee to the crotch and yell until one of the greaser car-monkeys that hung around the garage showed up to finish the job.

Mark played the gentleman again when we arrived. He got out of the car, walked around to my side, opened the door, and offered his hand to help me out. We stood face to face on the curb, my heart fluttering at the proximity. He was close enough for me to feel the heat of his body and my head started to tilt expectantly. As I moved toward him, I could see a fuzzy shape over his shoulder. It stood on the second step of the staircase that climbed the outside of the garage and the romance suddenly was sucked out of the moment.

Virginia was watching us. I stiffened, locked in her despairing gaze. Mark immediately noticed.

"I'm sorry, I thought that . . ." He pulled back. "Old habits again, you're going to think I'm some kind of a jerk."

Fate was conspiring against tonight being anything more than an innocent evening out and now Virginia Beal was in on the scheme. By the time the awkwardness had passed, her apparition had faded away. I did my best to recover gracefully.

"You're not a jerk, I had a great time."

"A great time but . . ."

"Mark, there are no buts." I gave a quick kiss on the cheek. "Go home before you catch cold. Nobody trusts a sick doctor."

"All right, I'll call you. Next time we'll go somewhere less stuffy. You can set the itinerary."

He waited at the curb with the car running until I reached the top of the stairs. No guy had ever done that for me before. I was grinning and unlocking my door when I felt a presence looming behind me. I let out a disgusted sigh.

"Virginia, we definitely have to talk about your timing." I turned around, but it wasn't Virginia.

21

"Oh crap, Scott . . ."

"Funny thing happened to me tonight, Mel. I had a date with this girl, I even took a couple hours off so I didn't have to rush off to work, you know—make things a little more casual and everything. But when I got to her place to pick her up, guess what?"

"Oh God, Scott, I'm sorry." I could see the muscles in his jaw working. I hated when he did that, it made my molars hurt.

"You know, I've been stood up before, Mel. I'm an adult, I can take it. I just didn't expect it from you."

I could hear Voe scratching at the door; as if things weren't bad enough without a cat competing for my attention.

"I didn't mean to."

"I understand, you *accidentally* stood me up. It happens to me all the time, hell, sometimes I hardly can get through a day without promising I'll do ten things that I just blow off."

"Scott."

"Who's your friend with the fancy car?"

The scratching became fiercer. "Look, let's not do this on the doorstep. Come inside where we can talk."

"You sure you've got the time? I mean maybe another fellow's got your eleven o'clock time slot booked?"

That was enough. Regardless if he was hurt or not I wasn't putting up with that kind of accusation.

"Scott, cut the crap and get inside this apartment right now or I swear to you I'll call your mother and tell her what kind of lewd insinuations you've been making."

He hesitated for a second and then cursed under his breath. "Fine."

I opened the door and Voe trundled out under my feet, nearly tripping me as I felt for the light switch. "Have a seat, Scott. You know where the beer is."

"I think I drank enough already. I don't want to wake up with a hangover wondering if you actually said something or if it was the booze."

"Suit yourself. I'm having one. Hell, I might have three or four before this night's over." I opened the refrigerator and grabbed a bottle about the same time that Voe opened his mouth.

"We need to talk."

It's one thing to be the only one who can understand cats, but another to have said beast start talking to you in front of other people. The experience really messes with your head and my poor abused brain really didn't need any extra messing.

"When did you get a cat?"

"He's a stray. I just kind of took him in."

"Mel, we need to talk now!" Voe repeated.

"You feed him people food? I've seen dogs beg but never a cat." Scott reached down and puckered his lips, making a kissy sound. "Come here fella, come here—"

Voe shot Scott the cat version of a dirty look, an expression I'd become increasingly familiar with. "Wow, an intellectual, how charming. I'm sure if I could understand a word he was saying I'd be so taken with his wit I could barely stop despising him. Would you mind putting wunderkind out so we can discuss important issues?"

I glared at Voe. "He's not too friendly with people he doesn't know. Uh, let me lock him in the bedroom where he won't be underfoot."

I scooped Voe and carried him, squirming, across the living room and to my room. "Look, just cool it. I've got enough trouble to deal with for one night and I don't need you adding drama!" I tossed him on the bed and shut the door just in time to foil his escape. It's just like me to have three male egos to deal with at the same time. I returned to the kitchen, retrieved my beer from the counter, and grabbed a church key from the drawer before taking a seat across from Scott.

"I'm really sorry, Scott. I didn't mean to stand you up. Whether you believe it or not I swear it's the honest truth."

"So, I should feel better because you didn't *mean* to dump me for another guy?"

"Whoa, let's get something straight here. There is no dumping because to dump someone you've got to be involved with them."

My kitchen was so cold that if I didn't know better I would have sworn Virginia and Death both had arrived simultaneously to make a foursome for bridge. Scott stared at his folded hands as he spoke.

"I see. Well, shouldn't be any surprise. I mean I'm a cop, it's kind of ironic that I didn't catch on to all the clues." When his eyes came up they were damp but an angry fire burned behind them. "So, tell me. Did you string me on just to satisfy your morbid little homicide fan hobby or was I the back-up guy until someone better came along?"

I wanted to hate him for saying that. I wanted to fold my arms, rear back, and ask what gave him the right to say that sort of crap to me. But then I wasn't sure he didn't have me nailed. The part about him being my backup was bullshit, but what he said about getting information on murders . . . I'd have a hard time denying that charge. So I just sat there looking stupid until he stood and pushed in his chair.

"See you around, Mel."

The door closed but I didn't move. A guy I'd known all my life was walking away and I just sat there, fingering my beer bottle. In a few minutes, Voe hopped up on the table.

I didn't stop staring at the kitchen door. "How the hell did you get out?"

"You've got rotten latches. Look, there's something important I've got to tell you."

"What, that you're irritating? You don't have to tell me that, I figured it out on my own. I figured something else out too, men are nothing but trouble. Exasperating, self-centered, dim-witted, little . . ." I stood, kicked the chair, and started toward my room with Voe in pursuit.

"You remember when I said two men went into Alfonzo's house the night he was killed? That man was one of them."

I stopped. "Who, the guy who just stormed off? You're telling me Scott had something to do with the death of your former owner?"

"No. And he wasn't my *owner*. We went through this before."

"Get off the feline pride kick and explain yourself, Voe. Who the hell are you talking about?"

"The guy in the car, the one who dropped you off."

"Mark?"

"I don't know his name. I told you, you're the first human I even knew had a name."

I sat down hard. No chair required, right there in the middle of the living room floor. In a second Voe was looking me in the eye.

"Mel? Are you all right?"

"Do I look all right?"

Voe sat. "Uh, no. I thought you'd be happy."

"Why should I be happy? The guy I just decided I could fall

in love with turns out to be involved in a murder and I'm supposed to be happy?"

Voe sat. "No, I guess not."

"Men are nothing but trouble, Voe."

"You already said that."

"It deserves saying twice."

22

After the news about Mark, I couldn't sleep. I lay awake staring at the shadows the TV antennas on the roof next door cast on my wall and listening to the murmur of ghost voices. Hearing the dead isn't comforting and they don't make very good company in times of need. Reminders that everything has a mortal end can't be comforting.

And insomnia offers an inordinate amount of time to consider the events of your life. For me, that mostly involved wondering how the hell Mark was linked with Alfonzo Arnie's death. I toyed with the possibility that Voe was wrong about Mark being at Arnie's house. Hell, until we discovered each other he didn't even realize people were sentient. It wouldn't be so surprising if he couldn't tell one human from the next. It was a possibility, if I distorted the odds enough and forgot the fact there was no reason Voe would make that particular mistake. I mean, I'm no cat, but I certainly can tell a tabby from a Siamese.

Possibilities and arguments against them raced around in ugly circles in my head until I finally sat up in bed. Voe was sitting in a pool of moonlight, staring out the window with glassy-eyed fascination. He was so intent that he didn't notice me getting out of bed. I startled him when I settled on the floor by his side and his head snapped around toward me.

"You're sure it was Mark?"

Voe played down the fact he'd been caught unaware by licking his paw before he returned to his vigil. "No doubt."

179

"Go over what happened that night one more time."

Voe looked at me, his phosphorescent eyes catching the moonlight that filtered into the room. "Alfonzo opened the door to let me out for my nightly stroll at the normal time. When I went out, there were two men coming up the walk, an old man with a beard and the one that dropped you off tonight. They stood outside yammering for awhile but since there was nothing unusual about that kind of thing I didn't pay any attention. I just went about my business. When I came back to the house, Alfonzo didn't come to the door to let me in; I pawed and scratched and called but nothing so I settled down in the bushes to think. After I'd been sitting there for awhile, a man comes out of the house, but this is a new guy, not one of the two that I saw earlier. I recognized him because he came to the house a lot; a dark-haired guy that always smelled bad. He looked angry and he slammed the door and took off in his car leaving me hiding under the bushes."

Voe returned to staring out the window, his eyes still glowing in the darkness. "And that's everything."

"I see."

"I'm sorry the killer had to be this man you're infatuated with."

"I'm not infatuated." I sighed and leaned back on one elbow, looking out at the blind night sky. "It's just, well, I hoped—"

"There's an old cat saying, 'Only trust a human male whose back you can see.' "

I glanced at Voe. "Kinda fatalistic, don't you think?"

"When you've known enough human males you get to be fatalistic, I guess."

"Yeah, but that sounds like something I'd say and I'm no joy to be around." I puzzled over his advice for a moment. "Voe, are there any old cat sayings about human women?"

He contemplated the night sky for a long moment. "Actually,

I can't think of any."

"Odd." I took a deep breath and got to my feet, "Well, I'm not going to sit here wallowing in what Mark possibly did or didn't do, I'm going to find out for sure."

"You know the sun's not coming up for a long time, don't you?"

I pulled a fresh pair of underwear out of my dresser and headed for the closet. "I can't sleep so I might as well have insomnia in the Mercy Hospital's parking lot."

When I started toward the bathroom, Voe had returned to intently staring at the night sky. He seemed so enthralled that I had to take another look. Outside, the moon peeked through the slate gray clouds.

"What are you watching, anyway?"

"I'm admiring the hanging of the stars and watching the comings and goings, that's all."

I settled on the floor and leaned back against the side of my bed. "I just see clouds and the moon."

"You're not looking right."

I snorted. "Okay, so how should I look at the sky to see these marvelous things?"

He chastened me with a stern look. "First you need to realize there's a time and a place for sarcasm. After you've got the hang of that, take a deep breath, clear your mind, and accept that just because you can't explain something doesn't preclude it from existing."

I tried to relax and to let thoughts of Mark's betrayal pass out of my mind. It seemed like an eon before the dialogue inside my head stopped. When I opened my eyes again, the night sky had come alive. The city's artificial glow gave way and the heavens swam with lights. Stars gathered in great shoals that undulated and migrated across the void of outer space toward some unknowably distant shore. Occasionally, one of these orbs would separate from its school, darting down toward the ground with the brilliance of a shooting star. For once, I found myself out of witty retorts. I watched for minutes with my mouth hanging open before I managed to speak.

"What is it?"

"The workings of the universe."

He acted like he was telling me the weather or something just as mundane.

"Workings of the universe? What's that supposed to mean?"

"Think of the lights in the sky as windows into a million rooms in a million houses with locked doors. If you look at them right, you can see into places you're not supposed to be and if you learn where to find the keys, you can even get inside."

"It's beautiful."

"It's not beautiful or ugly; it's just the way the world works."

"Why haven't I ever seen it before? Does this happen all the time or is tonight special?"

"It's new to you. I remember when I was a kitten—it seemed incomprehensible and amazing then. Eventually you'll get used to it; you'll learn to read which doors are opening and which ones are closing. If you study hard enough you'll even be able to tell when something enters or exits." He fixed me with a steady stare. "Things aren't as neat and close-ended as you thought, are they?"

He was mocking humanity again and it might have been appropriate. The skies were filled with wonders and nobody so much as noticed. I didn't even have the will to feel superior; after all, I'd thought Mark might be the perfect man and look where that'd landed me. I forced myself to turn away from the lightshow and started for the bathroom again.

"Still going?"

"Weren't you the one who was reminding me how important it was for me to find Alfonzo's killer and solve Death's case?

Time of Death

Mark lied to me about knowing Alfonzo; he might be hiding something more serious."

"What are you going to do, pound on his door until he lets you in and gives you the answers you want?"

"Actually, I'd planned something a little more mortifying."

I didn't wait around to debate Voe. I only had about five hours to get ready.

I didn't feel like messing with the Pontiac and my poor LaSalle still was up on a lift, so I had to improvise. I left a note on Manny's desk and took the keys to the '38 Reo tow truck he parked in the lot beside the garage. Something about driving a mechanical monstrosity felt appropriate: Mel, the avenging angel, astride her diesel-belching warhorse, bound for Sisters of Mercy Hospital to exact vengeance. It felt refreshing; I hadn't driven anything as big as the Rio since my adolescent days when I stole a milk truck from the high school parking lot. That scandal still carries enough potency to make my mother blanch. Nothing like a good memory to get a girl through the headache that results from a sleepless night.

I got a lot of looks sitting outside the hospital. The tow truck dominated all the other vehicles in the parking lot. Initially the casual onlooker probably assumed one of the hospital staff got overzealous and the repo man had shown up to claim the creditor's due. Seeing a woman behind the wheel probably upset their sense of all that was right in the world. A balding guy with glasses became so befuddled he walked into a light post. It should have been funny.

About eight thirty Mark drove his little red sport car into the lot and found his reserved parking space. Most people I know are up before the sun, but apparently doctors keep more relaxed hours. Just another rotten thing about the way life is geared. I yanked up on the truck's stiff door handle and pushed the door

183

open with my foot, then stepped out onto the running board to watch Mark step out of his car.

"Tell me about Alfonzo Arnie, Mark," I yelled across the lot.

He looked up from locking his car door. His casual smile had gone; this morning he wore an expression of confusion and shock. "Mel?"

"Yeah, it's Mel. Now that we've established my identity, let's move on to a more interesting subject. I've got an idea, how about the exact nature of your relationship with Alfonzo Arnie?"

People were stopping to gawk and the idea of being shown up in front of the staff seemed to bug him. I can't help it if the sight of a girl hanging on the door of a wrecker with hot coals smoldering in her eyes is more interesting than clocking in for a day's work.

Mark glanced around the lot. "Uh, look, maybe we can talk about this later?"

"I've got time right now. Hell, I've got all the time in the world, Mark. I've got hours and hours of time and nothing to do but talk."

He started walking toward me. "Look, I'm not sure what you're talking about but I don't know any Alfred Arnold or whatever his—"

"Alfonzo Arnie, Mark, and don't even try to bullshit me. A good friend of mine saw you go into his house." I glanced at the growing crowd and then back at Mark. "Would you like to guess what happened to Arnie that night or should I explain it to you in great detail?"

He closed the distance between us. The look of embarrassment he wore combined with fear and he lowered his voice. "Okay, we can talk. Why don't we take my car down to—"

"Oh, I don't think so. Remember when you said I could choose the venue for our next outing? Well, I'm choosing and I'm driving so get in."

I clambered back inside the wrecker, slammed the door, and reached across the half mile of bench seat to unlock the passenger side. It was very satisfying to see the good doctor nearly fall as he scrambled into the Reo. The wrecker exhaled a cloud of black smoke and lurched violently. I urged the stick into first gear and we started across the parking lot at a slow lope.

"I really don't appreciate you showing me up in front of my coworkers."

"And I don't appreciate you forgetting to tell me that you associate with bookies who've recently shown up with their throats cut," I interjected. "So why don't we can the hurt feelings crap and get down to explanations? How is it you wound up visiting someone like Alfonzo Arnie in the first place? Did you try to rob him to fund your fancy car and membership in that mausoleum of a club you belong to? Or was it something else?"

"I can't believe you're accusing me like this."

"Answer the damned question, Mark!" I snapped.

He stared out the passenger window. "I didn't try to rob him."

"Then what was it? Why were you there?"

"It's—it's embarrassing."

"Embarrassing? Is it more embarrassing than going to the chair on a murder wrap?"

He drew a deep breath and looked at me. In the hard morning light I could see dampness in the corners of his eyes.

"I went to Arnie to place bets, okay? It's a problem I've had for a long time. You wondered why I didn't think I could live up to what my father did, why my mother didn't accept me? Now you know. I've been trying to kick the habit but recently I haven't been doing such a great job at that. I went to Arnie to put a couple of bets down, that's all."

The truck had slowed to an idle. It rolled across the empty lot toward the street while I looked at Mark. "My friend said you showed up with an old man."

"His name's Ernie. I met him at the club and we started talking about the horses. I figured I finally had something in common with someone, you know? Next thing we're taking a ride out to the suburbs."

"You didn't kill Arnie?"

"I can't believe you'd think I'd kill someone. I just put a couple of bets down, just a few hundred bucks on horse races, that's all."

"But you knew he was dead."

"I saw the story in the paper."

"Why didn't you talk to the police?"

His Adam's apple worked up and down rapidly as he swallowed. "Because I didn't know anything and if I'd gone to the police the hospital board would have found out and fired me. I've worked my whole life to live up to my father's reputation. The last thing I need is to get canned for gambling. Then I would be a total failure."

I eased back in the truck's uncomfortable seat and stared at the morning sky. He'd talked about living up to his dad's reputation at the club. Parental expectations complicated everything. I felt the touch of his hand on mine; he was leaning toward me with a stricken look on his face.

"I swear, Mel, I didn't have anything to do with this Arnie guy's murder. Don't you believe me?"

I tried to rub the gravel out of my eyes. My head had started to pound.

"I want to believe you, Mark. The problem is that means I have to trust that you're telling me the whole truth and the only thing I know for sure is that you've withheld things from me in the past."

"I've made a lot of mistakes, Mel. But I'm not a killer." He looked small and dejected. "I never thought you'd think that of me. I thought we really connected last night. Maybe that's just another thing I've been wrong about."

I wanted to grab him by the shoulders and scream that we'd more than connected. I wanted to expel all the unanswered questions from my head and throw away every iota of suspicion. But I couldn't, not yet.

"Mark, I'd like to believe you but you're going to have to prove yourself."

He nodded. "I understand. I just want you to trust me again."

I should have left it at that: a rational commitment to see how things worked out. Instead I kissed him: his lips were warm and soft and the pounding in my head dissipated into pounding of my heart. When our lips parted, I turned the truck around and dropped Mark off by his car. I watched him in the mirror until I turned out of the lot and headed for the street. On the way home I saw Virginia standing in the shadow of a tree by the roadside, her transparent form hugging the shadows where the morning sun hadn't quite chased away night's shadows. I stopped the truck and watched until her form dissolved into nothingness.

A half block from the garage is Midtown Baked Goods. It's an evil place, a nondescript storefront that, every morning, perfumes the entire block with the scent of doughnuts and fresh rolls. It's one reason I have so much trouble keeping a little black dress that fits. There are benefits, though. A bag of fresh glazed, still oven warm, would go a long way toward making my impromptu borrowing of Manny's truck all right. After pissing Scott off and practically accusing Mark of murder, I needed to curry as much favor as I could muster. I walked the uneven sidewalk between the bakery and garage with a bag of doughnuts in hand and mind filled with questions.

If Mark was telling the truth—and God, I hoped he was telling the truth—he'd left the house on Woodford before Alfonzo had been murdered. That left Vince as the likely killer, a conclusion I would eagerly accept. The script played out logically: Arnie had the ten grand the pair accumulated buried in his backyard, their partnership had gone sour, Morello decided he deserved the cash, and in his rush to get the money he'd cut his partner's throat. His attempt at running me off the road and threatening me at the drugstore proved his psychotic tendencies and made a nice bow to decorate the package. The problem was proving my theory well enough that the cops would arrest Morello. Oh, and there was the matter of fitting Death's little problem into the equation. With five days left in the year, I didn't have time to sort through the facts. My next move had to be dangerous.

23

Just to be sure my arrival would be a surprise I parked a block down from Morello's rat-hole and walked. The neighborhood was colorful, if you found poverty and suffering colorful. Still, children played on the streets. I passed a game of stickball and it made me think about Scott. For half a block I wondered what he might be doing and for the next half block I relived the evening I'd ruined our friendship. We'd had spats before, but nothing this serious. In the past, grand and heartfelt apologies had brought him back, but nothing like this had ever happened before. Maybe it was best for us to part. Maybe I'd done him a favor by removing myself from his life so he could find that cop's wife he deserved. Life had gotten way too complicated.

I stopped at the corner of West Fillmore Street, checking to make sure there were no witnesses when I pulled the .25 from my pocket. I clicked the safety to the off position and worked the action to chamber a round. Unlike the night I'd run into Fleck, I meant to be ready for any extracurricular activities Morello had in mind. I slid the gun back into my pocket and started south.

The plan was simple: confront Morello with Arnie's ledger and demand he translate the names of everyone who owed them enough money to make murdering his partner worthwhile. In exchange, I'd give up the box of cash and good old Vince could buy his way out of trouble with the Mob. In the process I'd suggest I'd decided he couldn't be the killer. Hopefully the thought of getting the money back and putting some poor sap in my sights would tantalize him into mistakenly linking himself to the murder and the theft of Death's mask. Perhaps *scheme* would be a better term for what I hoped to pull off; it reflects the lack of control I had over the situation a lot better. Either Morello killed Alfonzo Arnie or Mark was lying. I didn't want to contemplate that possibility.

In spite of my plan, climbing Morello's front steps felt wrong. This was the lion's den and I was waltzing in with a porterhouse strapped to my ass, calling "Here kitty-kitty." The pistol in my pocket fortified my resolve a little, but it didn't eliminate the possibility of this whole thing ending horribly. I stood at the foot of the steps, surveying the house for signs of movement. The shades hung limp and the windows were dark so I started climbing.

The two halves of the double shared the porch, and lumber sat stacked on the right side. Apparently, the landlord meant to repair the burned-out side of the building. Countering that potential of renewal was the rusty NO TRESPASSING sign nailed to the sheet of plywood that sealed Number 19's front door. The slumlord who owned this place didn't intend to fix it up anytime soon because he'd seen it necessary to seal it up and mark it out of bounds to squatters.

My hand slid into my coat pocket, finding the butt of the pistol before I knocked. I didn't have to think about the action. My finger slid inside the trigger guard and I lifted the gun slightly so I could draw quickly if needed. Readiness for violence was becoming natural; I'd transformed into something that I wouldn't have recognized a year ago. For a frantic moment my brain recoiled from the present, searching for a time when I hadn't, at least under the prattle of everyday life, been thinking about murder and death. My assertive side shoved the worry away; I couldn't afford distractions.

The sounds of neighborhood life began to encroach on the porch: a dog barked, in the distance a crow cawed, and the breeze rattled the NO TRESPASSING sign. Something was wrong. I knocked harder and the world grew still. Everything paused.

I backed down the steps until I could see the upstairs windows. The blinds were pulled like before. Maybe one of them was open a little more; I couldn't be certain. The only sure thing was the absolute stillness that'd seized the neighborhood. I eased the pistol out of my coat pocket and started around the house.

This time I chose Morello's side of the double. I hugged the foundation, staying below the sightlines the tall windows offered as I made my way to the backyard. If Vince was playing hide-and-seek I wasn't going to concede the game.

I peeked around the corner of the house. The backyard hadn't improved since the last time I'd seen it. Obviously Morello wasn't worried about impressing me when I showed up. One thing had changed, though. This time Morello's back door stood open.

I slid around the corner, staying flat against the siding and ducking under another window. I tried to remember the layout of the kitchen: a table sat in the middle and a chair by that, both of them under a bare bulb, but where was the doorway into the rest of the house? Manny's interference had prevented me getting a good enough look. I couldn't remember *if* there'd been another doorway let alone its position. I'd have to find out when I reached the kitchen door.

Three steps led from the weedy lot to the decaying concrete stoop. I eased up the first two and paused to listen: nothing. I raised my gun, letting it rest by my ear while I gathered myself, and then I moved.

I pivoted into the doorway with my pistol leading the way. Two shapes confronted me. Morello stood by the toppled chair.

His arms were pinned and his body was turned toward the door. I'd seen Morello furious and now I got to see him wearing an expression of utter shock. The second figure stood behind Morello. He wore a black overcoat, a scarf pulled up over his nose, and a hat pulled down to the point where it nearly met the scarf. The only features I could make out were his eyes and the knife he held at Morello's throat.

"Let him go!" I bellowed, as if the purpose of my arrival had been to save Morello. I should have welcomed seeing him get his comeuppance; instead I was calling off his attacker. Irony loves me.

The man behind Morello didn't find my savior act convincing. He drew the short, business-like blade across Morello's throat with the ease and precision of an expert.

For a second everything was still. The mysterious man stared at me and I stared back. Morello didn't move; the shocked expression he'd been wearing when I burst into the room remained fixed. I tried to remember Manny's shooting lessons: don't tense up, slow my breath, stay focused on the target, and stay calm. Yeah, I bet Manny never held a gun on a knife-wielding lunatic.

"Morello, move away from him," I barked.

He didn't flinch. His expression didn't even change.

"Morello, I said step away."

Morello started to move. He slowly slumped to one side. It was like a film running at the wrong speed; his motions seemed unnatural and his gaze unfocused. On the other hand, the man with the knife wasn't anywhere near as slow when he bolted for the door that led to the house's interior.

The gunshot seemed to snap everything back from the weird edge of reality. Morello fell on the toppled chair, crushing it under his body. Shards of plaster flew from the wall where my shot had gone wide. Checking Morello would have to wait; I hurtled through the kitchen after his assailant.

I rounded the kitchen doorway and ran into what once had been a grand sitting room. My focus narrowed on the man in the overcoat, heading out the front door. I pulled the trigger and my second shot caught him in the side, spinning him around. He stumbled out of view; then there was the sound of scattering lumber as he fell. I approached slowly, keeping my gun ready. When I swung around the doorframe, I found my target sprawled among the two-by-fours, writhing.

"Don't move, buddy. I swear I'll shoot you again."

He squirmed and I sympathized. I'd had a bullet in my shoulder and nearly three weeks later it still hurt. This wasn't the time to feel sorry; I needed to think about my next move. A cop would have cuffs and a car radio. I had a gun and no plan. Hopefully I could find a phone in Morello's place so I could call the police.

"Get up, we're going inside."

He didn't move; I couldn't even tell if he was breathing. Maybe the bullet hit something vital and killed him. I took a half-step toward the man and regretted it almost instantly.

He chucked one of the two by fours in my direction and it hit me on the inside of the right ankle. The pain was intense and my gun went off, blowing a chunk out of the porch. I recovered just in time for my friend to catch me across the chin with a punch that jarred my molars and bloodied my lower lip. I stumbled backward and probably would have wound up on the ground if I hadn't crashed into one of the columns that supported the porch's roof. The force knocked the wind out of my lungs. This time I wasn't going to let some jerk pound me without paying a price. I snapped my arm up, leveling the .25 and getting ready to squeeze off another round. My friend had bolted.

I scrambled over the tangle of boards and leaned over the

porch railing but he'd disappeared. He'd probably run around to the back of the building and the alley beyond the yard. It didn't really matter. With my head ringing from a right hook, and the issue of the battered ankle, I'd never catch up. I headed back into the house, wiping my busted lip and cursing.

The blood pooling around Vince made me realize what Alfonzo Arnie's kitchen must have looked like the night he was murdered. Morello's lifeblood had poured out on the dirty hardwood, flowing across its uneven surface at the whims of gravity and the building's crumbling foundation. I choked back the urge to vomit; the taste of bile and my own blood was in my mouth and I had to leave the room before I lost composure. I found a telephone in the parlor of the once-great house and I dialed the police.

24

The ride to the hospital wasn't voluntary. A uniform insisted and when I started to complain he made it clear he didn't care what I wanted. I sat on the sideboard while the attendant knelt in front of me, cleaning my bloodied lip with an alcohol doused gauze pad. It stung but thinking about what happened to Morello kept me from caring.

My mind kept replaying an irritatingly irrational scene. In it Morello slowly toppled after having his throat sliced. He didn't fight or flail; he just fell over in slow motion. I didn't know how he should have fallen but I did know that what happened just felt wrong. It'd played out too slow, like the world had been turned down from 78 to 33 rpm. Everything in the world with the exception of Morello's killer and me, which made things even more wrong. When we reached the hospital the attendant didn't even bother to ask if I needed to ride in on the gurney, he just hopped down and offered a hand to help me down.

"I'm not sure where you should wait," he said, slamming the ambulance door. "I guess one of the exam rooms."

"Why? I've got a busted lip and a bruised ankle." I glanced down at my foot. "Crap, and a pair of ruined stockings!"

"How is she?"

The question came in a familiar voice. Rolland had a real knack for being in the wrong place when I least needed him there.

"I'm fine."

Rolland stood just inside the hospital doors with his pipe in the corner of his mouth and a very serious look on his face.

"I was just telling the attendant I'm fit to go home."

"Uh-huh. I'll take her from here." He took my arm and we started walking across the lobby. "That was bad business you got mixed up in, Melody. You could have gotten seriously hurt."

"Well, I didn't."

"God favors the foolhardy," he said without looking up or breaking stride. "The chapel is unoccupied; I think we can use it."

The voices of the dead had started to seep up from the morgue again and they were playing hell with my sense of security. Religion could only make things worse.

"It's a little late to offer prayers for me, don't you think?"

Jokes always fall flat with Rolland. He kept walking, past the statue of the nun, right through the little ghost girl playing her eternal game of hopscotch, and down a side hall to a darkened room with two pews and a stained-glass window that silhouetted a crucifix. He settled me in one of the pews and closed the double doors, shutting out the sounds of life. Unfortunately, no door could turn the wailing of the dead.

"Melody, we discussed this whole detective fantasy less than two weeks ago."

"Actually, it's been more than two weeks."

His expression remained unchanged. I tell you the man is utterly immune to humor.

"Since you recall it so well you'll remember that I warned you about getting mixed up in this sort of thing. It's dangerous and you have no business muddling about with police business."

I knew it was dangerous but he didn't have the slightest idea just how much it *was* my business. I swallowed the urge to tell him, staring at the red carpet and trying to shut out the cries and pleas from the morgue.

"Tell me what you saw."

My head came up, was he asking me about the thing with Morello moving so slow or the ghosts or something else entirely? I opted for playing dumb instead of taking a wild guess.

"What I saw?"

"Yes, what happened to Vince Morello?"

Ah, he just wanted the normal cop stuff. Actually that was less of a relief than I would have thought. Still the question irked me.

"Oh, now I'm useful?"

"Melody, I'm trying to help you."

"Frankly, I think you're trying to help *you*." I met his eyes. His expression was as passive as ever. "One more notch in Detective Rolland's badge and maybe he'll get a bigger Christmas bonus next year. Isn't that the way it works?"

He drew on his pipe, the sweet smell of the smoke penetrating the alcohol scent that clung to my nostrils. "When I first met you, I thought you probably were another juvenile heading for prison or an early casket. Since I knew your mother and what sort of woman she is, I hoped my instincts were wrong."

"Oh, please don't try to guilt me. If Mom can't do it you're not going to have any luck."

"I'm not trying to make you do or feel anything, Melody. I'm just asking you to think about something. Your mother already lost a husband; she doesn't need to lose a daughter too. If you keep this up she will." He took his pipe out of his mouth and leaned in close. "I agreed to try to steer you in the right direction and I've done what I can. I just ask you to think about the consequences of your actions before you make your next decision."

We sat in silence for a long time. Well, he did, and I sat contemplating what he said while fighting off intruding voices of the dead. His point was irritatingly valid. I'd never thought much about Mom except when she got in the way of my doing what I felt was right. We bumped heads, we'd always been opposites and that meant fights were inevitable, but there always had been Dad to pull things together again. Since he died, Mom and I had been heading in opposite directions and there wasn't anyone to intercede.

"I went to Morello's house to have him translate a book. I think I dropped it in the kitchen of his house."

"What kind of book?"

"A ledger. I think it was a record of the people who owed him and Alfonzo Arnie money."

The pipe returned to Rolland's mouth. "Who is Alfonzo Arnie?"

"He lived out in Sunnyvale, at the corner of Woodford and Vine. His body was found on November first. Somebody had slashed his throat."

Rolland sat back in the pew, chewing his pipe. "Sounds like a trend."

Something about Rolland's statement caused the cogs in my mind to loosen. Maybe that's why cops work in pairs, maybe playing off each other helps jar ideas loose. Arnie and Morello had died the same way but I knew one more person who'd had her throat slit: Virginia Beal. I stifled the urge to blurt out my realization. My interest in Morello and Arnie ended with finding Death's missing property. If this had strictly been about their murder Rolland could have the honors of seeing justice done. I'd promised Virginia that I'd personally catch her killer and I meant to fulfill that promise. I kept my questions to Arnie and Morello.

"So, you think the same person killed both men?"

Rolland kept chewing his pipe stem. "Tell me everything that happened today."

"I knocked on the door but nobody answered so I went around back. When I got there, the kitchen door was standing open and when I went inside, this guy in a black overcoat was attacking Morello."

"Did you see his face?"

"He had a scarf pulled over it."

"Maybe there'll be prints."

"Ah, he was wearing gloves."

Rolland exhaled a cloud of smoke and looked me over. "You shot at him?"

"Are you asking me or accusing me of a crime?" I was halfway joking.

"The uniform radioed that there was a bullet hole in the kitchen wall. Morello's gun hadn't been fired and his killer used a knife."

I nodded. "I shot at him in the kitchen and missed but the second time I hit him." One of Rolland's eyebrows cocked prompting me to continue. "I chased him through the house and put a slug in his side as he was going out the front door."

"I need to get you a badge," Rolland mused, tapping the mouthpiece of his pipe against his bottom lip. "So, what would you do now, detective?"

"Put out the word for all the local hospitals to watch for gunshot wounds."

"And?"

I didn't have an answer for that question so he favored me with his own.

"Advise inquisitive members of the public not to get involved because their interference could prevent the authorities from performing their duties and might be construed as a prosecutable offense."

"Ah, I see. Back on the sidelines, kid, let the big boys take care of this."

"Melody."

"I know, you promised Mom. You've made your point."

"I doubt that." He stood with a weary groan. "But I've done what I can. How's the shoulder?"

"It hurts."

"You should get more rest. Stay in bed for a day or two. Let that uncle of yours take care of you."

"Yeah, sure." I slumped back into the pew and listened as he left. He might have made his point about Mom, but if he thought I'd sit out solving Death's case, especially when it looked like it might be linked to Virginia's, he'd really started to slip.

I stared at the crucifix for a few moments, debating the implications of Morello's death. He'd been exonerated from Alfonzo Arnie's murder in the worst possible way. I almost felt sorry for accusing him. In my old calculations, Vince's death would have left the blame on Mark, but now there was an extenuating factor. Virginia's death happened long before Mark met Arnie and there was no connection between Mark's gambling debts and a dead hooker. There was, however, a connection between the three killings: each of them had been dispatched by having their throats slit.

A chill seized me. I'd seen the man who'd killed all three of them. I'd shot him and nearly captured him. I cursed in spite of being in a chapel, then I realized something. Everyone who'd died since November 1 shared the same hell: being trapped in their corpses instead of passing on to the great beyond. That meant Morello would be trapped inside *his* body and being trapped meant he wasn't beyond being questioned by someone who could speak to the dead. Maybe he could give me some kind of information about his killer. I forgot my sore ankle and ran for the morgue.

25

The elevator might as well have stopped at hell's waiting room as the hospital basement. The voices of the dead reached a terrible crescendo, nearly drowning out the sound of "When the Swallows Come Back to Capistrano" that played through a tiny speaker in the ceiling. The cries, screams, howls, wails, and constant pleading got inside my skull and echoed around until I could barely stand them. My palms started sweating in spite of the fact my fingers were so cold they'd gone numb. The elevator stopped and I braced myself: it felt like standing in the tracks waiting for a freight train. The wait wasn't long.

My preparations weren't nearly enough. The sorrow of so many trapped souls crushed my defenses. I steadied myself against the wall of the elevator to keep my knees from buckling. The noise was horrendous: like every power tool in Manny's garage running full bore. The agony of the dead bored into my brain in spite of the fact I'd clamped my hands over my ears to seal it out. I took a tentative step into the hallway, and then another, leaning into my strides until I'd gained enough momentum to carry me to the corner. But the dead weren't done tormenting me. They had a surprise waiting.

Over the past eight years I'd gotten accustomed to seeing ghosts. I'd run into all varieties: shadows, cold spots, effigies that seemed unaware of my existence, and even a few spirits who'd spend the afternoon discussing their lives when I had the patience to listen. Every one of these encounters had been unique except for one feature: I'd only met solitary spirits. In my experience, ghosts didn't congregate. In fact, I didn't have any evidence they noticed each other anymore than most people noticed them. If you would have asked me, I would have sworn there was no such thing as a crowd of ghosts. Rounding the corner into the hallway outside the morgue showed me I needed to rethink my assumptions.

Ghosts pushed through each other in the confined space. They passed through walls, erupted from the floor, fell through the ceiling, and floated in the air like spectral dust motes. Their wails mirrored the despair of the trapped souls in the morgue. They clamored and cried, all the while looming and dissipating.

I pushed through the first shadowy rank. The spirits of the dead weren't a physical barrier, but passing through them pulled me deeper into an abyssal sadness from which I couldn't conceive escaping. All I knew was I had to get through quickly or I'd drown in their misery. I pushed and stumbled forward and as I penetrated the shades I became aware of something solid and alive standing in my path. Two men stood outside the morgue and as I got closer, they started moving toward me. Warm relief flowed into my heart; one of them was Scott.

I could see his lips moving but his voice got overwhelmed by the noise. The only thing that came across was his expression. It wasn't pleased. He started speaking again, his mouth working purposefully, as if the message he needed to convey was important and unhappy. I decided I'd tell him what I wanted if he couldn't cut through the crosstalk.

"I've got to get in there."

Immediately I wondered if I'd just screamed over a din only I heard. He didn't look impressed by the urgency of my mission. Instead he grabbed my arm and started to haul me in the opposite direction.

"Scott, let go! I need to see Morello."

He didn't react. Okay, not the way I wanted; he pulled harder. We had passed the elevator and turned down a series of industrial-looking hallways before the voices of the dead quieted enough for me to make out Scott's muttering.

"Stop fighting, Melody." He yanked me around another corner. We were headed for a pair of windowless doors and Scott's attitude told me I didn't want to go there.

"Let me go!"

He shoved me ahead of him and took up a position in the middle of the hallway to block me. I straightened my coat and rubbed the kink he'd yanked in my shoulder.

"What the hell's wrong with you, Scott?"

"Nothing's wrong with me. I've just clued in to a few hard facts about the world, that's all."

I started to chastise, but I couldn't work up the fire. "I understand you're disappointed with me, Scott. I'm disappointed with myself too. But you've got to understand that I need to get in that room. It's really important."

"Important? You know, it's funny how everything you want is important while everyone else is just kind of along for the ride. When you wanted to see Virginia Beal's file it was important, when you wanted me to run Morello's plate it was important, and now you want to get into the morgue and, what a surprise, it's important."

"Scott—"

He held up a hand.

"If you try to get into that morgue again I'll arrest you for criminal trespassing and interfering with an ongoing police investigation. Do you understand that? Because it's *important* that you do."

"I don't have time for your bruised ego." I tried to push by Scott but he caught me and cranked me around toward the doors. "Stop it!"

My yelling and flailing was pointless. I wasn't going to fight him off. He rushed me through the door and we burst out into the cold daylight of the hospital's back parking lot among the Dumpsters. I struggled free of his grip and straightened myself. He stood outside the door, his arms folded across his chest and his scowl set. I slung my purse strap over my shoulder and tried to give him an equally rude look.

"I never thought our friendship would end, Scott."

"Yeah, me either." He straightened his hat and tucked his tie back into his jacket. "Consider me not running you in a tribute to what we had."

He turned and went back into the hospital, the doors slamming heavily behind him. When those doors shut I lost my chance to question Morello. There was no way I'd get through Scott and his buddies in blue. I screamed as loud as I could and then kicked one of the Dumpsters for emphasis. My foot instantly went numb which probably was a blessing since it meant I couldn't feel the toes I'd just mangled.

26

Sometimes bad days can be fixed with a pint of ice cream: if your boss was a jerk from open to close, if you got snubbed by the cute guy you've been stalking for a month, or if you're on the way to an interview and you get caught in the rain without an umbrella. Any of those can be cured, or at least mitigated, with generous application of rocky road. Today demanded something stronger.

Today required an absolute, industrial-strength, junk food binge. I stopped at Mill Street Market on my way home and blew half a week's paycheck on stuff that probably had the power to rot my vital organs before it was even unwrapped. I had chocolate candies, crème-filled snack cakes, and a head-sized bag of potato chips to balance out the sugar with an equally potent dose of sodium. Voe sauntered into the kitchen as I unloaded sacks. I'd been frustrated when I got home and, apparently, the noise of me banging around the kitchen disturbed his afternoon beauty rest. He blinked, yawned, and gave me a quizzical look.

"What are you doing home? I thought you were going to shake down that what's-his-name guy, not go shopping."

"Morello's dead." I hobbled over to the refrigerator, regretting my rash decision to take on a Dumpster. When I turned back to my pile of groceries, Voe's sleepiness had disappeared.

"You *killed* him?"

He seemed genuinely shocked. The thought of me offing Morello might have scared him. He probably figured I'd finally gone totally insane and started killing the people who upset me. In a perverse way, it felt good to see an animal who took such pleasure in being in control pitched from his throne. If I'd been in a playful mood I would have left him guessing, but the concept of playfulness seemed to have taken a permanent sabbatical from my life.

"I didn't kill him." I pulled out a beer; it was afternoon, close enough to cocktail hour considering how the day had been going. "Some freak in a black overcoat slit his throat before I got a chance to talk to him."

"This is bad," Voe ruminated.

I popped the cap off my bottle. "You think so? I figured it just was some version of good I wasn't acquainted with."

"You don't have to get smart with me about it." Voe settled on the floor. "It's not my fault."

"I know." I grabbed the chocolates from my pile of junk food and sat.

"What are you going to do now?"

"Eat M&M'S."

"I meant about finding the mask."

"I knew what you meant the first time you asked." I tore a bag of candy open and poured a handful.

The kitchen fell silent except for the crunching of colorful candy shells and the put-putting of the garage's air compressor coming up through the floorboards. Too many doors had been closed. The year was running out and my one suspect had met with the same gruesome end as the man I'd assumed he murdered. Life's boot prints were all over my butt.

"Mel, are you giving up?"

Voe had moved around the table and was peering at me. He looked like a needy child and that made me feel guilty.

"Honestly, I don't know. I thought I had this all figured out but now . . ."

Where should I turn now? What piece of flawed intuition would I follow into the next blind alley? Maybe Scott and Rolland were right and I should have stuck to working the counter at Beeman's Drugs. Maybe Death had made a mistake by choosing me as his champion. I'd started to believe maybe I'd managed to get in the way just enough to prevent anyone who could unravel this case from having enough time left to do it. Voe interrupted my self-flagellation with another question.

"What about your doctor friend? He visited the house the night of Arnie's murder. Isn't he still a suspect?"

The answer was yes. Ever since Morello's murder I'd been turning that particular thought over in my head. The problem was I believed Mark and worse yet I didn't *want* to think he was anything *but* innocent.

"It's not Mark. It's someone else, this weirdo in the overcoat. Maybe that guy has some kind of connection with the mobsters Morello owed protection money. Maybe both Morello and Arnie having their throats slashed is just a coincidence." I dumped the rest of the M&M'S on the tabletop and tore into the bag of chips. "God, I wish Scott wasn't being such an asshole. I could use someone watching the hospital for people arriving with gunshot wounds."

Voe tilted his head slightly. The action conveyed a mingled sense of curiosity and dread. "Should I ask what that means?"

"No." I fingered through the candies scattered on the tabletop, sorting them by color. "It's a shame. Just when the world is coming to an end I start to get the hang of life. I found a cute guy and came into more cash than most people make in half a decade, all that was left was wrapping up this screwy errand Death sent me on and things would have been set."

"There's still hope."

I snorted at Voe's proposition.

"You're forgetting, I've been shown what the future holds: an eternity of imprisonment in a rotting corpse lies ahead for every man, woman, and child on the planet. I'm not the kind of girl who can ignore that, elope with Dr. Right, and then fly off for a honeymoon in Acapulco with that kind of thing running around in the back of her mind."

I sat crunching and listening to the guys working downstairs. I wished I could have forgotten about everything and gone on with my life. I didn't want to think about Death's mask, Alfonzo Arnie, or Vince Morello anymore. Laughter drifted in with the sounds of power tools. Downstairs a practical joke had probably just been played. Hell, all of humanity probably was joking and going on with life, totally oblivious to the cliff they were heading toward. God, it'd be great to be that blissfully ignorant. I'd trade it for angst ridden and impotent without a second thought.

"Maybe you should relax. There's still time, you might come up with an idea about what to do next."

"Maybe." I let out a disgusted breath. "I don't know, Voe. All these doubts keep running through my mind. What if I'd showed up a half hour earlier? If Morello were alive he might have provided the information I needed. What if I hadn't insisted on chasing down Virginia's killer? If Death chose someone with real talent the case might be solved by now. Even when the doubts disappear, I can't stop thinking about the fact that Virginia Beal, Alfonzo Arnie, and Vince Morello all died the same way: their throats were slashed and they were left to bleed to death. Even though none of them were very good people, they didn't deserve to go like that."

Running through the names started the morning's events replaying in my mind. There was something terribly wrong with what had happened. Aside from my witnessing a murder, time had seemed to be off kilter. I fixed my cat friend with a stare.

"Voe, what can make time slow down?"

"You mean aside from being locked up alone in a tiny apartment?"

"You're funny; remind me to laugh after the urge to strangle you passes. I mean actual time running like at a tenth normal speed. Do you know anything that could do that?"

"I'm sure there are lots of things." He stopped talking without answering the question.

"Specifics?"

"Well, it'd be something unnatural."

"See, that's not really an answer. It's more like stating the obvious." Something occurred to me. "You don't know, do you?"

"I know more about the way the world really works than you'll ever know!" he snapped.

"Yeah, maybe, but when it comes to this time mess you're totally at a loss."

"I'm never at a loss."

"Voe."

"All right, fine, I don't know." His tail flicked. "There, are you happy?"

In spite of the horrors encroaching around me, I had to snicker. Hey, I had a choice of finding some humor in the situation or going nuts so I chose humor. Besides, when life kicks me around I kick somebody else. It isn't a nice philosophy but it does get me through some tough times.

"Mr. Genius, the cat with all the answers, doesn't know?"

"I already *said* I didn't."

"Wow, how does it feel to be just as ignorant as one of us poor, dumb humans?"

Voe didn't seem to appreciate our solidarity. He hopped off the table and stalked toward the living room with his tail held disdainfully high.

"I don't have to put up with being ridiculed."

"Oh, come on Voe! I'll make it up to you. Come on, we can take turns wearing the dunce cap!"

He'd rounded the corner and he didn't come back. With the cat gone, I was left to my snack food and consternation. At least teasing Voe provided a momentary distraction from my misery. I grabbed another handful of chips.

27

Two days left in 1952 and I'd practically given up. Morello had been autopsied, a horrible thought considering his living soul was trapped inside his body while the coroner took it apart with knives and saws. In the end, he'd paid a higher price for his crimes than could be remotely considered appropriate. Soon everyone would share his fate. Humanity stood on the threshold of a world of living death; at midnight on New Year's Eve we'd step through the doorway and it'd become permanent.

In the midst of my consternation over finding Morello's killer, Mark called. He sounded weary. Apparently, the doctor business had been kicking him around; he went on about the late nights he'd been pulling and apologized several times for not calling sooner. It'd been three days since the incident in the hospital lot and if circumstances were different, I would have made him pay a premium for ignoring me. As things stood, I wouldn't have been good company even if he'd been the most attentive fellow in the world. Who can be enthused about a new love interest when they're contemplating the ruin of human kind? It kind of kills the romantic buzz.

So when Mark asked me to a movie, I considered turning him down. If I hadn't known about what the future held for humankind, this date would have been a first step toward earning my trust again. Doubtless it would lead to a more significant date on New Year's Eve and, perhaps, a kiss as the clock struck midnight. These were the small steps toward reconciliation, the only sort of steps I would have been willing to take. I started to deflect the suggestion, but he insisted and I started to feel the condemned deserve at least one more night on the town. I didn't have any other courses of action; why not pretend everything would be okay? Why not dress up and cuddle in a theatre as if we could have a normal life? At least the pretense would distract me from the ugliness of a future that seemed more inevitable all the time. We agreed on the seven o'clock showing of *Bloodhounds of Broadway* at the Montana Theatre and then Mark was off on his rounds again. I spent the rest of the evening and most of the next day moping, finally rousting myself to get ready to go out around four o'clock in the evening.

When I decided on the career of crack detective I didn't think about the potential impact it'd have on my makeup palette. Before, I'd weighed rouge color against skin tone, I'd debated nail polish as a complement to wardrobe, and I'd even thought about hair dye, but I never thought I'd be worrying about concealing bruises and gashes. I still like to put time into getting made up, but when hiding genuine battle scars is added to the process, the time invested goes up exponentially. It took twice as much foundation and powder to hide the bruises around my mouth and applying lipstick over a busted lip is nearly as agonizing as waxing your legs, but the end product is nowhere near as satisfying. Then there were the shoes. Out of the dozens of pairs I own, only one didn't put too much pressure on my banged ankle or pinch the toes I'd jammed while trying to punt a Dumpster. I ended up looking presentable: red dress, black flats, stylish hat, and a sequined clutch. You'd never know I'd shot a man and had the daylights beat out of me days earlier.

My black swing coat was becoming the outerwear of choice. It looked good but it also let me slide the .25 inside a pocket without hinting I was armed. It gave me pause to think that a pistol had become one of my most important accessories. It ranked right up there with earrings and bracelets in the pecking order. I pocketed it just before going out the door and took one last turn in the mirror to make sure it didn't affect the fall of my coat.

I fixed the coat's collar and glanced at Voe who lay draped over the back of my well-worn sofa. "You know, the girl's the one who's supposed to keep the guy waiting."

He raised his head and opened his eyes a little more than a squint. "I have no idea what you're talking about."

"It's too hard to explain." I glanced at the clock above my tiny television. "The short version is Mark should have been here five minutes ago. The weather's bad, though."

"Ah, I see. Well, I guess that's the way it goes." Voe yawned.

"What's that supposed to mean?"

"Oh, nothing."

That set my teeth on edge. "Don't 'nothing' me, cat."

"Well, it's just that I thought I remembered you saying something about not falling for this man's lines again but here you are, waiting."

God, I hate justifying myself to a housecat. I'd definitely give up talking to cats for being unaware just how skeptically Voe regarded my decisions.

"We worked things out, okay?" I checked the clock again. "Besides, I told you I trust him. If he said he'll be here, then he will."

"Whatever. I just thought I'd point out that you'd gone back on what you said before."

I went to the closet and retrieved my gloves. "You're just bent because you don't like Mark."

"You're right, I don't like him. But that has nothing to do with you breaking all your lovely rules."

Did he smirk? Can a cat smirk? I was about to lay into him

with a lecture about "my lovely rules" when the phone rang.

"This isn't over," I growled and then headed for the kitchen. My heart sank when I heard who was on the other end of the line.

"I'm really sorry, Mel." I could hear what I'd come to know was the sound of the hospital in the background. "Some idiot drove a truck through a guardrail and I need to stick around until everything's settled down."

"It's okay, I understand. So, no movie I guess." I could sense Voe putting on a smarmy expression but I refused to look.

"No, I don't want work getting in the way of our evening. This shouldn't take too long. Why don't you catch a cab down to the theatre and I promise I'll be there in time for the next showing."

"Are you sure? The roads aren't going to get any better and that car of yours doesn't like snow."

"I insist." The din behind Mark grew. "Better go, I'll see you in front of the theatre in about an hour."

I hung up and turned to Voe. "Work kept him so stow your assumptions before I put you out in the snow."

He dropped off the back of the sofa and silently slunk out of the room while I called a cab.

The roads were rotten. A trip from the garage to Main Street normally took less than twenty minutes, but snow and slush turned it into a forty-minute slog. I checked my watch as I stepped out of the cab; it was ten till seven. If Mark hadn't been delayed at work, we'd already have our popcorn and be settling into a cozy spot in the theatre. Thoughts of being snug with Mark staved off the cold and made standing amid the big snowflakes feel wonderful. I unsnapped my purse and started to dig for change.

"What do I owe you?" I asked, finally finding my wallet.

The cabbie didn't answer and when I looked up from pulling out bills my eyes were drawn to something hovering just an inch in front of my nose.

A cluster of flakes had stopped in midcourse to hang barely an inch from the tip of my nose instead of spiraling to the ground. I blinked and refocused my gaze; all the snow had stopped. Snowflakes hung in the sky like stars; impossibly motionless against an urban backdrop. The snow wasn't the only thing affected. The city stood still and the silence was eerily familiar. I'd felt the same sensation standing outside Morello's door, an unnatural calm that quelled normality. This was much more than an unnatural hush.

The crush of patrons who, moments ago, had been heading for the theatre doors stood silent and immobile. To my left, a man's lips remained attached to the cloud of cigarette smoke he'd been exhaling, another's hand halted in the midst of brushing snow from his hat, and two women bent together with one's lips frozen around the juicy tidbit of gossip she'd been sharing when the world wound down. Even the neon lights around the Montana's marquee had stopped; they cast an unhealthy blue-green glow on the coming attractions posters, making *The Member of the Wedding* look more like a Vincent Price flick than a romantic comedy.

Peripherally, I caught a movement. With everything stopped, motion seemed aggressive and I immediately pivoted to face it. An old man was crossing the street. I take that back. *Old* was too generous a term; it suited the codgers who hung around the Moose Lodge or haggled over the cost of a quart of oil with Manny. This guy was *ancient*. The weight of years had stretched his body until it looked thin enough to snap. His skin was gray compared to the white of the snow and it seemed poorly tailored to his frame, sagging in loose folds over his bones. Mangy strands of unkempt hair fell about his shoulders and swayed lifelessly as he walked. The robe he wore almost matched his pallor: moldering with no hint that it'd ever been remotely attractive. Like the man's skin, the robe was oversized and where it hung open it revealed that, in spite of the cold, he wasn't wearing anything under its folds.

The nakedness repulsed me but it didn't top the strangeness hit list. That credit went to the hourglass he carried. His right arm was extended, and he held the glass turned on its side, stopping the flow of sand. He casually strolled across the frozen street as I watched and seeing the scene made me feel like I might have finally lost my tenuous grip on sanity. Apparently it wasn't a shared feeling; he kept coming as if there wasn't anything patently insane about the entire situation. When one of his bare feet reached the sidewalk I snapped out of my stupor. Without thinking, my hand went to the pocket of my coat and the pistol came out in a smooth, automatic motion.

"Stop right there!" I hollered. The contents of my purse scattered on the pavement as I squared with my target in the way I'd been taught.

The old man froze.

"What the hell's going on here?" Having the gun separating us steadied my nerves nearly as effectively as a stiff drink. "Don't bother playing stupid, old man. I'm in no mood to screw around."

The tone of his reply wasn't fearful; I'd classify it more along the lines of bemused.

"You're outside the normal realm." His liver-spotted brow furrowed. "Who's shepherding you, girl?"

"Shepherding?" I had the gun so I didn't intend on letting him dictate how this conversation would go. "Answer the question!"

It didn't look like my fury intimidated the old man. Then

again, it was hard to read any emotion in those droopy, watery eyes.

"If you insist, I will amuse you, then you will answer my question. I have interrupted the due course of my life to intercede at this place and time."

He looked satisfied with that answer. I wasn't and I didn't bother making nice about it.

"What the hell is that supposed to mean?"

"I answered your question, now you will answer mine. Who is your sponsor, is it Long Black Thomas?"

The silence of the city had become unnerving. I meant to address the similarities it had with a certain recent event. "You were on West Fillmore Street the day Vince Morello was murdered. Who is this Thomas guy? Your partner? Is he the guy with the knife?"

"Your failure to fully grasp the situation is tedious." He took another step toward me. "I will admit to being present when Mr. Morello's time came. Having certain—talents—makes the elimination of untidy details very convenient."

Yes, it would be convenient. Stop time, slit a throat, walk away, and then start the clock again. Your enemies drop dead and you're nowhere near the scene of the crime. Damned perfect.

"Who is your shepherd, girl? Maybe you know him by another name? Perhaps Mort?"

I responded reflexively. "You're talking about Death."

"Ah, curt and simple. That suits his style. That is, of course, implying an animated corpse can *have* style." He'd crested the curb and was standing on the sidewalk.

"I said stay where you are! I won't hesitate putting a bullet in you, old man."

"Come, come girl. Let's not be foolish. I don't have forever."

As he said that I realized the snow had started moving again, nowhere near as fast as it should but moving nonetheless. Apparently this freak's power, though impressive, wasn't limitless. That spark of hope outshone his dread banter and assertions. If his power was finite, I had a chance and that's all I needed. Courage flooded into my body and sarcastic Mel returned to her full glory.

"Let me guess; now I've become an untidy detail that needs to be eliminated. Right?"

"Bravo, my dear. There is a complication, though, because we shouldn't even be having this conversation. You should be a part of the urban statuary." He nodded to the slow motion cityscape around us. "Unfortunately, it appears the alliance you've formed has complicated matters significantly."

He stepped past a man who was locked in the process of feeding a parking meter. The window of opportunity was open, but narrowly. I'd practiced shooting cans off a fence left-handed. I hadn't tried shooting psychopaths intermingled with crowds of innocent bystanders. One mistake and I'd be explaining myself to the hanging judge. When it came time to pull the trigger my aim would have to be perfect. Until that time arrived, I meant to make him think seriously about pushing my hand.

"Don't you think it's kind of stupid to walk up on a woman who's pointing a gun at you, old man?"

"Come now, do you really believe shooting me will do a bit of good?"

"I'd rather not be forced to find out."

"Then, by all means don't."

"Oh yes, perfectly reasonable. I'll put my gun down and let you walk up and do whatever horrible thing you'd like. Sounds great!"

The warning went unheeded. He took another step and I pulled the trigger. The .25 spat fire and a spent cartridge ricocheted off the cabbie's outstretched hand before falling into the gutter. I did my best to absorb the gun's kick with my weak arm while readying for a second shot. The slug punched a hole just to the right of the old man's sternum, but no blood came from the wound. Instead, a stream of white sand poured out of the hole. The old man swayed, barely flinching to register the hit.

"I told you it was pointless."

Before I got a chance to respond, someone grabbed me from behind. Experience is a good teacher, though. My elbow caught him in the stomach, giving me enough time to spin around. He was inside the arc of my gun hand and as I came around he caught my wrist, forcing the pistol up. God, it would have been good to have a right elbow to plant in his gut. I tried, but the sling restrained my motion and the blow came up woefully short. The man in the black overcoat spun me into a rough embrace, and then shook the pistol from my grip, letting it fall in the snow at my feet while I kicked and fought.

"Such a commotion." The old man's face was impassive. He didn't seem to care enough about my being subdued to waste the energy on a smile. "There's a saying in the game of chess: the king may be the thing, but the pawns decide the outcome of the game. It seems Death has lost both pawn and game."

"I'm nobody's pawn!" I screamed.

The old man shook his head. "Don't be insulted. You'd be surprised how many great men and women are the tools of forces beyond their comprehension. They play their part without even being aware of that fact. You should take solace in knowing you've at least glimpsed the greater truth, even if it was in failure."

I'm not a good loser. While granddad was lording it over me, I noticed his buddy's grip had loosened just enough for me to give him a good elbow poke. It landed in his ribs, about where I'd shot him. He winced and let go of me. Well, until he shouldered me into the side of the cab.

I caught a glimpse of the knife. It flickered as it came out, reflecting the cold light of the streets before being slammed home. The sensation was so cold I instinctively sucked in a deep breath. Fleck's bullet had burned into my body, an angry intruder that eagerly ate into my flesh. The knife was insidious, so keen it almost didn't hurt. When I let the air out of my lungs there was a troubling gurgle deep in my chest. Through the tears that filled my eyes I saw the face of my attacker and when I did, I wanted to go ahead and die.

Mark's eyes didn't seem sad: they were empty. The scarf that had disguised him had fallen away during the struggle and now we were face to face, him holding the handle of the knife that was meant to kill me. He pulled the blade out and I instantly felt the warm rush of blood spreading and sticking my dress to my body. I clamped a hand over the wound; somewhere I heard that was the right thing to do though I don't remember where. Mark took a step backward into the slowly accelerating world, watching as I slumped against the cab for support.

"It's a shame our little tryst had to end like this." He took out a handkerchief and casually cleaned the blade of his knife before snapping the blade closed and returning it to the pocket of his coat. "We might have made a good couple. We could have had something. It's too bad it didn't work out."

I wanted to tell him where he could put his opinions about what kind of couple we could have made. I would have liked to inscribe the message on a bullet and deliver it airmail. Unfortunately my body refused to obey my will and the details of the world were getting soupy. All I could manage was to stay upright and watch as he casually strolled off into a nearby alley.

"A shame indeed." The old man bent and picked my pistol from the snow, holding it with two fingers until he'd dropped it into my pocket. "I would like to say it's been a pleasure meeting you but I don't like to lie. When you're returned to the void, tell your friend his gambit failed and in a little more than twenty-four hours he'll be out of a job."

"Kiss my ass," I managed just before breaking into a painful coughing jag.

"I'd be careful. Most people like their last words to be somewhat more memorable than an impotent threat. Good-bye."

With a flick, he turned the hourglass upright and the world exploded with sound and motion. He'd disappeared, gone into the fury of human activity.

"Lady?" The cabbie withdrew his outstretched arm and leaned his head out the window. "Are you all right?"

I struggled to maintain my tenuous balance. "No."

"You need to go to the hospital or something?"

"God, no." Yeah, that'd be great. Mark could knock me off in private. I kept a hand clamped over my chest to stem the blood flow but it still oozed between my fingers in time with my pulse. I grabbed my purse from the ground, opened the taxi door, and tumbled into the back seat. "Just take me home."

"Miss, you really look like you ought to—"

"I said take me home!" Forcing the words out made me dizzy and nauseous. "Please."

We pulled away from the curb and he drove in silence. I felt him looking at me in the rearview mirror but I didn't care. Instead, I focused on the steady advance of the cab's meter. It might as well have been ticking away the seconds remaining in my life. When we stopped in front of the garage, I forced a handful of bills into the driver's hand. They were bloodstained but I couldn't make myself care. The world had started going dim and I needed to get to the apartment.

I fell halfway up the steps and slid all the way to the ground. It hurt even more than it should have. For a few seconds I lay, watching the snow spiraling down from the slate sky. Blood had run down past the waistband of my dress and it was plastering my once frilly slip to my legs. I never imagined a human being could bleed so much without dying. I clamped my weak hand over the wound, turned onto my side, and clambered on hands and knees to the top of the steps. It took three tries to get my key into the lock and another two to open the door.

Voe exploded out onto the stoop the moment I pushed the door to. His voice intruded on the encroaching darkness. It sounded frightened and small.

"Mel? Oh, Mel, you're hurt!"

He climbed over me as I crawled over the threshold. Some display of compassion. I didn't have the energy to insult him for his disrespect.

"I'm sorry."

That's all I got out. No soliloquy, no grand and important last observations on life, just a stupid apology. The old man was right. I should have spent some time thinking about my last words. Then again what could be a better summary of my life than an anemic expression of regret?

"Stay here, I'm going to get help."

Voe hopped over me and dashed out the door into the snow. The world had grown colder and dimmer and I found myself hoping he'd run off to find a new life free of the pain that humanity brought. He deserved that after suffering through losing Arnie. Maybe there'd be another hot Persian to entice him somewhere in the neighborhood. As I lay, the thoughts of Voe finding happiness ruminating, a sound drifted in on the chilly air.

First it reminded me of a siren, but then it grew throaty and mournful. There were words mixed into the wail, I think. They were so alien that not only didn't they have meaning; their very sound was beyond my ability to imitate. I strained against the

fatigue that was settling over my body to turn my head toward
the open door.

Voe was silhouetted against the falling snow. He tilted his
head back and sang his strange lament into the night—and the
night responded. There was a sound on the wind. Not distant
cars or the mournful whistle of a train, something utterly alien.
I lay, listening to the exchange: Voe would cry piteously and in a
few moments the reply would come. Consciousness waxed and
waned and with it all notions of linear time. I don't know how
long it was before Voe scampered back inside to take a place by
my ear.

"Try to relax," he advised.

"I'll do my best." Another fit of coughing interrupted; this
time it came with the taste of blood. That certainly couldn't be
a good sign. "Voe, I want you to know I'm really glad we got to
know each other even if it was just for a little bit."

"Hush!" he hissed. "People just don't know how to keep their
mouths shut!"

Great, here I am ready to pour out my heart and I'm being
shushed by a tabby. I was thinking of a pithy response. Okay,
actually I was thinking how tired I'd gotten, but I'm sure if I
didn't have an extra hole poked in my body I would have
delivered a crushing retort that would have set the feline back a
few lives. As it was, I just breathed heavily until I became aware
something had arrived.

I say something because someone didn't seem to fit. A figure
stepped through the open door. It stood no taller than the coun-
tertop in spite of being almost broad enough to fill the doorway.
In the poor light all I could make out was shaggy hair that
almost formed a mane. Its voice was female, but the shape
definitely wasn't feminine.

"Who called me?"

"I did," Voe replied.

"A cat?" The creature seemed put off. "I've come all this way for a cat?"

"Yes, my friend needs your help."

The creature let out a snort. "Your 'friend' doesn't need my help. She's got no mark. Let her do her own stitch work." The creature started to skulk off.

"I can pay," Voe said.

That stopped the thing from exiting. "Since when do cats pay for anything?"

"I'll make an exception this time." Voe settled by my ear.

"And what do you have that's worth my time, cat?"

"Fresh eggs." Voe leaned over me, whispering. "Please tell me you've got eggs in that food box of yours."

I would have answered but to be honest I had no idea if I had eggs or not. Groceries weren't exactly the utmost thing on my mind. Consciousness was enough of a struggle.

"Eggs?" The creature froze in the doorway, its head cocked to indicate Voe's offer had piqued an interest. "How many?"

"Three."

"You insult me!" the creature bellowed.

"All right, I'll raise it to four, but that's all."

The creature seemed to chew the price. "They're not sparrow's eggs or something like that, are they?"

"They're good, white hen's eggs." Voe's tail swished. "So do we have a deal or do I need to call someone else?"

"Someone else? You couldn't find another flesh-mender if you hollered all night long." The creature stumped forward and the floor vibrated with each heavy step. I'd nearly drifted off when a callused hand gripped my chin and turned my face upward.

I was staring at a yellow-eyed thing. Wild, red hair encircled a ruddy round face. The nose was squashed almost to the point of looking like a pig's snout and two stubby tusks jutted from its lower jaw. It turned my head roughly, inspecting me in a way I've seen Manny look over a punctured tire. When it released my chin, my head bounced on the linoleum. I started to complain about the rough treatment but the words were driven out of me when the creature shoved a finger into my wound. I gasped and squirmed but couldn't escape the rough inspection.

"Seven eggs, this will take a good bit of twine to bind."

"Fine." There was a worried sound to Voe's voice. That didn't do much for my confidence.

"Good. It's a deal!"

The creature's voice boomed and in a moment it was gripping my chin and forcing me to look at its ugly face again. A fire burned behind its eyes like embers, burned down but hot enough to singe. The stare got inside my head and everything became disconnected. Nothing was important anymore. Not murders. Not cases. Nothing mattered.

"Sleep, I have work to do."

The rough edges of the creature's voice were gone and all I wanted to do was obey. So I did.

28

I don't know what time it was when I opened my eyes. All I can say is that I felt like a car had parked on my ribcage. Assembling the facts took a moment. I'd moved from the kitchen to my bedroom, judging by the swath of ceiling overhead. I ran my left hand across my stomach and found the bloody clothes I'd been wearing were gone. That was a little disconcerting since I didn't remember undressing or being undressed. I continued, moving from my navel and over the ridge formed by the bottom of my ribcage until my fingers found something foreign to worry. A rough cord pierced my skin, cinching the knife wound closed. The sensation of feeling the stitching and puckered skin was shocking and revolting and I tried to sit up. It didn't take long to realize sitting up was a mistake. My ribs ached worse than when Mark had stabbed me and lightheadedness instantly fouled my vision. The room swam sickeningly, forcing me to flop down on my pillow again.

"That wasn't very smart."

I opened an eye to see Voe reclining on the headboard, looking down at me. Inside I bet he was laughing. If he had lips I'm sure they'd be curled into a smug, self-satisfied smirk.

"Thanks, the crushing agony wasn't quite enough to let me know that."

"Just trying to help."

My mind leapt from verbal sparring with a cat to the fact a strange creature had just stitched my insides back together.

"What was that—thing? Is it gone?"

"Not so loud. Not everyone is as willing to forgive your rudeness as I am." Voe stood and stretched before gently dropping onto my pillow. "You might be the first human to ever receive the gentle attention of a troll."

I chuckled and my aching ribs made me regret it. "Come on now, don't screw with me. A troll? Like those ugly dolls with the frizzy hair?"

"If I had *any* idea what you were talking about I'm sure I'd be telling you not to make the comparison."

His tone didn't crack. I raised my head slightly.

"You're serious?"

"That a troll sewed you up? I wouldn't have told you that if I wasn't." He settled beside me. "They are some of the best healers in the world. Maybe it's all the digging around in the dirt they do. You know, all those herbs and roots and stuff?"

Now a new terror possessed me. I scanned the darkened room. "Is it still here?"

"Is what still here?"

"The troll, is it still roaming around here, somewhere?"

"Okay, a little etiquette lesson: *she* not *it.*" There was disgust in Voe's voice that his feline face was incapable of expressing.

"Etiquette? What the hell are you talking about?"

"I mean your old world, the one where you could get away with thinking that the only creatures with feelings were human, is gone. In your *new* world that sort of ignorance is going to get you into a lot of trouble."

The new world sounded more like the old one than Voe apparently realized, but then I'd never told him about the ghosts.

"All right, fine. Give me a break, before now I didn't even know there *were* trolls let alone he and she trolls."

"Really?"

The troll's entrance was preceded by the sound of her heavy

footsteps. Through the gloom of my darkened room, I could see she wasn't looking at me. She was admiring a white oval that she held between stubby thumb and forefinger. It was an egg. She inspected it over as if it was a rare jewel while she spoke.

"You don't know about trolls? Didn't your mother prepare you to go out into the world? Or do humans simply cast their children out leaving the witty to survive and the foolish to perish?"

The last thing Mom would have taught me about was trolls. I'm pretty sure she'd lump them in the same category as ghosts: a topic to be avoided.

"Uh, she just read me stories. 'The Billy Goats Gruff' and things like that." I stopped to think over the possibility I'd just committed another faux pas. I can be sensitive when I feel like it. "But I suppose that's probably not a very flattering portrayal."

"I don't know." The troll took a seat on the stool I use when I'm applying makeup. Her fiery eyes met mine in an intent stare. "Never heard it, how does it go?"

I glanced at Voe and he let out a sigh, resting his chin on his crossed paws. "Don't look at me. You got yourself into this mess."

Having a friend jump in to save you is wonderful, absolutely wonderful.

"It's, well, it's a kid's story. Really it's dumb."

The troll sniffed the egg and then popped it into her mouth. The crunching made me shudder. I had to look away to avoid a more open display of disgust.

"I don't mind dumb. Sometimes the dumb things can be more revealing than the brilliant ones. The truth hides under stupidity like juicy things hide under rocks."

"Okay. Well . . ." I grabbed for a chance at salvation. "You know, I just realized I don't know your name."

"Why do you want my name?"

There was a note of open suspicion in the troll's voice. Could trolls even be suspicious? If she could be offended by my ignorance of social niceties, I guess anything was possible. I eased myself into a sitting position, propping my back against the headboard and trying not to wince at the pain.

"I'd just like to know what to call you."

"She doesn't know any magic," Voe interjected, giving me a lazy glance. "If there's one thing for certain, it's that she's not going to lay any sort of spell on you."

I wasn't sure about all the implications of Voe's statement, but I was sure it was at least partially slanderous. Still, he was vouching for me—kind of.

"I promise; I just want to get to know you better."

"Pierhind."

"That's a very pretty name." There wasn't any harm in lying. "My name's Mel. Thank you for saving my life, Pierhind."

"You don't know much, do you?" She popped the egg she'd been examining into her mouth.

I answered before Voe had a chance to comment. "I've been told that before and it's becoming obvious that it's true."

Pierhind hopped off the stool and approached my bed, chewing noisily. "Let's just see how little you know. Earlier I told you that you got no mark, do you know what that means?"

"No."

She looked at Voe and snorted. "She is dense."

Again I jumped in before the cat had a chance. "Yes, I'm dense. So what does my not having a 'mark' mean?"

"It means your name's been erased from Death's rolls. He doesn't want you," Voe responded.

She leaned in closer. "Exactly. The Black Robe's got no claim on you. Most everything carries a little candle right here."

Pierhind reached out and touched my forehead with her index finger. It felt like being poked with a broomstick. Less than a month ago Death had touched me in the same spot. "When the candle burns out it's time to dig a hole."

The night on the plane of ash raced back into my mind. "That's what Death said; that he renounced his claim on me."

"You never told me that." Voe rose to a sitting position. "If Death has given up his claim that means you can't die."

"Right, and that's why the hole didn't bleed you dry," the troll confirmed.

Pierhind pulled at my covers and I had to fight to keep them at collarbone level. "Hey, do you mind?"

"Mind what? I don't mind checking my work."

She pulled at the covers again. This was becoming a real wrestling match and I was getting the impression there was no way I could match strength against the troll.

"I don't exactly feel like baring my ever-loving all in front of everyone!" I yanked the covers from Pierhind's hands and turned away in spite of the horrible pain it caused.

"It's not like I didn't see whatever you're trying to hide." Pierhind leaned on the edge of the bed. She smelled like mildew and raw eggs. "Who do you think did the stitch work on that stab wound?"

I braced myself. Having a troll see me naked wasn't the worst thing that had happened to me. Hell, it wasn't even in the top ten. I sat up again and let go of the blanket. For the first time I saw the wound that'd laid me low.

Just below my right breast was a line of neat stitches. I ran my finger along them, feeling the rough texture of whatever Pierhind used to sew up the gash. I wouldn't have thought the troll's stubby fingers could have done such fine work.

"Took a long needle to get down inside that hole. Big open wounds are better; you can get down in them to work." Pierhind reached over and touched the cut. "This just may be the best work I ever did, and for seven measly chicken eggs."

I nodded. "You did a great job."

"I know. Like the cat said, you won't find a better flesh-knitter in a hundred miles."

I felt the wound again. "Pierhind, I was thinking about what you said about me being dense. What would you think about teaching me a few things?"

Her wooly eyebrows bunched. "I think you're too squeamish even to learn how to sew up wounds and set bones. I hate to think what might happen if I tried to show you how to deal with the vile stuff."

"I don't want to learn medicine. I want to learn about the world, the real world, the world I've been blind to for most of my life."

Pierhind rubbed her chin; it sounded like sandpaper on stone. "That's a lot to teach."

Voe stood. "Mel, what are you doing?"

"I'm trying to be less ignorant. You said I better learn something or I'd be in trouble, so that's what I'm doing." I turned my attention back to Pierhind. "I'd be willing to pay for your tutoring."

"Pay?"

The mercenary quality crept back into the troll's voice and Voe quickly interjected himself.

"Whoa, hang on. I think you must be running a fever or something, Mel. I can teach you. You don't need to spend money on her when you should be spending it on me!"

"Just the other day you admitted there were things you didn't understand; maybe she does." I looked over Voe to the troll. "I'll give you half a dozen eggs for each lesson."

The fire danced in Pierhind's eyes. "Half a dozen, that's six eggs just for telling you how things are?"

"Right. You give me one lesson a week. I want to know

everything you know about the world. After each lesson I'll pay you."

"Mel, come on," Voe pleaded.

"You've got a deal." Pierhind rubbed her meaty hands together.

"Good, we can start with a short lesson tonight."

"Wonderful, get your lessons. I'll just starve when you've given all our food away," Voe snarled.

He jumped off the bed and skulked out of the room, muttering. I could tell his pride was hurt though I couldn't be sure why. When lacking information I fall back on humor, or a rude approximation of it. I called after him.

"Oh, take it easy, Voe. You could stand to lose a few pounds!"

When he didn't answer, I figured I'd have to patch things up once the lesson had ended. I needed to arm myself against Mark and the geezer, not smooth Voe's ruffled fur. I turned my attention to Pierhind. "Okay, tonight I met a strange old man."

She shrugged. "There are lots of strange old men in the world."

"Not like this one. He could stop time, at least for a while."

"Ah, I know the one. He's called Jack of the Wheel."

"The wheel?"

"The Wheel of the Year. He's not always old." Pierhind paused, her jaw working as if she had to physically chew the thoughts before putting words to them. "He is tied to the passing year. As the year grows old, so does Jack. When the old year ends, he dies, and is reborn with the new."

"Dies . . ." That linked to what the old man said in front of the theatre. "When this Jack dies, is Death himself involved?"

"Death has a bony hand in every death. He exists to see the end of all things. It's his sole purpose and only concern."

"What if Death couldn't fulfill his part?"

Pierhind's jaw worked harder. "I never thought about that. I mean, I guess the cycle would be broken. Jack couldn't be reborn if he never died."

I drew a deep, painful breath. Solving a mystery is supposed to feel good, not frightening. Death told me if he didn't get his mask back before the year ended he'd cease to exist. That meant dear old Jack would be immortal and some perverse version of 1952 would go on forever.

"Pierhind, is there a special place where this whole death of the old year, birth of the new ceremony has to be performed?"

"There are very few places it can occur. The changing of the year can only happen where the ley lines cross in just the right way."

"Ley lines?"

"Ley lines are currents of power that flow through the land. Where they intersect marvelous things are possible."

"Where do they cross?"

I was so anxious that I forgot I'd just been sewn up. I rocked forward to better hear her response and the result felt worse than getting stabbed. I sucked in a deep breath and held it, squeezing my eyes closed until tears welled up and ran down my cheeks. When I finally let my breath out again, it escaped in ragged pants. It didn't help when Pierhind started snickering.

"Them stitches don't like to be agitated."

"Yeah, I got that." I tried to breathe normally and take the pain. Focusing on the score I had to settle with Mark helped. "What about this spot where the ley lines cross?"

Pierhind's reply didn't do much to make me feel better. "Only the Map Maker can tell you that."

"Then where is the Map Maker?"

Pierhind shook her head. "Again, I don't know."

"Great, then we're screwed." I laid my head back against the headboard and closed my eyes.

"You give up too easy. You got a cat."

I opened my eyes. "So?"

"So ask him to find the Map Maker."

I sat up again. "Huh?"

Pierhind shook her head. "Here's another thing to remember about the world, child. When you need a wound sewed up, call a troll. When you need to find a way into somewhere you're not allowed, call a cat."

I swung my legs over the edge of the bed and gingerly took a step toward the door. The world had gone from dim and fuzzy to immediate, crisp, and filled with aches. I shuffled into the living room, doing my best to avoid any movement that might twist or bind my stitches. Moonlight sifted in through the blinds, painting the space with stark stripes of dark and light. Voe sat on the back of the couch, his tail wrapped around his haunches and his head turned away.

"Uh, Voe?"

Nothing. He was being difficult. His version of difficult was worse than my mother's.

"Voe?" I hobbled across the room and found a place to lean against the back of the couch. I could see his eyes crack open. "You're not mad at me, are you?"

"Why on earth would I be mad?"

Cats really do sarcasm well. I consider myself practically a professional at the art of thinly veiled mockery, yet even I could take lessons from Voe.

"Well, I mean that comment about not feeding you. You know that was just a joke, don't you? I never really would let you go hungry."

"Oh, but I do need to lose a few pounds, don't I?"

"See, that was part of the joke." I laughed and it didn't sound remotely convincing. "Honestly you're svelte and slim, the very model of a hot cat on the town!"

"Your attempts at flattery are almost as pathetic as your attempts at wit. It's obvious that you figured out you need me and now you're afraid I won't help because you mistreated me."

I closed my eyes and hung my head. "I need your help, please don't be petty."

"I'm never petty."

His statement had a frightening coldness to it. "Then you'll help?"

"If you'll admit you were wrong."

I nodded. "Yes, I was wrong."

"And you're not moving the troll in?" He eyed me. "There's barely enough room for the two of us, let alone her."

"I never intended to move Pierhind in. Where did you get that idea?"

"Well, you're giving all our food away. Who knows where the bargaining might have ended?"

"I'm not giving *all* our food away. Voe, I promise I'll go hungry before you do." I was getting tired. Whether the reason was the arguing, the bazaar-style trading, or the fact I'd just had my insides stitched back in place was debatable. "Look, if you want you can have tuna every night. Please help me."

"Okay, I'll do it."

Finally. "All right, we need to find somebody called the Map Maker. Pierhind says you might know where to go."

"I do."

"Great, I'll get my coat."

"No use." Voe stretched and yawned.

"What do you mean it's no use? You said you knew how to find this map person."

"Patience."

"Patience? You'll think patience when I kick you so hard your tail falls off! What the hell do you mean telling me to be patient? Don't you understand how important this is?"

He looked at me without flinching. "I understand. But to

235

find the Map Maker the moon needs to be full and it won't be until tomorrow night."

I shuffled over to the blinds and parted them with my fingers. The moon showed bright above the rooftops. "Tomorrow's New Year's Eve, Voe."

"Then I recommend you say goodnight to Pierhind and get some sleep."

29

To most people December 31 was just another Wednesday. They went to work or the market, got ready for parties, and generally stuck to their routines as if their eternal souls weren't less than twenty-four hours from the edge of peril. I watched through the window of Beeman's, leaning on the counter and thinking over my plan as the seconds ticked by.

My eyes burned with fatigue. Pierhind had left around two in the morning and in spite of Voe's admonitions, I didn't do a lot of sleeping after that. When my ribs weren't throbbing, my head pounded. When the pain paused, I couldn't stop thinking about meeting this Map Maker and then trying to find Mark before it was too late. Tonight everything had to go perfectly or the whole game was lost and it'd been a long time since anything had gone perfectly.

I thought about keeping the drugstore closed and devoting the day to watching Mark. But I couldn't afford to slip up and reveal myself before I knew the meeting place. If Mark found I'd survived and alerted his aged buddy, they might be able to take some kind of countermeasures. The risk wasn't worth taking. One thing I'd learned is that a bad situation can always get worse. Right now Mark was ignorant of the fact I'd survived being stabbed and that gave me an advantage I intended to exploit.

Pierhind's stitches itched. I rubbed them absentmindedly through my dress as I watched people pass the store. The swelling around her handiwork had started to fade. In a day or two, it'd probably be impossible to see the wound. She'd warned me that the pain would remain. Apparently, muscles didn't knit together without complaining but eventually I'd be able to stretch and bend without having the wind knocked out of me by a pang. I doubted if the emotional aches would ever subside.

How could I have been so stupid? I'd fallen for Mark twice, even after I knew he'd lied to me about knowing Arnie. My willingness to give him a second chance would have killed me if it hadn't been for the fact Death didn't want anything to do with me. The drugstore's door jingled open, and I looked up to see Rolland strolling toward me.

"Morning, Melody." There was a happy lilt in his voice and a smile on his thin face. "You'll notice I left the 'good' off in deference to your nocturnal leanings."

"I'll make sure to give you a gold star." I straightened and did my best to hide the pangs that squeezed my ribcage. "To what blessed event do I owe the pleasure of this visit? I want to make sure I avoid repeating it in the future."

"You make me sound like the harbinger of bad news!"

"You have to admit our past hasn't exactly been roses and chocolates."

He chuckled. That wasn't something I heard from Rolland often.

"I'll concede that point. Actually, I came in to buy a tin of Edgeworth and share a little good news."

I surveyed the tobacco display; his brand would have to be on the top shelf. I pushed the rolling ladder along its track and kicked the brake in place before starting to climb. Each rung was a new adventure in pain.

"We've found your friend."

"What friend would that be? I've got so many admirers I lose track." I paused to catch my breath at the top rung.

"Richard Fleck."

I turned to look at Rolland in spite of the pain. I'd almost forgotten Fleck. Rolland stared at me, fishing his pipe out of his jacket pocket while he waited for a response.

"Then arrest him." I grabbed a tin of tobacco and started back down the ladder.

"We will. Scott's on stakeout; when Fleck shows up we'll give him an unpleasant New Year's present. I wanted to give you a chance to prepare to do your part in getting him off the street."

I sat the tin on the counter and rang it up. "I thought my part was staying out of your way like a good civilian."

"It is, until a court date is set. Among the charges he'll be facing is attempted murder. You'll have to testify." He looked up from his pipe. "Are you up to that?"

"Are you sure you want me in the courtroom? I wouldn't want to foul things up like I've been doing." It was a low blow but I didn't feel very amiable.

"I think you'll do fine as long as you don't decide to crack wise with the judge." He was giving me his stern schoolmarm look, staring over his glasses.

"I promise I won't smart off. Does that make you feel better?"

"Loads." He pushed a dollar bill across the counter for his tobacco.

I started making change and thinking. "Rolland, how's Scott?"

"How should he be?"

"I don't know." Why did Rolland have to make this hard? Was it some kind of man thing? "I just wondered if he'd said anything."

"Anything about the fight you two had?" He took his change. "What was it about, anyway?"

"Nothing."

"If it was nothing you wouldn't have asked about him."

239

"Do you do this detective thing all the time or do you take time off?"

He smiled. "It helps pass the time. You didn't answer the question."

"All right, save the bright lights and thumb screws." I pushed the register drawer closed. "I told him that I wasn't interested in dating him and that I liked him as a friend."

"Ouch." Rolland dropped the change into his pants pocket. "Well, as far as I can tell he's not frothing at the mouth or plotting your demise. I guess that means he's taking it about as well as can be expected. He'll get over it. Give him time."

"You think he'll forgive me?"

"I'm not exactly a charter member of the lonely hearts club, Melody. In case you didn't know, I live in a one-room walkup with a pair of lovebirds that don't get along. He drinks too much and she's making time with a starling on the side."

I laughed against my will. "That's really sad."

"I don't know, it's better than television."

"Why didn't you ever get married?" It was a personal question, but it stopped me from worrying about tonight. Besides, Rolland dug into my personal life so I couldn't really be blamed for doing the same to him.

"If you want to know the truth, I waited too long and the moment passed."

"Career got in the way?"

"No. The girl got away. By the time I was ready she was taken."

"You could have tried to woo her away."

He tucked the tin of tobacco into his coat pocket and shook his head. "Take care, Melody. I'll be in touch about the trial."

I watched him walk out. He stopped under the store's awning, cupping his hand against the wind as he touched a match to his pipe, then puffed a few times before stepping out into the sunlight. I couldn't help wondering about Rolland and his mystery woman. Part of me could picture him as a devoted husband. A bookish man, smoking his pipe while reading the paper. Three kids with their toys scattered across the family room floor and a wife knitting an afghan. It felt sad that he'd traded that life for bachelorhood. I think fatherhood would have suited him.

30

I closed the drugstore early and Voe and I were on the road by four thirty. On Voe's instructions we headed out of the city and drove toward Sunnyvale. The sun hovered close to the rooftops, occasionally throwing the car into mock-nighttime to remind me time was running out. Voe didn't look any more comfortable on this car ride than he had during his first. Maybe running through a hedgerow and almost crashing into a one-story rambler had soured him on automobiles. When the urban landscape gave way and we passed into suburbia, I finally asked some of the questions that'd been building up in my head.

"Where, exactly, does this Map Maker live, anyway?"

"Nowhere around here."

Less than a month ago I would have slammed on the brakes after that revelation. Experience taught me the cat was leaving a lot of information out. I shot him a glance.

"This is one of those 'gotcha' things, isn't it? You're baiting me so you can tell me what an idiot I am when I flip out."

"You're finally catching on."

He sounded impressed but I knew better than to get smug. "Thank you. So, where is the Map Maker?"

"Not far from my old neighborhood there's a dirt road. That's where we'll find the gateway that leads to the Map Maker."

"This sounds too easy."

"It won't be easy at all. The Map Maker is deadly, he's every bit as much a killer as your doctor friend."

"You can stop calling Mark my friend. If I had him here I'd personally strangle him without the slightest bit of remorse."

"Keep that attitude in mind when you think about the Map Maker."

"So, if he's such a killer how do we convince him to help us? Should I stop to pick up a dozen eggs or something like that?"

"You're not dealing with a troll, Mel. There are no bargains and there's nothing you can barter for the information we need."

"You're making it sound damn near hopeless." I blew out a disgusted breath that fogged the windshield. "How the hell am I supposed to make this jerk cooperate if I don't have any leverage?"

"By being resourceful and smart."

I glanced at Voe. "Did you just imply I had the smarts and resourcefulness to fool the Map Maker into doing what we want?"

He didn't look at me. "Something like that."

"I think that's the first time you've actually complimented me. Now I'm really scared."

About a quarter mile past the entrance to Sunnyvale, a dirt track left the road and headed out into the thickets. The sun had vanished and the countryside was a study in black and white: skeletal trees rendered against snow. We bumped along the road, the car bucking uncomfortably as we traversed potholes and wallows on our way to our destination. After about ten brutal minutes, my headlights fell on a rusty gate. Beyond the barrier the trees closed in on the roadway, showing that no motorized vehicle had gone farther than this point in a very long time. From now on it would be ugly footwork. Voe hopped onto the dashboard and assessed the situation.

"Up the hill there's an abandoned house. That's where we'll find the gateway."

I opened the door and Voe jumped out. His dark shape

instantly blended with the weeds and briars that poked out of the snow and if it weren't for his talking, I doubt I would have found him again.

"The moon will be right soon." He'd already passed the gate and was bounding up the path. "We need to hurry."

I rolled my eyes, as if I could hurry through the brush in the dark. Sometimes I think Voe forgot he was talking to a person, not another cat. That might have been a compliment but it led him to impossible assumptions about what I could and couldn't do. While he headed up the hill, I grabbed a flashlight from the glove compartment. The undergrowth clawed at my legs as I headed for the gate. The intellectuals at The Quarter like to ramble on about agrarian values and how America is losing its connection to the soil. They talk about returning to the land but after a few seconds of fighting burs and briars I knew the country life wasn't for me. I'm an unabashed fan of concrete; in fact I'm pretty sure mankind invented cities to keep nature in all its scratching, biting glory at bay. But there wasn't time to contemplate the shortcomings of country life. Voe had nearly gotten out of earshot and if I waited too long I might never catch up.

The terrain would have been hard to navigate even without the ankle-twisting hillocks of grass and greenbrier tripwires. I fell a half-dozen steps after slithering between the gate slats, and by the time I righted myself, I couldn't hear Voe's banter. The roadbed climbed steadily, cresting in what seemed to be an impenetrable wall of brambles. Thorns had cut my palms and the cold made them sting furiously. I took a moment to wipe the blood on my coat before retrieving my flashlight. In the light I could make out Voe's tracks leading through the brush and over the hill, but my feline friend was nowhere in sight. I stumbled to my feet, brushed myself off, and got moving.

I fought through the weeds at the top of the hill and emerged into a small clearing. The sky was perfectly clear. Millions of stars dusted its black velvet hems, shimmering slightly as if the winter evening left them shivering. The lights of the city shown on the northern horizon as a reminder of all I'd left behind. Compared to the stars, the city's glow looked sickly and yellow, a poisonous radiation seeping into the nighttime sky. It looked pretty but I still would have done just about anything to have a little of the city's light to dispel the darkness.

An angular, black shape cut into the sky. The outline of a swayback roof attested to the fact that I stood in front of some kind of building. I raised my light and the beam illuminated the overgrown corpse of a house.

Decades ago, the clapboards had given up the notion of being any color but weathered gray. They hung loose in places, leaving gaps my flashlight refused to penetrate. A fallen-down porch jutted out from the front of the building; its roof collapsed on one end owing to the tree that had fallen on it. Through the maze of timbers and branches, I could make out a gaping doorway and Voe sat at its threshold.

"You'll find the gateway on the second floor."

"You say that like you're not going to be there with me."

"I'm not."

"Whoa, I thought you were here to be my guide. You know, we're talking about Mel the lout who knows nothing about how the world really works here. I'm going to need all the help I can get!"

"I know and you're right. The problem is this only will work for one of us and that one has to be you."

I squinted at Voe. "Are you saying that this gate is specially tuned to work only for me?"

"Of course I'm not. What, do you think somebody came out here to set your own personal portal? Don't be stupid!"

I wasn't sure whether I should be relieved or pissed. For the moment I opted for just staying confused.

"So why, exactly, can't you come along?"

"We really don't have time for a tutorial session."

"I don't care; I'm not walking in there if you don't explain this to me."

"Fine." Voe hopped off the porch and settled uncomfortably in the snow. "Do you remember when I said that this only would work tonight, with the full moon? Well, actually it works best at midnight on the night of a full moon."

"But we can't wait until midnight."

"Exactly. Which means the portal isn't at full strength."

"I see. That means only one of us can use it. That doesn't explain why you shouldn't go, though."

"I'm a cat; there are certain things I just won't do."

"You're full of shit, Voe." I tucked the light under an arm and pulled my pistol out to check the clip. "But I don't have time to argue."

"That gun won't do you any good, Mel."

"You never know, it might. Besides, I'd rather be ready than sorry." I flicked the safety off and collected my light, pointing it into the building. "So, what does this gate look like?"

"It's on the second floor; you'll know it when you see it."

That didn't make me feel any better. I ducked under the front edge of the porch's collapsed roof and clambered up the slick boards to the threshold of the open door.

"Mel."

I turned; Voe was sitting at my heel and the flashlight set his eyes alight. "What?"

"Be careful."

I smiled. "I'll do my best. Keep the car warm."

I stepped through the door and into the remains of a small room. The floor sloped away from me at an angle that made me feel slightly drunk. The walls had been plastered, but now most of it lay on the floor in heaps and the bare lathing gave the room a skeletal feel. I'd heard stories about people leaving the countryside to work factory jobs but until this moment I'd never really thought about what they left behind. There might be houses like this all around the country, little ghost residences overtaken by weeds and beaten down by time until all memory of the people who'd lived in them disappeared. All that remained was the corpse of the life they abandoned. Another ten years and this house would be a heap of rotten lumber in the middle of a second-growth forest. That is, if some developer didn't bulldoze the place to build another subdivision first. I swept the light around the room; in the far corner a staircase led up to the second floor and Voe's gateway. I swallowed hard and started up.

The stairs emptied into a tight hallway and I swung my light around to get a feel for my surroundings. The hallway could have been claustrophobic but for the fact that the tree that'd crushed the porch on the lower floor had also taken out the end of the hallway. My light fell on the tops of trees instead of a wall. Saplings pushed in through the gaping wound, their bare branches clawing at the remains of the floral wallpaper and scraping the bare lathing of the ceiling. The fallen tree had knocked the house off its foundation and the hallway pitched toward the destruction. I leaned against the decaying wall for moral support as I addressed the two doors to my right.

The first door opened into an empty room. Its broken window looked out over the porch toward the drive where my car was parked. Once it might have been a nice bedroom. Maybe the kids slept there, waking up each morning to the crowing of a rooster and sun rising across the family's fields. Life on the farm might have been damn bucolic before it all caved in but I didn't have time to mourn the bygone era. One more doorway demanded my attention.

It might have been grandstanding to kick the door in but it sure felt great. I burst into the room with my pistol leveled, but there weren't any targets. In the process of crushing the far end of the house, the tree had removed part of the roof. I stood in a room that was open to the sky. The moon had crested the tree line and its full face stared down on where I stood, intense enough to make the flashlight I carried unnecessary. There were no doorways: no burning portals or gaping inter-dimensional maws leading to the nether realm of the famed Map Maker. Aside from me, the only thing inside was a badly weathered full-length mirror the former inhabitants hadn't seen fit to take when they abandoned their agrarian lives.

I lowered my pistol and cursed. What the hell was this? Had Mark and his friend gotten here first? Maybe they'd hedged their bets and decided to close off the only portal that would leave them vulnerable. I kicked a branch across the room and it ricocheted off the base of the mirror. The silvery surface flashed as it shuddered, reflecting the light of the moon. I slowly crossed the room, pistol raised again, watching the glassy surface.

This had to be the gateway, disguised as a weather-worn mirror in a collapsing house. It was too *Alice in Wonderland* not to be the gateway! I drew a steadying breath and reached out with my gun to poke the silvery surface. The pistol's nose bounced off the hard glass just like it should have.

"Damn it!" I screamed at the sky, and then kicked a piece of loose plaster.

Where the hell was this gate? How could I find and deal with the Map Maker if I couldn't even figure out how to get to his realm? Obviously Voe had misjudged my intelligence back in the car because this riddle was kicking my ass. I leaned against a wall and crossed my arms, feeling defeated. What could I do now? Go downstairs and ask Voe if he would come up to help me find the missing portal? Yes, that was an option. It tasted a lot like cod liver oil, but I couldn't think of any appealing ideas. I started to stand but the edge of my coat was glued to the wall. At first I assumed I'd caught myself on a nail. The place was devastated enough that there had to be a million opportunities for tetanus lying about. I yanked again but the cloth didn't tear loose; it actually seemed even more attached to the wall than before. I swiveled and shined my light down toward the tail of my coat to see something . . . utterly impossible.

The mirror cast a reflection on the wall, a rectangle of moonlight slightly smaller than a door. That wasn't amazing in itself. Any mirror will reflect light; it's what they do. The marvelous thing was how the moonlight moved and rippled around the spot my coat had touched, spreading out in concentric circles that marched toward the edge of the lighted patch. The material had passed through the plane of the wall, disappearing beneath its shimmering surface. I poked the wall with the nose of my gun. The waves were more intense, spreading out from the barrel until they reached the edge of the light pool where they rebounded and redoubled.

I pushed with the gun and it sank, passing through the plaster and disappearing. I could feel a steady tug. Like my coat, once the nose of the gun had passed through the wall it began to be drawn in by a force that couldn't be resisted. This was magic quicksand; just trying to fight the pull made my wrist hurt. It had to be the gateway and that meant there wasn't any point in resisting because I needed to go through. So I relaxed and let the gun sink further into the wall. When my knuckles touched the rippling light the cold of the night air disappeared, replaced by a strange tingle that felt like what white noise ought to. I took a deep breath, closed my eyes, and leaned into the wall.

For a second, I floated in a sea of static. Current flowed over my body, snapping between my fingers and nipping at my earlobes as I tumbled. I held my breath. I might have been able to breathe but I wasn't sure and the worst possible scenario seemed to be making the wrong assumption. My lungs started to ache for air, tears began to flow from the corners of my eyes, and the taste of pennies filled my mouth. Then it was over. My left toe caught something soft and then I stumbled free of the prickly cocoon. The air was warm, heavy with moisture, and smelled of mold. I opened my eyes to absolute bewilderment.

The rotting bedroom had disappeared. At first I thought I'd stepped out of the gateway with my nose almost pressed against a wall, but as my eyes adjusted to the gloom I recognized the rough surface as bark. I'm sure there had never been a tree the size of the one I stood facing, or at least until that moment I was sure of that fact. My eyes couldn't find the edges of the trunk; it spread out until it disappeared into the haze at the limits of my vision. I followed the stalk upward to the first spreading branches. They looked as wide as city streets and hung with swaths of gray-green moss from which condensation dripped. Droplets fell from the tree, pattering on the leaf litter like a slow rain. That was where any semblance to a forest in my world ended.

The air was horribly still. There were no birds in the branches of the giant tree, or maybe none that wanted to give away their location by singing. In fact, nothing moved. There were no skittering rodents in the leaves, no insects whirring or chirruping, the only living thing seemed to be me.

"Hello?" I tilted my head back and yelled louder. "Hello, is anyone here? I'm here to see the Map Maker."

The fog smothered my voice; it disappeared into the hidden vastness of the landscape without the courtesy of an echo. This kind of quiet unnerved me. Growing up in a city, surrounded by hundreds of people and enveloped in the noise of their lives, silence is anathema. It only happens when something's horribly wrong. I was getting the feeling this world was no different. In the silence something terrible lurked, and I had no doubt it was the Map Maker.

I took a few paces away from the tree. The fog rushed in to soften its trunk until it might have been a stone wall to my eyes. Details had a way of disappearing in this place. Everything seemed out of focus. I swept my light around to survey my surroundings, but the beam stabbed out into the mist and died before it struck anything. I looked around, the ground sloped away from the tree in irregular lumps, piled deep with moldering leaves that had fallen from the invisible branches overhead. I turned and swung my light around until it fell on a slightly luminescent patch of fog.

A shimmering rectangle hovered a few inches above the ground. Its surface swam with the sort of rainbows that oil makes on a puddle. This had to be the opposite end of the gateway. I carefully brushed my fingers across its surface, but unlike the gateway in the abandoned house, they didn't penetrate or stick. The surface was solidified fog, elastic enough to stretch without allowing my hand to penetrate when I pushed.

This had to be what Voe meant when he said the gateway wouldn't be at full strength before midnight on the night of a full moon. Maybe, right now, the gateway was like a car with its battery being charged. I managed to get through in one direction; now I'd have to wait to get back home. The two big questions were how long until I could return and how the hell to find the Map Maker. I contemplated that question and as I did the silvery disk's sheen dimmed under a looming shadow.

At first, the thing in the mist seemed human, but by the dim beam of my flashlight that visage fell away. Its misshapen head sprouted clusters of gleaming, black eyes arranged around a horrid, pulsating maw. It raised a pair of hairy limbs to fend off the light. They were long, gnarled, and sprouted from the same side of the beast's torso. At the end of both were huge, three-fingered claws. The two opposite arms—if that wasn't too human a term—supported the creature in an apelike manner. It shrieked and bolted back toward the tree, mounting the huge trunk and bounding up its surface faster than I could have sprinted across flat ground. I stumbled backward, trying to keep my light trained on the beast but in seconds it'd disappeared into the mist.

The massive limbs overhead shook, leaving me to guess what the thing might be doing. I pointed my gun into the mist, as if I could have hit anything. Now I longed for the oppressive silence. I desperately wanted to be the only thing in existence.

"Are you lost, child?"

The voice came from everywhere. It left me turning in circles, sweeping the fog with my light in search of its source. It wasn't a question of concern; the thing was taunting me.

"I'm not lost; I came here to find the one called the Map Maker."

The tree limbs shook. The creature had shifted positions, probably sizing me up. I tried to track its motion, but with the fog it was pointless.

"Who are you and what do you want?"

"That's none of your business."

"If you want answers it is." Deep in the fog bank I heard something heavy land in the leaves. I pivoted my light toward the sound and waited. "You see, I am the Map Maker."

Now I understood why Voe didn't want to come through the portal. The charge thing gave him adequate excuse but aside from that, what sane creature would willingly face this hideous thing? Its every word dripped with malice. There was no doubt that, given the chance, the Map Maker would do something terrible to me. I didn't want to contemplate the extent of what it could do; I needed to stay focused on the reason I'd come through the mirror passage and pray I lived long enough to get back through again.

"Then we have business. I need information about ley lines."

Through the fog I caught motion. An almost human shape lingered just outside the range of my light. I could hear the sound of the Map Maker's breathing.

"Ley lines, why would someone like you need to know about ley lines?"

"That's my business. You don't need to know."

"But I do, that is if you want answers to your questions."

"I don't have time for games."

"You'll make time. No one comes to me if they're not desperate and the desperate are in no position to make demands. Besides, I get so little news and so little company in this lonely place. Is it so much to ask for a little companionship?"

For once I'd like to go into a situation *with* the power. The last thing this creep wanted was companionship. Still, he was right about my desperation. "I need to know what locations in the Pittsburgh area are suitable for the ceremony that marks the end of the year."

The Map Maker let out a wheezing laugh. "That happens in every squalid little home through the city. That's not why you need to know the ley lines. Be specific, girl. I want details."

I drew in a deep breath of dank air. "I need to know the location that's suitable for the death of the old year."

"And why?"

"Because I need to make sure it ends like it's supposed to."

"See, was that so hard?"

I didn't need to put up with smugness. "I told you what you wanted to know, now answer my question."

A long limb extended through the fog and the Map Maker splayed his hooked fingers. Silk threads spanned between their tips forming a fine web that glistened and pulsed with firefly light. "The lines are many, child. Each one pulses with power:

power to create, power to destroy, so many different possibilities."

The lines were obvious. Each strand of silk glowed, forming what I assumed was an individual ley line. They crossed and recrossed each other but a definite epicenter existed. That had to be the spot where the changing of the year would occur. There was an issue, though.

"There are no points of reference. How do I know how these lines relate to the physical world?"

The hand withdrew into the fog. "That is troublesome. You told me where you needed to be but you didn't reveal exactly what part you will play in this yearend drama."

"Wait a minute, you only gave me part of the information I needed."

"Yes, that's true." The creature's voice dripped with insincerity. "Are you the executioner? Has Death farmed out his dirty work to the highest bidder? Perhaps it's a lark? It would be wonderful to see an entire year snuffed out in the span of a second."

I swallowed my ire. "Like I told you before, I need to be there to make sure everything goes as planned."

"Why wouldn't it? Is there something afoot? Some terrible flaw in the cosmic order?"

"I'd love to tell you, but you haven't answered my last question."

That felt nice. The creature moved a little closer. His claw extended again; this time there were more threads. A pair of them snaked in gentle curves, joining in to form a point that I recognized as the confluence of the Allegheny and Monongahela rivers. The triangle of ground between the two would be Point Park and just north of that, the confluence of ley lines intersected.

"That has to be near Allegheny Cemetery." My mind raced.

A clock tower stood just inside the Butler Street gates. What better place to greet the New Year by preventing it being born? "That's got to be the place."

As the riddle unwound, a disturbing fact intruded. The Map Maker stood closer to me. I hadn't noticed him move; it must have happened while I deciphered the map he'd spun. Now one of his hands rested in the leaves less than a pace to my left and another was inching closer to my right foot. The sight of long, clawed fingers gave me chills. There was no way this could be good. I stepped backward trying to be nonchalant.

"Well, thanks for the information. I'd better get going—"

"Why leave now? We're only just starting to get acquainted."

"Yeah, it's a shame, isn't it? Unfortunately I've got to meet someone. Maybe some other time?" I took another step backward.

"It's disturbing how manners have declined over the eons. It seems like all of my guests are so rude nowadays. They come pleading, or worse, demanding my help, and when they've gotten what they want they think they can just flit off."

"That must be awful." If I remembered, the entrance to the gateway was to my left. I started to curve my retreat in that direction. Hopefully the thing had recharged enough for a return trip.

"Your concern is touching, but it's misplaced. In the end they see it my way."

He raked the ground with his claws, clearing away the leaves. Muscular roots snaked across the ground, pushing down between jumbled masses of bones. Empty sockets stared up at me. Jawbones gaped in wordless agony. Arms, stripped bare of muscle, lay locked in their final, futile struggle. The massive tree grew on the bodies of the Map Maker's victims and it was clear he meant me to be the latest addition to his macabre compost heap.

To my right, the Map Maker's hand darted for my neck, scattering leaves into the foggy air. I'd prepared and dropped to my knees as his claws sang over my head. I rolled and brought the gun up alongside my flashlight, firing at the Map Maker. I couldn't tell if the bullet found its mark. The creature leapt into the branches.

I scrambled to my feet, keeping my eyes on the foggy sky. Leaves spiraled down as the Map Maker moved about but I couldn't fix the bastard's position. I scrambled toward the gateway, stumbling over roots and God knows what else, while I kept watching for my assailant's next attack.

"You don't really think you can get through that gateway before I catch you?"

The creature's mocking tone prompted me to take a blind shot into the tree's boughs. His laughter told me just how fruitless the urge had been. Still it felt better than just standing around, waiting to be snatched up.

"Maybe I'll wait until you almost touch the gateway before I grab you." He'd moved. The voice was almost overhead. "To be so close to escape and to fail, wouldn't that be pathetic?"

"Very." I kept sliding toward the mirror. "You could show what a good sport you are and let me actually touch it."

"That *would* be cruel. After all, soon you'll be tied to this place forever, a part of it, unable to be severed from it for all eternity. Just like me."

Hmm, out of the mouths of hideous, slobbering, bloodthirsty monsters. I stopped retreating. "I have an idea of my own."

"Really? How intriguing. Please, share."

"How about we stop playing this moronic game of hide-and-seek?" I held up my gun. "This thing's no good against you, I know that."

"Brave and smart. Quite exceptional." The limbs moved under the creature's weight. "Go on, what do you propose?"

I dropped the pistol into my coat pocket. "You come down and show yourself to me. I'd like to see the one who beat me before I die."

"That would be a noble gesture on my part, wouldn't it?" He laughed.

"Yeah, it would be."

The limb overhead swayed and a dark shape dropped to the ground. As it did I took one more step toward the mirror. The Map Maker looked like the ugly offspring of a man and a spider. The wiry hair that covered his bare body glistened with beads of condensation. The flesh that covered his lopsided head bore gray blotches and resembled leather. Set in that head were shiny button eyes, black and pupil-less. The head was mounted on narrow shoulders from which the first set of horrible, gangly arms extended. Below the first set of arms, sprouting unceremoniously from about the armpits was another pair of equally nasty appendages. I hated my idea of facing this monster more every moment.

"Behold your doom!"

The mandibles worked but I couldn't be sure if all the fluttering and gyrating was for the purpose of forming words or if he was salivating at the thought of making a meal of me. I didn't plan on finding out. I brought my flashlight up and snapped it on. The beam caught those glassy eyes flush and the Map Maker squealed and recoiled. I bolted for the mirror but he was just as fast as I feared.

Clawed fingers wrapped around my waist just as I got to the edge of the silver disk. I tried to bring the light to bear again but a backhand sent it sailing into the fog. Maybe that was for the best. The gloom helped hide the Map Maker's hideousness. I could hear him breathing as he drew closer. A claw touched my chin, turning my face toward his.

"You will suffer for that."

"I don't think so."

Most of the time I moan over my constant fight for a trim figure but this day I was more than happy for every extra pound. I threw my weight toward the gateway and caught the Map Maker off guard. His knuckles broke the plane of the silvery disk. I could feel him fighting the inexorable pull of the gateway.

"When you said you were tied to this place, how literal were you being?"

The creature answered with a frantic shriek. His fingers loosened but he couldn't withdraw the hand that had held me. My back had passed the gate's plane and I lay, Fay Wray style, in the creature's hand. That's where the similarities ended. There definitely wasn't a weird love affair going on.

"You bitch!" the Map Maker snarled, yanking its trapped appendage.

"I'll take that to mean you were being pretty literal. You know, my uncle once told me a joke that reminds me of this predicament. Let's see if I can remember it: do you know the difference between involved and committed? In a bacon and egg dinner the chicken is involved but the pig is committed."

"You'll never see your world again!"

The monster lunged at me, his mandibles spread and dripping venom. I leaned away from the attack and he struck the shimmering surface of the gateway face first. He tried to extricate his trapped mandibles, but the pull of the gateway was inescapable. Once something went in, it only could come out on the opposite end of the passage; there was no turning back. The Map Maker's insect eyes stared at me. They were unreadable; cold black beads glistening in the dim light of the netherworld. The flailing of his limbs slowed and then subsided. There would be no more threats. I relaxed into the electric sting of the gateway.

I reentered the abandoned house less gracefully than I'd

entered the Map Maker's world. I fell out of the rectangle of
moonlight, landing on the rotting floorboards butt first. Then
the gate disgorged the remains of my antagonist. I've seen apple-
sauce that was less pulverized. The sticky mess flowed across
the floor and spattered out of the wall in fitful coughs. If being
coated in monster guts wasn't bad enough, it made the floor so
slick I had to lean against the wall for support as I slipped into
the hallway and down the stairs.

"What happened to you?" Voe called up to me.

"I squashed a spider, a damn big spider."

"I knew this wouldn't work!"

There was genuine rage in Voe's voice. I'd heard him miffed
and afraid, but this was different.

"I didn't know you cared." I reached the ground floor and
paused to shake something sticky and nasty off my hand. "If
you think you could have done a better job, maybe you should
have tried yourself."

"No, it's not that." His voice softened. Now it was colored
with disappointment. "I just hoped you'd get the information
you needed. I guess our cause truly *is* lost, now."

"Don't be such a pessimist." I started for the sliver of light
that marked the decrepit building's exit. "They're meeting in
the clock tower just inside the Butler Street gates of Allegheny
Cemetery."

"But I thought you killed the Map Maker."

"He talked first. Then he got fresh. Don't ever get fresh with
me unless I give you permission."

We stumbled through the undergrowth; well, I stumbled and
Voe bounded, all the way to the car. It felt good to sit in familiar,
civilized surroundings. It didn't evoke such comfort when I got
a look at myself in the mirror. I pulled a handkerchief from my
purse and started mopping goo off my face.

"Next time I negotiate with some otherworldly nemesis,

remind me to bring a rain slicker or a change of clothes." I turned the key and the dashboard lights came on. My heart sank. We had less than an hour before midnight. "Fasten your seatbelt, Voe. It's time for some inspired driving."

31

Allegheny Cemetery is located outside the busiest part of the city; a good thing when you don't want to get caught up in amateur night shenanigans. On New Year's Eve, everybody suddenly comes to the conclusion they're endowed with a God-given gift to drive superbly while drunk. Personally, when I've overindulged I prefer stumbling home on foot, but I've known guys who held their liquor so well you'd hardly know they'd drunk the tavern dry. Some of them even had an innate knack for making it home without so much as denting a fender after a night bending a barstool. Those guys wouldn't dare put whitewall on pavement on New Year's Eve; maybe it's for the same reason trapeze artists don't go on stage with the clowns when the circus comes to town.

The wagon wined as we crossed the Allegheny River, her tires singing on the wet pavement. The north side went by in a blur, the lights of houses creating abstract color studies on the fogged car windows as I thought about what I might find at the cemetery. Mark and the old man would be in the clock tower. That had to be the pivot point of the ley lines in the Map Maker's web. All I had to do was figure out where and how to keep them from succeeding. That would be a lot easier if I had the slightest idea what damned gyrations they'd be going through to fulfill their unholy plan. Unfortunately, I was speeding into the situation blind. You'd think I'd get used to it eventually.

I skidded onto Butler Street and then eased up on the accelerator as I neared the cemetery gates. No sense in announcing my arrival with squalling tires. I cruised by the gates at ten miles per hour. Mark's red Jaguar sat in the lot beside the clock tower. I drove on for a half block and then parked along the curb.

Voe practically climbed across me to stand with his feet on the driver-side door. "So, what's our plan?"

I took my pistol out and refilled the clip. "I'm going up there to settle up with a couple acquaintances. I suggest you stay here and wait."

"Stay in the car? This is as much my problem as yours!" he whined.

I'd known Voe less than a month and I already hated when he whined. I checked the clock.

"What part of this is your problem?"

"The terrible things that you've seen happening to people might happen to animals too. That makes it my business."

I hadn't considered that possibility. He could be right; if animals were sentient beings they might suffer the same unending hell I'd witnessed in the morgue. Pierhind had said that Death saw to the end of all things, which would include animals, wouldn't it? It'd be closed-minded not to even consider the possibility. I had an out too. I slapped the clip into my pistol and eyed Voe.

"Death said I had to stop this thing. He didn't say anything about a cat being involved."

Voe's tail flicked while he worked out a way around my protest. The process didn't take long.

"Well, then I've just gotten used to you and I don't feel like having to break in a new human."

"Voe, that's flattering but it's also the biggest heap of bullshit I've ever heard."

"I don't bullshit. It's the truth."

"Oh, really?" His statement earned a smirk. "Fine, I guess you can come along. Just do me a favor and don't get underfoot, okay?"

I opened the door and Voe was out, heading toward the gates. "You act like I'm some kind of burden."

"Yeah, well let's just not find out exactly how much of a burden tonight. Okay?"

We crept along the tree-lined fence that surrounded the graveyard until we reached the cemetery gates. The clock tower looked like a castle, its crenellated shape cutting a dismal shadow out of the skyline and making the task ahead feel more daunting. The creeping sense of doom wasn't helped by the backlit clock face. It showed ten minutes remained in 1952! We didn't have much time to think.

I stopped at the corner of the gates, which stood open. Obviously Mark had connections with some coroner or undertaker who could get him keys. He'd unwittingly let his influence work in our favor.

"They're on the roof," Voe whispered from between my feet.

"How do you know?"

"Somebody moved up there." He looked up at me. "Some of us don't need a light to see at night."

"You're right, you're not a burden." I nodded toward the clock tower. "Let's try to get across the road without tipping our friend off. I think there's a door under that arcade."

I followed Voe's lead, dashing across the drive, through the Gothic gates, and into the lot behind the clock tower where Mark's car sat parked. The thought of dragging my keys across its glossy red hood played in my mind momentarily; unfortunately, there wasn't time to indulge my vindictive side. Spoiling his plans would have to be enough.

We passed under the arcade and I started to feel safer under its vaulted roof. No one on the roof could see us now and I could use every advantage available. I grabbed the ornate brass door handle and pulled; the door didn't budge.

"Crap, they locked it."

I pressed my face to the door's glass. The building apparently served as some kind of office for the cemetery. A pair of desks and a few chairs populated the interior. Across the room I could see light seeping under a closed door, but nothing moved. I doubted Mark would hang out in the lobby while the clock ran down on his victory. We needed to get to the roof and there wasn't time to skulk around the building looking for another entrance. So much for stealth. I balled a fist around the gun in my pocket.

"Turn your face away, Voe."

I've seen movie crooks break out a window while barely making a sound. In reality it doesn't work that way. Maybe it seems worse when you're the one trying to be quiet but the glass breaking, falling on the marble floor inside the building, and scattering everywhere, certainly seemed pretty damn loud. I reached through the jagged hole in the shattered pane and turned the doorknob. No sense in concealing my pistol anymore. I eased the safety off and we crossed the room.

The only exit from the room, aside from where we'd broken in, was the door bearing a sign that read MAINTENANCE. The light escaping under the door spilled across the marble floor in a soft arc that didn't give a clue to what might be happening beyond. I paused, held my breath, and listened. Nothing, no rushing feet or sounds of alarm to indicate Mark and the old man were onto us. Maybe they hadn't heard the breaking glass. I pushed through the door, keeping my pistol ready.

Inside a spiraling staircase led upward. I pulled the door closed, sealing us in with the sounds of the tower's massive clockworks. Overhead gears and cogs growled and the time-keeping mechanisms rattled and clinked. The din covered my footsteps on the metal stairs, making me as silent as Voe while we ascended toward the roof.

The clockworks dominated the fourth floor of the tower. Machinery murmured and groaned, grinding out the unfaltering pace of time. A greased shaft extended from the mass of gears and weights, passing through the glass panes of the tower clock face holding the clock's massive hands. They'd mark the passing of the old year without fanfare or even pausing in their toil. A ladder led up from the clockworks, ending in a metal trapdoor that let out onto the roof. I glanced at my companion.

"Unless you can grow opposable thumbs it looks like we have to part company."

Voe circled, staring up at the door.

"Take it easy; I've got this thing handled. Just don't get your tail caught in a gear and I'll be right back."

He sat and curled his tail around his haunches. "Don't get cocky."

I grabbed the ladder and started climbing until Voe spoke.

"Good luck, Mel. I know you'll stop them."

I smiled. "With that kind of faith behind me, how could I fail?"

I climbed to the top of the ladder. The padlock dangled unlocked and hanging by its hasp, more evidence we were in the right place. I put a shoulder against the door and gave a slow, steady push. It rose, revealing first the roof, then the parapets, and then a robed figure looking out over the city. I laid the door back as quietly as I could. Mark wasn't on the roof, a disturbing fact I didn't have time to worry over at the moment. I pulled myself onto the roof and pointed my gun at the old man's back.

"Okay, don't move. And this time I mean it."

He turned and though I'd tried to steal myself for the

potential of violence I wasn't prepared for what I saw. He'd aged since the night in front of the theatre. His skin had become so translucent that he looked like a skeleton. The hair that had curled over his shoulders had fallen out except for mangy patches that clung to his skull in irregular clumps. The wisps of beard that remained hung around drooping lips that showed long yellowing teeth. I couldn't tell if he wore a smile or a snarl as he looked me over.

"Miss Rush, I wish I could say it was a pleasure."

Aging hadn't changed his voice. It still had all the melodious charm of a rusted hinge.

"What a shame, and I tried so hard to please."

"At least you impress. For instance, I greatly admire your tenacity. It's, perhaps, humanity's only redeeming trait and you possess it in such abundance."

"Yeah, thanks. Speaking of humanity, or the lack thereof, where's your lackey? I'd like to say hello."

"He's around somewhere." He nodded to the pistol. "Are we playing the same game again? You already know that gun is useless."

"Consider it my security blanket. Besides, you might survive but I guarantee I'll make one hell of a mess of you by the time you get to me."

He didn't look impressed but he also didn't seem eager to come after me. I took advantage of his hesitance to take a quick look around the roof. "So, really, where is your servant?"

"I sent the doctor on an errand so that I could enjoy a little privacy and take in the sights of the last year."

With a shaking hand he gestured out over Butler Street. From our rooftop vantage the city looked like a model. Miniature trees spread out from the clock tower; on the Butler Street side they were bathed in the milky glow of the streetlights. Beyond that freight cars clustered in the rail yard, huddling on the edge of open countryside as they waited for the dawn of 1953. To the south the darkness of the cemetery eventually gave way to the lights of greater Pittsburgh. By now the clubs and bars were filled with revelers. They were raising glasses to their doom and didn't even realize it. I needed to keep the old man busy while I sorted out what to do.

"Explain something to me. When you introduced Mark to Alfonzo Arnie did you know the two of you were going to kill him, or did the idea come to you later?"

"My dear child, I didn't introduce Dr. James to Mr. Arnie. I'm afraid when the doctor said he'd never met Mr. Arnie he wasn't quite being honest. They knew each other long before Dr. James and I became acquainted. In fact, the doctor introduced *me* to Mr. Arnie."

"So at least Mark was telling the truth about his gambling problems."

"Yes, he owed Mr. Arnie a rather large sum; enough that Mr. Morello would have become involved in short order. The death of Mr. Arnie turned out to be mutually beneficial."

It had started to be obvious I'd have an easier time counting the truths Mark had told than it would be to track the number of times he'd lied.

"So Mark got out of his debt but you got something a lot more valuable, didn't you?"

His drooping lips tightened into an unhealthy smirk. "I knew you were smarter than the doctor supposed. Please, enlighten me. What have you deduced?"

"You convinced Mark to kill Arnie. Whether he knew the real reason or not, I'm not sure, but I know that your plan was to draw Death to Arnie's house where you could steal his mask. If you could keep the mask until after midnight on New Year's Eve you'd avoid dying and being reborn. In effect, you'd be immortal. How am I doing?"

"Very impressive, however there is one flaw."

"Mel!" I heard Voe call up from the gear room. I didn't exactly have time to provide an update on my progress.

"What flaw?"

"I didn't convince your precious doctor to kill. He'd done it once before and willingly participated again."

"Virginia—"

Before I could say more, a hand grabbed my arm. The pistol discharged before it was knocked from my hand and the old man spun and stumbled. My practice had paid off. In spite of the interfering blow, I'd still scored a hit. I would have congratulated myself if it wasn't for the familiar blade pressed against my throat. I did manage to be sarcastic.

"Honey, you're late. We started without you."

Mark shook me violently. The nice-guy persona was like his doctor's coat: easily taken off when it suited his needs. Now the kindhearted doctor disguise had fallen away and the hatred burning behind his eyes was clearly visible. When I looked away from Mark, I saw my bullet had cut through the old man's cheek. Sand poured out of the wound like it had when I shot him in front of the theatre.

The old man wheezed out a laugh. "Yes, your knight is a cold-blooded killer. Do you feel foolish, realizing the man you believed you might have spent the rest of your life with kills for pleasure? The first time Dr. James killed was in a squalid alley."

"Virginia Beal." I felt like vomiting.

"Was that her name?" the old man asked.

"Yes, that was her," I whispered.

Mark spoke in a voice that was as cold and hard as the knife he carried. "Whores don't have names."

The old man chuckled. "You can see he possessed the sort of cruel cunning required for this little endeavor. His ruthlessness turned out to be quite an asset."

I took over the narrative.

"You introduced yourself to Mark at his club and you pitched your proposal. After that night you two were allies."

"Correct, I told him about the possibility of defeating Death and the necessity to sacrifice some poor soul in order to draw the grizzly bastard out into the open . . . and the doctor took the initiative."

Mark took the old man's cue. He seemed to luxuriate in my despair.

"I told your hooker friend that I'd lift her out of the hellish life she'd fallen into but I never promised she'd enjoy the process." Mark pressed his cheek to mine. "She never saw it coming. I don't even think she saw me before I'd cut her throat."

"She didn't."

The old man continued. "If he hadn't been such an anxious student we would have taken Death's mask that night. Unfortunately, the girl crossed over too quickly. Death came and went before even I could slow the process. We had to bide our time until Mr. Arnie."

Sickness washed over me. The man Virginia pined to find was Mark. She'd expected a savior and gotten a murderer. I wanted to weep, to fall on the ground and scream until I couldn't anymore. But I'd made a promise to Virginia and breaking down didn't fulfill that promise. I had to stay smart and work through this. I swallowed against the hard edge of the blade. Mark was a pawn and a distraction; the old man had to be my target.

"All right, you've got the mask and that'll stop you from being reborn. From here it looks like rebirth would be a lot better than eternity looking like a corpse."

The old man's self-satisfied smirk waned. "And I had such high hopes for you. I shouldn't be surprised; in the end you're just as ignorant as the rest of humanity. You can't possibly know what it is to be everything to everyone. I encompass all existence for every living thing on this pathetic planet. Can you imagine what it's like to know all and, as a part of that all, know that in the brief span of one year you'll be erased and reduced to nothingness? Can you imagine knowing there are only two truly seminal events in the year's calendar: your birth and your death? I am all powerful yet my life is arbitrarily ended by the machinations of an unthinking universe."

"So you did something about it." I didn't wait for a response. "What if I want to stop you?"

The question prompted Mark to press the knife harder against my neck. I eyed the old man.

"You want to clue your patsy in on how things work?"

"What are you talking about?" Mark glanced between the old man and me.

The old man sighed. "Remember when you stabbed her before?"

"She got lucky. The blade probably deflected off a rib and missed the heart."

"Your blade didn't miss. Death wants no part of her. You could slice her throat ten times and she'd still live." The old man approached. "Death isn't the only one who can dole out favors."

He brought a hand up to his cheek, letting sand fill his palm. Then he blew. The sensation was like having salt thrown in my eyes and poured down my throat. It stung ferociously and tears streamed down my cheeks.

"Now time itself won't touch you. Because of my influence, you'll be a lovely young woman a hundred years from now. A thousand years and you'll barely remember this night, but you'll remain the same woman who stood here with a knife pressed to her throat while the world changed around her."

"Wait a minute," Mark protested. "You promised I'd be

spared growing old, why are you blessing her when I have to wait?"

I coughed the last remnants of sand out of my throat. "Maybe you need to get a new contract."

Mark shook me. I could feel his knife biting into the skin of my neck.

"Don't let her get to you." The old man's voice was stern. "You will receive exactly what I promised once our task is finished."

"So that's how he bought you. You get eternal youth in exchange for being his little slasher—some deal. So, is it a permanent job or a one-time contract deal?"

"Don't shortchange me, Mel. It's more than just staying young and pretty." He pulled me close, breathing his vile words into my ear. "Together he and I are going to defeat Death. That's something no doctor could claim to have accomplished. Even my old man couldn't say he'd actually stared the specter of Death in the face and defeated it."

I blinked the last bits of sand out of my eyes. "Is that what this is all about? To you this is some kind of stupid competition for the respect of your dead parents? Mark, do you know what kind of immortality your friend is offering humanity? It's not life unending, it's living death!"

The clockwork below our feet gave off a tangible shudder and the tired tones of the Westminster chime began echoing across the graveyard. I'd heard those notes ten thousand times from just as many clocks and they'd been so ubiquitous that I barely noticed them. Now they were the most important sounds in the world. I struggled against Mark's hold but I couldn't break free.

"Mark, you don't realize what you're doing! Let me go!"

"I'm afraid you'll find Dr. James is quite dedicated to our shared goal." The old man strolled back to the parapet. "He's filled with gusto and desire, so eager to make something of himself, so ready to reach out for the reigns of fate. Perhaps he'll give you some of his attention after this is over. Perhaps he'll dissect you. I wonder what it will be like living through eternity severed limb from eternally young limb."

The chimes stopped and the first toll of midnight began.

"Mark, please listen!"

"Shut up, Mel," he growled.

Second bell.

I struggled and pleaded. "Virginia Beal trusted you, Mark. She's still searching for you even after her death. That has to touch something inside you!"

Third bell.

"None of it matters." The old man pulled something from his robes. It resembled a carnival mask in the shape of a scarlet skeletal face with dribs of gold and silver paint for accent. "The time has come for the sands of time to crush Death." Fourth bell. "The wheel of the year has turned for the last time!"

Fifth bell.

"Mark!"

He stood impassive, his blade biting into my neck as he watched his master.

Sixth bell.

"Let her go and drop the knife!"

Mark jerked around bringing me with him. Rolland stood by the trapdoor with his revolver drawn and leveled. I never thought I'd feel good about seeing the bastard.

Seventh bell.

"Shoot the old man, Rolland!" I screamed as Mark hauled me in front of him as a shield.

Eighth bell.

"Surely your mentor taught you only the initiated can see what's happening here, child." The old man laughed. "Needless to say that doesn't include this simpleton policeman."

Ninth bell.

"Put the knife down." Rolland pulled the hammer on his gun back.

Tenth bell.

There was only one way to end this. I yanked into the knife, turning out of my coat as the blade slid across my throat. The pain was intense and I could feel the warmth of blood streaming down my chest as I fell forward. My gun lay between Mark's feet and I aimed myself for it as I went down. Before I reached the roof, Rolland's gun went off and Mark jerked as the bullet struck.

Eleventh bell.

Reality slowed and as Mark fell away from me I brought my pistol up and fired. The old man shrieked and recoiled as my round reduced his hand to a cloud of sand. The death mask flipped over the edge of the roof and disappeared into the darkness.

Twelfth bell.

A pressure wave washed over the rooftop as reality slowed to a stop. Only the ones the old man had called "the initiated" moved. Mark coughed and squirmed in the snow while the old man wailed and cowered against the stonework. I lay on my side, blood gushing out of my wounded throat in strong throbs. As I looked on, a great black figure ascended.

At first, Death resembled the insubstantial specter I'd met the day Fleck shot me. Evil black smoke boiled up over the crenellated wall that surrounded the clock tower roof, pouring through the gaps in the way and onto the snowy rooftop. Amid the smoke, the gold and crimson mask that the old man treasured bobbed like a cork floating on turbulent waters. The mask rose and rotated, until it found a place to take hold and then the smoke began to solidify.

Flowing waves of sackcloth spread out from the mask, rippling and flapping as they reached for their full length. Bones formed from the air: first a ribcage, then arms, and finally clutching hands. The robes drew up into ultimate darkness, deeper and colder than any night. Great, blue-black wings spread out from Death's shoulders, their tips spanning wider than the roof and blotting out the lights of the city. The mask receded into a cowl until all that remained visible was the starlight glint of two eyes. When Death spoke there was no malice or contempt in his voice.

"The wheel has turned again and the time has come. *Vetus annus est mortuus.*"

"No—"

The old man raised his fingerless hand in defense and tried to crawl away but as he did his body began to disintegrate. He fought to raise limbs that fell apart, dissolving into rivulets of sand. Before he'd traveled the length of three steps, all that remained was a cloud of dust in the cold air. From that cloud, a single spark emerged. It ascended and then sailed away into the night sky. As it vanished, I thought I heard the sound of a baby's crying on the wind.

Death glided toward me. "Melody Rush, you have succeeded in restoring order." He knelt over Mark's body and extended a skeletal hand.

"Great, now humanity can all go about dying in the appropriate manner; just wonderful." Things were getting fuzzy and my head wasn't feeling so good.

"It is the way of things. Only you stand outside the order."

"Yeah, I know." I felt dizzy and weak. Mark lay at Death's feet, convulsing as his blood spread, staining the snow. "What about him?"

"His time has not come." Death's wings unfurled. "Rest well, Melody Rush. You will not see me again."

With a single wing beat Death lifted from the rooftop. He turned a half circle, and then sailed away over the cemetery. Soon I couldn't pick his form out of the night sky. I rested my head against the roof, closed my eyes, then opened them to find Rolland hovering over me.

32

Happily, I didn't wake the next time to a good-looking doctor standing over my hospital bed. I don't think I ever want to see a handsome doctor again. The empty room and the hum of medical equipment were comforting enough. I settled back on my uncomfortable bed and pathetic pillow and reached a hand up to feel my throat. Compared to Pierhind's work, the stitches felt ugly. Who would have thought I'd be longing for a troll's medical attention over the best the city had to offer?

The door opened and I fully expected to hear the beginnings of one of my mom's sermons on how my bad choices led to this unfortunate situation. Instead it was Rolland. He wore a dark overcoat and carried his hat. He didn't look stern, instead he looked a little like he'd just been introduced to someone he kind of feared.

"I know, I'm in trouble for messing around with police business. Let me heal up and then you can cuff me and drag me over whatever kettle of coals you want to concoct."

I closed my eyes and waited for the lecture. He surprised me.

"I've seen cuts like the one you got but I've never seen anyone walk away from one."

He surely wasn't going to let me off easy. I pushed.

"Yes, and if I'd only learn to be more responsible and lady-like these things wouldn't happen to me. Go ahead; get it out of your system."

"I'm not here to lecture you, Mel."

I opened my eyes. "What did you call me?"

"I called you 'Mel.' I figure you're nearly thirty now, you ought to be able to decide what you want to be called. If that's 'Mel' then I should start respecting your wishes."

"Okay, what's going on?" I ran through the list of things that didn't seem to be right. One stood out. "Where's Mom? Is something wrong with her?"

Rolland settled in a chair beside the bed. "She's fine. Well, that's relatively speaking. I asked her to let you have a few days to recover before she visits."

"That's nice but you'll excuse my saying the Rolland I know not only would have driven my mother to the hospital but also read off my list of offenses to make sure Mom didn't miss the good ones."

"What can I say? I'm a changed man. I'm on your side."

"Yeah, right. You better pull the other leg or I'll wind up walking in circles."

"Okay, I'll be absolutely honest. I think you made some bad decisions. But who would have guessed that James guy was a psychotic flake. He had a respectable job and seemed on the level. I never would have pinned him as a head case and it's my job to pick them out of the crowd."

I thought back to New Year's Eve and what Death had said. "He survived?"

"Yes."

"Where is he now?"

"Does it matter?"

"It does to me."

"He's in the infirmary at Eastern State. They'll patch him up and then he'll stand trial on three charges of murder and one attempted murder."

Somehow it seemed nonsensical to send a guy to the hospital in order to get him healthy for the chair. A lot of life didn't make much sense, though.

"How did you find me on that rooftop?"

"We found that red sports car that belonged to James. I didn't know you were on the roof until I stuck my head through that trapdoor."

"So, how did you know to look for Mark's car?"

"Fleck talked. Under Scott's interrogation he told us Virginia Beal worked for him as a streetwalker and that she'd been hanging around a big money doctor named James. It took a little research, but we were lucky; there was only one Dr. James in the Pittsburgh area."

"I guess I owe Scott."

Rolland leaned forward, putting an elbow on his knee and steadying his chin in his palm.

"Does that mean you've decided to apologize to the boy?"

"Apologize is a very strong word."

"True. The question is whether it's the right word."

I leaned back on my pillow. "I don't know, Rolland. What should I do?"

"Hold on." He sat up. "Let me get my notepad. I need to remember this day. You are asking me how to run your life, aren't you?"

It's hard to backpedal while in a hospital bed. "I don't need you to tell me how to *run* my life, Rolland. I just want a little advice, that's all."

"Still, *you* asking for advice ought to be some kind of national holiday."

"Forget I asked; just forget it. Okay?"

"I can't; it's indelibly seared into my brain."

"Don't make me call an orderly. I swear I'll have you thrown out."

"Sorry. Don't do anything drastic!" He held up his hands, laughing all the while. "Scott should be by anytime now. He needed to do some paperwork but he said he'd visit."

"Rolland, no! I don't know what to say to him!"

There was a rap at the door and Scott stuck his head inside. Rolland patted my hand and stood. "I'd suggest you think fast. I'll get out of the way."

I wanted to latch onto Rolland's hand, but it probably would have just added to my embarrassment. Rolland winked at me, and then opened the door. Scott stood just outside. His clothes looked like he'd slept in them and there were dark circles under his eyes.

"She's tired, so go easy on her, huh?" Rolland advised, patting Scott on the shoulder and stepping out into the hallway. I waited until the door closed. Now it was just me and my former old buddy. I swallowed hard and wondered how ugly this would get. Scott had every right to make a scene. I just hoped he wouldn't.

I stared at the foot of my bed instead of making eye contact. "If you want to give me an 'I told you so' you can save it."

It was the first time in my life I'd ever been shy about staring Scott down no matter how wrong I was. "I know: I blew it, I made a stupid choice, and I probably got what I deserved."

"Mel." Scott's voice sounded small and hesitant. I looked up at him. Up close he looked even more haggard. His complexion was pale and his normally smooth chin sported a day's worth of stubble. "About the other night, I didn't have any right to say the things I said. I was sore and I shot my mouth off. I'm sorry."

"Whoa, it might be the drugs they've got me on but did you just apologize to me because I stood you up for a guy who turned out to be a class-A psychopath?"

"I don't know if I'd put it like that—"

I cut in. "No, but I will. Scott, I should have talked to you a long time ago. I should have told you that I'd gotten the impression you wanted more from our relationship than I did. I owe you the apology and I'll understand if you turn it down."

"I don't want to turn it down. I've been going insane since that night. It's as much my fault as anyone's that you wound up mixed up with Morello, Arnie, and Fleck. I have a responsibility as a cop. I'm supposed to keep people safe, even when they really want to get into trouble. I let you down."

"You couldn't have kept me out of Virginia Beal's case if you wanted to." I could feel my lips twisting into a smirk. "You know me better than just about anyone in the world, Scott. What are the odds of keeping me from doing something I'm really bent on?"

"Pretty long." He laughed and it sounded wonderful.

"So, no hard feelings?"

"None."

"Still friends?"

"You'll have to try harder than this to get rid of me."

The tension drained from my temples. "Good, I hope it's a long time before I nearly blow our friendship again."

"Yeah, well, you still owe me two meals and don't think getting shot and having your throat cut will get you off the hook."

"Don't worry, I promise I'll pay up with interest as soon as I'm out of here."

We talked for an hour: laughing over the old days and commiserating over the time we'd lost in the past month. When Scott left I felt exhausted. I slept better that night than I had in weeks and I dreamed of playing stickball in the old neighborhood.

It took nearly a week for me to get on my feet and even then my doctor objected. Luckily, he reconsidered when I made it clear tying me to the bed would be a noisy and embarrassing affair. I think, in the end, he would have been happy for me to bleed out in the hallway. If he only knew that wouldn't do any good.

Healing without supernatural aid was a frustrating pain in the butt. Small accomplishments built on each other until I could imagine regaining my liberty. When I conquered the hallway outside my room I set my aim for a trip around the floor and when I'd mastered that, I felt strong enough for something a little more profound.

With my mother and Manny in tow I hobbled to the elevator and pressed the down button. I needed to go to the morgue for absolute proof the nightmare had ended. I hadn't heard the wails of desperation from my room but I needed to witness the silence of the corpses in the morgue drawers. Mom didn't understand why I needed to visit the morgue and, frankly, I didn't try to explain it to her. She stood at the back of the elevator with her arms crossed and her bottom lip pushed out.

"This isn't healthy. Getting exercise is one thing but why do you have to be so . . . morbid?"

Mom really didn't know morbid. Morbid is working for Death. By comparison, this was tame. The floor indicator inched toward the basement and I felt an upwelling of uncertainty. What if the fix hadn't worked? What if the door opened to a chorus of imprisoned souls? The tension needed dissipation and for me that means talking.

"You're feeding Voe twice a day, aren't you?"

Good old Mom. Her focus turned as smartly as I expected. "Melody, you've asked me about that animal a dozen times. If I raised a daughter I certainly can handle a cat."

"Oh, I don't know. You're always moaning about how bad I came out."

"Melody Rush!" Mom hissed as Manny tried to stifle a chuckle.

Oh, I pitied Voe. Then again, maybe some time with Mom

would make him more grateful when I finally got released from my antiseptic prison. I toned down the snarky banter a half notch.

"Just humor me, Mom."

"Yes, I feed him twice a day. He's got to be the most spoiled cat I've ever met."

"You won't get an argument on that point."

The elevator stopped along with my breathing. The doors jerked mechanically, and then slid apart. The inrush of pain I feared never came. The hallway outside the elevator stood quiet and empty. Mom peered over my shoulder, pinned to the wall by her squeamishness. Sometimes fright can be helpful, especially when it ensured I wouldn't have Mom at my elbow all the way to the morgue. I stepped over the threshold and looked back into the car. Since I knew she wouldn't step out of the car there wasn't any reason I shouldn't take the chance to rib her a little.

"Are you coming, Mom?"

"Your uncle can go with you. I won't have any part of supporting this unhealthy fixation."

I shrugged and the motion reminded me not to be too comfortable in my recovery. Mom and I were diametrically opposed and equally stubborn. I had to respect that.

"Come on, Manny, let's go." I hooked an arm in my uncle's and started walking toward the morgue doors. As I walked, I detected a slight hesitation in Manny's stride. It almost felt like I was pulling him along with me.

"You can wait in the hallway if you want," I suggested as we rounded the corner.

"I'm not afraid."

The forcefulness of his reply accused me of questioning his manhood.

"I didn't say you're afraid of anything, Manny. It's a morgue and I just thought you might want to wait outside."

He didn't answer my statement. Instead he sped up until he was leading me. When we reached the doors he opened them and stepped aside to let me through first. Manny could be a perfect gentleman when he wasn't being a total clod. On rare occasions like today he found a way to combine both.

We stepped into the cold of the morgue, drawing the attention of two men in hospital greens. One was a gray-headed white man and the other a black man with a clipboard. Behind them a man lay on the examination table, his body opened from collar bone to navel. The older of the two looked at his companion, prompting the man to speak. His voice was a deep baritone that seemed too warm for the room.

"May I help you?"

I smiled, not so much at the question as at the fact that their charge wasn't crying out in desperation. There wasn't a sound. Death had come and gone and his duty to the deceased had been discharged without fail.

"I think we took a wrong turn." I turned my eyes on the pair. "Sorry to interrupt."

When I got Manny outside the morgue, his color had drained away. I patted his shoulder. "I'm glad I had you along for support. I don't know what I would have done without you!"

"Shut up," he mumbled, the green in his face accented by the fluorescent lighting.

"Oh come on, lighten up! You know I'm kidding you." I punched him in the shoulder. "Seriously, I couldn't have gotten by without you."

His face brightened and some of its color returned. "Really?"

"Yeah." I hugged him. It was good to be engulfed in the warm comforting scent of cheap cologne and grease. "Hey, do you think you could do something for me?"

"Sure, I guess."

"I hid something at the garage and I'd like you to put it to good use."

On January 23 the hospital declared me fit for release. Manny drove me across town to Mom's house and for the first time in a long time I didn't feel the slightest pang of regret at seeing her waiting on the front step. I got out of the car, stepping into the lovely crispness of the winter air, and started making my way up the walk before Manny's sense of responsibility had him hanging onto my arm. Regardless of what my uncle thought, I didn't need a crutch, human or otherwise.

"I'm glad you're here; that cat of yours is about to drive me insane." Mom held out her arms and hugged me. "How are you feeling, dear?"

"Wonderful." Mom waited, expecting my usual sarcasm. She wasn't going to get it; at least not today. "So, how about I take a certain feline off your hands?"

Mom opened the door and I'd barely stepped over the threshold when Voe leapt into my arms. I'd never heard him purr before. It was a beautiful sound.

"I thought you'd never save me from this place!" He nuzzled his head under my chin. "Don't ever do this to me again!"

"I see how it is." Mom stood, watching with a little smile playing across her face. "Some of us get affection, the rest are barely worthy of contempt!"

Voe pushed his head harder into my chin. "If you only knew what I went through with that woman!"

"He's a one-person cat." I hefted Voe onto my shoulder, enjoying his steady rumble. "Thanks for taking care of him, Mom. I know he can be a handful."

"A handful?" Voe murmured.

I jostled Voe to make him shut up.

"Well, usually you don't want my help. At least this time I got to make some kind of contribution."

That's my mom. Subtext: if you're going to wreck your life at least I can feed the cat. This was how our truce worked and for once I was okay with that.

"Well, I need to get home." I hugged her against Voe's complaints. "Thanks again, Mom. Maybe we can go shopping this Saturday?"

She blinked. "You're giving up part of your weekend to be with your mother?"

"Yes, I am. This is where you're supposed to say 'that sounds like a great idea.' " I headed out the door. "I'll see you Saturday morning."

"Oh, to be free of that place!" Voe said, hanging onto my shoulder as we descended the driveway toward my uncle's waiting car. He called back to Mom derisively. "So long, you old bat! I hope you choke on that stale, dry cat food you've been forcing on me!"

"Voe! That's my mom you're talking about!"

"So?"

"So cut her some slack or I'm going to switch you over to kibble."

He fell silent until we climbed into the car. I dumped him into the back seat, settled in, and then waved to Mom as Manny pulled away from the curb. Before we'd reached the end of the block, something intruded on my mind.

"Manny, I wondered if you could drive me by Homewood Cemetery before we go back to the garage?"

He glanced at me. "You sure you ought to exert yourself? The doctor did say to take it easy."

"I promise I'll go right to bed when I get home. I just want to see her grave."

He sighed in a way that let me know he'd given in.

"I guess it can't do any harm. I can't imagine spending all

that money on someone you never even met."

Again I found myself stopping just short of honesty. Seeing the dead meant having to lie to everyone to avoid being considered crazy. It felt lonely. The only solution was feeling my way around the edges of the truth.

"I feel like we knew each other. Besides, everyone should have at least one mourner, don't you think? Wouldn't you want someone to visit your grave, even if it was a stranger?"

He shrugged, looking uncomfortable. "I don't think it'd matter. I mean when you're gone you're gone, right?"

I patted his shoulder. "Don't be so sure, Manny."

Homewood Cemetery wasn't like Allegheny. It has all the funerary basics: chapel, Gothic wrought iron fencing, winding roads leading through wooded grounds, and hundreds of graves. The difference is that Allegheny has been swallowed by the city while Homewood hangs onto its relative pastoral isolation. Whether the city ever will overtake the rolling hills around its borders, I can't say but I guess I'll find out. The world seems to shrink every day.

Manny parked along one of the curving roadways and I stepped out onto the snow, poking my head over the back seat to where Voe sat sunbathing on the rear window deck. "You want to come along?"

Voe looked at me as if I'd asked if he'd like to take a bath in mud.

"Uh, no thanks to getting my fur wet and ice-caked by walking around in the snow and cold."

Manny watched me talking to the cat and felt compelled to interject.

"For company you ought to get a dog."

I was glad Voe couldn't understand Manny. I smirked at what the feline didn't know.

"You might be right."

"In the meantime, I guess I could come along."

"Manny, you don't have to—"

"I didn't say you were forcing me to go, did I? Besides, I ordered the stone and fished your money out of the oil barrel. I feel like I should be there for the inspection."

I waited for him to come around the front of the car and then let him take my arm. We climbed the snowy hillside, up from the road and through a row of bare trees into a field of tombstones. He led the way through the gravesites; a few transparent figures strolled among the stones. Maybe they were visiting loved ones or checking on their final resting place. I still had a lot left to learn about the dead and their habits.

We came to an opening and Manny stopped, nodding to a polished obelisk separated from the rest of the yard with neat, hip-high fencing. Outside the fence sat a mourner's bench behind which stood a freshly planted sapling. I released Manny's arm and walked ahead.

"This is lovely!"

"Well, I had money to work with and you said you wanted something special." He shook his head again. "I still can't imagine spending that much money to bury a stranger."

"Yeah, you mentioned that." I touched one of the sapling's bare branches. "What kind of tree is it?"

"Flowering cherry. The guy at the nursery said it'll be filled with pink blooms in the spring."

I nodded and patted its trunk. "I think she would have liked that. You did a great job."

He smiled. "So, think we ought to head back home so you can get warm and rest?"

"Actually, would you mind if I sit here for a few minutes?" He started to approach the bench. "Uh, alone, please?"

He hesitated and then poked his hands back in his pockets.

287

"Well, try not to take too long. You don't need to get a cold to go with everything else."

"Just a few minutes, I promise."

I watched him walk down the row of headstones until he'd ducked under the tree line, and then I settled on the bench and bundled my coat around my chin. Virginia's stone caught the fading winter sunlight, giving it back in a mellow yellow-gold sheen. I felt her but she didn't appear. Something about the sensation of her presence felt different, though. It seemed peaceful, like her search had ended. The irony wasn't lost on me: I'd let Virginia pass on to whatever lay beyond the grave and, in exchange, I'd never see that afterlife.

The wind brushed through the tombstones, sending sparkling swirls of snow dancing across the grounds. The flakes brushed my cheek and then went on, dancing past the bench and into a grove of pines. The snow kissed the pine boughs and hissed as it passed through the green needles. In spite of January's best efforts the pines never slumbered. Amid graves and winter's cold they went on, unchanged. I had a kinship with them; the calendar's march meant nothing to us. I drew a deep breath of the cold air and tried to take in the meaning but it didn't work.

"Rest well, Virginia." I stood, straightened my coat, and then headed back to the car feeling a little lighter.

ABOUT THE AUTHOR

Gary Madden is a technical writer working in the biomedical field. His horror and science fiction pieces have appeared in various print and electronic magazines and anthologies. Gary grew up in Indiana where he still lives and his love of writing evolved out of his love of the Midwest and its people.